# Courage

## Book One

# Lions of God Trilogy

Lloyd D. Frazier

COURAGE – BOOK ONE – LIONS OF GOD TRILOGY
www.lionsofgod.com

Published by ApogeeINVENT – American Falls, ID

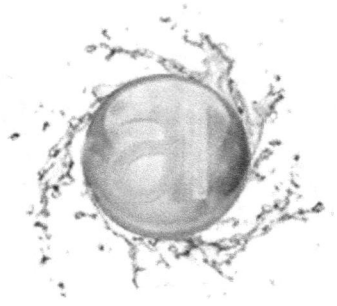

www.apogeeinvent.com

Author Lloyd D. Frazier
Editor Lindsey Winsemius
Cover design & illustrations Andrew Frey

First Edition November 2013
ISBN: 0615920993
ISBN-13: 978-0-615-92099-3

To my daughter Jade,

may the Light of Heaven shine upon you

even in your darkest days.

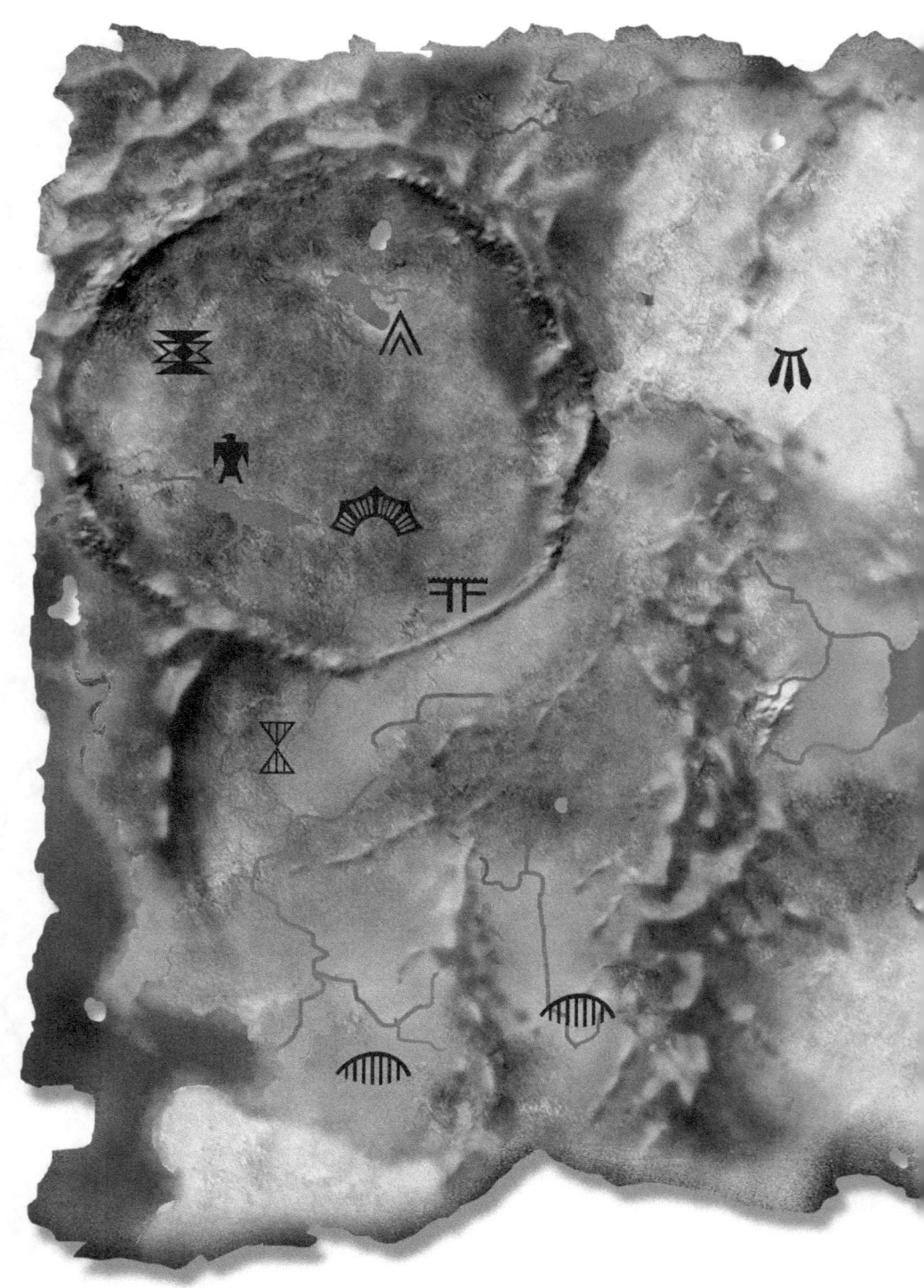

# The Areli Nation

Talseabus

Talberte

Talbaralisa

Taltarie

Zuya Savannah

Megiddo Jungle

Southern Marshes

Great Wall

# ACKNOWLEDGMENTS

You would think that writing a complete novel would be the hard part, but I find words are not adequate to express my gratitude for all the people who have helped me fulfill a dream or convey the depth of emotion I feel at this works completion. The two years it has taken me to conceptualize, plan, and write this novel have been two of the hardest years of my life. But I have never quit nor given up on anything that was important to me. As the saying goes, it is not how many times you fall down but how many times you get back up that counts. This book is a testament to that fact. I would like to thank my wife Kiesha, for, to put it bluntly, "putting up with me," while I talked obsessively about the grand fantasy playing out in my head. Or while I was so engrossed in my own thoughts and daydreams that I completely blocked out the reality that was around me. She is simply amazing. I would also like to thank my brother Joseph Frazier. He was the first to read the book in its entirety. He was also the first to take a financial risk besides myself to making my dream a reality. There is a lot more to creating a good book than simply writing it. This is where my brother's company ApogeeINVENT and his business partners entered into the picture. ApogeeINVENT provided me with a much needed editor, Lindsey Winsemius, who has done a fantastic job. She helped me take a good novel and make it great. Again thank you, Lindsey. ApogeeINVENT also provided me with a truly gifted artist, Andrew Frey, to do all the amazing artwork for my book. Thank you, ApogeeINVENT for all the other things you have done and will do in helping make this book a huge success. I would also like to thank all those people who have helped me become a better writer. First to every author I have ever read. You didn't know it but I was a student of yours. I would also like to thank every author who has published a book on writing. I have probably studied it in depth. I would like to thank the cast of Writing Excuses, Mary Robinette Kowal, Brandon Sanderson, Howard Taylor, and Dan Wells for taking the time to teach all us would be authors the art that is writing. I would also like to thank Brandon Sanderson for allowing his classes at BYU Provo to be recorded and posted to the web for free for someone like me who didn't get into BYU to still take his classes. And finally I would like to thank you, the reader, who has taken a risk on a new author. I hope the book captures your imagination the way it has captivated mine.

# PROLOGUE

Evil permeated the air. It lay so thick upon the land that the young boy bound to the altar choked on it. Rain falling from the broiling clouds above stung his face and body. He had been stripped down to nothing but his loin cloth. He strained against his bonds; the ropes cutting and burning the flesh of his wrists and ankles. His muscles corded and bunched with an effort that can only be found in the truly desperate. Lightning webbed and forked across the night sky followed by continuous sounds of rolling thunder that slammed into his body with such force that his ears rang and his bones rattled. The faces of his murderers were revealed with each flash of light.

The four men had captured him while he wandered the jungle on his spirit walk. They now stood proud at the four corners of the sacrificial altar—one for each limb. They too were clothed only in loin cloths. Tattoos covered their lean muscular bodies in dark twisted swirls that formed intricate patterns and symbols. The tattoos covering their faces and shaved heads formed demonic masks which only heightened the boy's fear. The men's eyes burned with hate and blood lust.

An old woman chanted in a language which caused excruciating pain that seared the boy's mind. As she chanted, she painted dark symbols across his body. Each symbol burned his flesh and its stink assaulted his nose. His throat and nose were raw and bleeding from the poisonous fumes that came from the stone goblet placed atop the altar above his head. The fumes seemed alive as they poured from the cup. They moved and flowed in unnatural ways; caressing his body, dancing over the symbols that the old woman was painting upon his flesh. The fumes would then return and force their way down his nose and throat, burning like acid within his lungs, causing him to cough up blood—which he would then spit at his captors.

The old woman's body was bent and twisted. Her flesh seemed to hang from her bones. Iron-gray hair sprouted wild and tangled from her scalp. Deep, cavernous wrinkles covered her face, and brown and broken teeth filled her cruel mouth. Her eyes were a solid, oily black which lacked any form of humanity. The warriors were demons wearing human skin and she was their master.

The old hag continued to chant even as she looked over the young boy's body, seeing that her work was almost finished. After a few final strokes of the brush she moved to the head of the altar and placed the brush down next to the stone goblet. The bristles were stained red from the blood contained within the goblet that she had used to paint the symbols upon the boy's now charred and bleeding flesh. With both hands she lifted the goblet up and then walked to the boy's side, her chanting growing louder and more insistent; as she raised the goblet up above her head her voice became a soul-wrenching shriek. Her words were in a language not meant for this mortal plane and it caused the earth to quake. She lowered the goblet and for the first time her eyes met the boy's, filling him with terror as an ugly smile split her face. Her eyes snapped to the warrior on the other side of the altar.

"You grab his head and plug his nose," she said, voice rasping like a snake slithering across gravel. She could have used her powers to force the boy's mouth open but it was far more satisfying to use their physical bodies.

The warrior grabbed the boy's head in a vice-like grip and viciously clamped his hand down upon the boy's nose. The hag moved closer and forced the boy's mouth open, then poured the tainted blood from the stone goblet down his throat, forcing him to drink. The boy struggled with every fiber of his being, but it was not enough as he was forced to swallow. Pain unlike anything the boy had ever felt before bloomed within his chest then quickly spread throughout his body. His very soul burned and a scream ripped forth from him that went on and on. The storm that raged above and all around them stilled and the earth grew quiet as if to listen in on the boy's final moments; making his cries ring out in the silent night. His body lifted up off the altar as his back arched until only his head and heels touched its surface. With a loud crack his spine broke and his body flopped back down to the altar. His screams were cut off by a black rancid liquid that filled his mouth and ran down his cheeks. His body stilled. Then his face fell lax as his eyes filmed over and became oily black like those of the old woman.

A look of pleasure and satisfaction twisted the old woman's face. "I have fulfilled my part, Akecheta, now it is your turn to fulfill yours; please me, and you will be richly rewarded. Fail me and I shall enjoy your screams for all eternity." This she said as she picked up the brush covered by the tainted blood and began sucking on it—savoring it.

The warrior that had gripped the boys head smiled wickedly. "It is an honor to serve you."

The old woman looked dispassionately at Akecheta; her eyes stripping away his flesh, seeing within his body, scrutinizing the demonic being that lay within. "Yes it is an honor to serve me, Akecheta, and serve me you shall." She pointed the brush at him. "There is much to be done. The one who sent me has decided it is time to take this world for his own, but in order to do that the Areli must be destroyed."

For a brief moment Akecheta fantasized about scores of Areli lying dead at his feet and his smile widened even more. "We shall burn their cities, and slaughter their people. Our altars will run red from the blood of their young, and our feet shall tread upon their bodies as we march forth to finally take this world for our own."

"Yes it shall be glorious," the old hag said contemptuously, "but first there is something that must be done. There will be a girl, a girl with green eyes. A child of the Second Realm, she will try to undo that which I have done this night. She must be captured and brought to me at all cost. This I have foreseen."

"Yes I know the one you speak of," Akecheta said. "It is no easy thing you ask."

"Gather the twelve and set them to this task."

"What of their so called Holy Daughter, and their Spirit Guide?" Akecheta asked.

"Capture the girl and bring her to me and I shall take care of those two; however, I will leave their High Chief to you."

"I hear that he is the finest warrior among all the Areli people; it shall be fun seeing the faces of his people as I strike him down before them."

"Akecheta."

"Yes?"

"The girl first, Akecheta, bring me the girl first. Then you may have your sport." The old hag said absently—having set the brush down, she was now running her aged and crooked fingers through the dead boy's hair.

Akecheta bowed silently then turned and started walking down the steps of their temple with the others, eager to fulfill his masters will.

The old decrepit body the devil Raum possessed had been a beautiful young woman just a few short weeks ago. She had only recently come to this world but already she was sick of the weak flesh she was forced to inhabit; their bodies withering like reeds from the dark powers that coursed through her. But when the girl with green eyes was brought before her that would all end. She would not take the girl back to the one who had sent her here like she had promised, but instead she would keep the girl's body for her own; possessing it, thereby taking its inherent powers. The girl's powers would be added to her own, making her powerful enough to rule worlds; powerful enough even to supplant the one who sent her. *Come, little girl, our destinies await.*

# CHAPTER 1

Jade sat under a massive tree, her back resting up against the slick bark. Her eyes were closed and her breathing slow and steady. She could hear the branches of the tree swaying in the light breeze. The thick foliage of the branches above broke up and gentled the rays from the bright sun. It was still hot and humid; it almost always was, even in the shade. The breeze rustling her chocolate-colored hair felt good, even cool, as it dried the perspiration on her face and arms.

Jade absently sucked on a long strand of hair, something her grandmother hated, and would often tell her to stop. So she would, but it wouldn't be long before the hair was back in her mouth. She didn't do it to defy her grandmother; it was just a habit she had developed as a little girl. It soothed her. She had begun doing it shortly after her mother was killed. Her mother and Jade had been out in the jungle beyond the Great Wall looking for a particular herb to add to their garden. A poisoned arrow shot from a Belial's War bow, pierced her mother's heart. Another arrow took her mother's totem, a Night Stag.

Jade had stood transfixed as she watched her mother die before her, blood pumping from her body and spilling across the ground. Then, in a panic, she had fled into the jungle, quickly becoming lost. The terror she had felt that day, wandering lost within the jungle, became etched permanently within her consciousness.

After that, her heart-broken father had drank strong spirits and raged on and off for months. Then came the quiet time when he would stand upon the Great Wall staring off into the jungle for hours—brooding. He was inconsolable, though his friends and loved ones tried. Then the day came when he had picked up his spear and entered the jungle with his totem Sisabil. He was never seen again.

After that she had gone to live with her grandmother. That had been when she was five.

By age 8, she would have had to go live with her grandmother anyway. Her innate powers were growing to the point where she needed constant monitoring; she was different from the rest of her people. All Areli had either dark brown or even black eyes, but the sclera of Jade's eyes were the color of life, a green found in the physical aura's of all living things, and her irises were a shimmering gold like her grandmother's.

Theirs were the same eyes as the Holy Mother who had come to them in the time of Great Sorrows, bringing life and health back to the Areli people—saving them from total destruction.

The Holy Mother fell in love with a young chief named Chikasha who became known as one of the greatest chiefs in tribal history. They had many sons but only one daughter. She too had eyes like her mother. Because of this, she had her mother's powers. So the Holy Mother taught her daughter the ways of life and healing. Then when the day came that the daughter had learned all that the Holy Mother was willing to teach, the Holy Mother left.

Several generations passed away as the daughter worked to bless the people the way her mother had, but as the years went by the daughter grew to understand why her mother had left. For though the daughter had grown through her childhood like any other, as time went by she seemed to age less and less; until the day came that she aged not at all. But all around her the people she had grown to love, her children and her children's children, grew old. Though she did all she could to prolong their lives, she could not stop time or death.

Then one day a great, great, great granddaughter was born who had green eyes, and so like her mother had done for her, she taught her grandchild to use her gifts to bless the people. Then when the granddaughter had learned all that the Holy Mother's daughter could teach her, she too left. Many in the tribe believed that she had gone to find her mother, and to this day this cycle has been repeated. Now Jade was being taught these things too.

Jade sighed. She knew she should be getting back to weeding the garden. Her grandmother would be back at any time and would not be pleased to see her just sitting there. Standing, Jade brushed herself off and made her way back out into the garden to kill the weeds. *Stinking weeds*, she thought. It seemed to never end. For each one killed, another sprang up to take its place.

She pulled on her leather gloves and got back to work. She did love the part of gardening where she could help things grow and witness the energies of life flowing through the plants that she helped sow; there was peace and contentment in it. She was also very proud of the fact that her and her grandmother's garden produced many more vegetables and healing plants than anybody else's. Even powerful earth and water crafters could not produce so much. She just didn't like all the weeding, hoeing, and other labor. But honestly, who did? Out of the corner of her eye she noticed that one of the tomato plants had muddy brown veins running throughout its aura.

"That wasn't there yesterday," she mumbled to herself.

Bending over, she examined the plant and saw tiny brown spots on its leaves which confirmed what was in the aura. A choke vine weed she must have missed the other day was growing up and around the plant. *Well that explains the plant's sickness,* she thought. Frowning in concentration she studied the plant's rather simple aura while running her hand over one of the leaves with brown spots. Then she studied the choke vine's aura.

The weed's aura was wrapped around the aura of the plant much like the physical weed was wrapped around it. Both the weed and its aura appeared to be trying to strangle the life from the plant. Her attention fixed firmly on the weed, she placed a finger on it and began to siphon off the colors of green and white from its aura; the colors of its physical life's energies. As she was siphoning off its energies, the weed began to wither and die. When she had siphoned off the last remaining bit, the weed disintegrated into a fine powder that floated to the earth around the plant.

Then she took one of the plant's leaves into her hand and began to pour all of the energies she had taken from the weed into the plant, adding to the plant's life energies. As she did this, the muddy brown streaks slowly began to shrink until they disappeared altogether. She looked over the plant again but this time all the brown spots were gone. The plant had even grown a couple of inches, its leaves now vibrant and healthy. She had a slight tremor in her hands from the effort she had just expended, having accidently given the plant some of her own energies as well.

She made her way down the rows, siphoning off the weeds' energies and transferring the energies to all the vegetables and healing herbs in the garden. She made sure she was more careful, even keeping a little bit of the siphoned-off energy for herself. Still the work was very tiring, and it didn't take long until the sweat started running down her face again. She wiped her forehead with the back of her arm; though it didn't do her much good since her arm was just as sweaty as her forehead. Some of the sweat dropped down into her eyes, stinging them. *Good thing I got back up when I did,* she thought, because she could now see her grandmother walking towards her. She had been gone most of the day in a closed meeting with High Chief Hiamovi and Alo, the Areli's head Spirit Guide.

Jade straightened, sighing when she saw her grandmother's face; she looked in her mid-twenties despite the fact that her grandmother was over three hundred years old. She did not look happy—in fact, Grandmother looked thunderous. When her grandmother looked like that, people tended to walk small. She was a formidable looking woman; beautiful, but formidable. She wasn't really all that tall but it seemed to Jade that her grandmother towered over them all. Sinopa, her grandmother's totem, was a sleek fire-tailed fox from the lands far north. He trotted next to her, tongue hanging as he panted.

She stopped a couple of feet away, putting her hands upon her hips, lips pursed, foot tapping. She seemed to study Jade for an eternity. Finally her face softened. "What am I going to do with you, child?"

"Do with me, Grandmother?" Jade said, feigning innocence.

"Don't play dumb. It doesn't become you."

Jade knew what that meeting had been about. "I'm not ready Grandmother. Don't make me go." She could feel the panic rising within her chest.

"You have to, Jade. You have put this day off long enough. If you were anyone else you would have been put out of the tribe the first time you refused to go."

Jade licked her lips, eyes glancing from side to side as if looking for somewhere to escape. She knew what her grandmother said was true. But she was who she was, after all. They couldn't kick her out of the tribe. They just couldn't.

"Jade, if it was just Chief Hiamovi saying you must go I would refuse because I believe you should not be pushed into this, but it isn't just Hiamovi who says you must go. Alo says you must go also. He has had a vision." This she said with a kind of finality.

"What did he see in his vision?"

At this question a look of profound worry crossed her grandmother's face and this more than anything scared her. If it was something that worried her grandmother enough to actually show on her face it must be downright scary. Jade had seen her grandmother calm and collected even under the most strenuous of circumstances.

"Never mind, that it is for me to worry about for now. Go get cleaned up," she said. Then when Jade just stood there her grandmother started making shooing motions towards her. "Go on, get."

"But Grandmother…" Jade protested.

"No buts! I said go!"

With that Jade turned on her heels and marched up to their large house, fists clenched and tears streaming down her face.

\*\*\*\*

Jade lay on her bed weeping tears of anger, frustration, and fear; thoughts racing through her head. The jungle had killed her parents and now it would kill her. Her own tribe, her own people, had turned against her. She would run away except that would require her to do exactly what she was trying to avoid, going back into the jungle. It wasn't like she could hide in the village because they would probably find her before the day was even done. She felt trapped. She was trapped. To run away—jungle. To refuse to go and be exiled—jungle. To go on her spirit walk—jungle. Every choice, every option led her straight into the jungle.

She'd known this day was coming but why did it have to be today? Didn't they know that it was the anniversary of her mother's death? Her death and the abandonment of her father still plagued her. It was something Jade could never forget, or forgive. It lurked in the back of her mind, waiting to strike like a deadly viper. The jungle claimed her parents and now it was going to claim her.

Sometime during her waking nightmare Jade became aware of her grandmother coming into her room and kneeling down beside her bed, slowly stroking her hair while making quiet soothing sounds. Sinopa, having jumped up onto the bed, nuzzled at her hand to get her to pet him. Slowly the weeping gentled and Jade began to pet Sinopa lightly, scratching behind his ears. Though she was not bonded to him she could sense his love and concern for her. Between that and the mild aura manipulation that her grandmother deftly worked upon her, she felt her fear retreat a little.

"Grandmother, what am I going to do?" Jade murmured.

"You are going to do what you must. I would not be forcing you into this if I didn't believe it was absolutely necessary. I will say this: you are far stronger then you know. You can do this," she said with a quiet, calm authority.

"Grandmother... Is it because of Alo's vision that I have to go now?" she whispered.

"Yes," her grandmother said simply.

"Will you tell it to me?" Jade said while she turned and sat up, swinging her feet over the edge of the bed to face her grandmother.

"No, it is Alo's to tell." She took Jade's hand in hers, eyes locking onto Jade's, seeing into her deepest being. "I will tell you this. You will survive your spirit walk. Alo says that this part of his vision is certain."

Jade felt her fear retreat a little more. If there was one thing Jade knew for certain it was that her grandmother never lied, and if Alo said he was sure, then he was sure. He had never been wrong as far as Jade knew. *Yes, yes I can do this*. Knowing that she would be successful and that she would return changed things. It didn't take away all her fear, but it was enough.

Her grandmother took out a small white cloth from one of her many pockets and handed it to Jade. Taking it, Jade wiped the tears from her eyes and face then blew her nose noisily into the cloth. This helped, drying the rest of her tears.

"Come on, let's get you ready," she said as she stood up from her crouching position; then helped Jade stand up also. Jade looked out her window and noticed that the day was almost through. She could see the sun peeking out through the storm clouds as it slowly sank below the tips of the trees, its powerful aura of light and life fading behind the horizon.

# CHAPTER 2

The bonfires burned bright, their light reflecting off the broken clouds above. The sun she had enjoyed earlier in the day had been a rare treat during the rainy season. Then as if in response to her plight the clouds had moved in as she had fled to her room. The storm that followed poured down sheets of rain while she had wept. The rain had been fierce but brief and the rest of the evening had been blessedly dry.

It had been several hours since Jade and her grandmother had left their home, and now it was truly deep in the night. While Jade did not require as much sleep as her fellow tribe members, she still felt tired. The events of the day seemed to weigh her down almost as if a mountain rested upon her back. Still, the festivities were incredibly impressive; any time her people gathered in large numbers it was a sight to behold. And because this was the Capital of the Areli Nation, it was no surprise when a few thousand people turned out for her send-off.

The Areli's Capital sat in the heart of the Megiddo Jungle with villages stretching every few miles from north to south. The villages were protected by the Great Wall, a towering barricade of stone that climbed over a hundred feet into the heavens. The wall spanned over a hundred miles, separating the east from the west.

The Areli stood as sentinels forming a living barricade to hold back the hordes of the hated Belial, and their Kaga masters (demons that possessed human flesh), from the rest of the world. It was a task given to them by the Holy Mother, and they would sacrifice their lives to see that task fulfilled.

Jade sat on a hard wooden chair with no cushions or padding for comfort. Even worse, she was placed up on a stage that held the three thrones of tribal leadership where everybody could see her. In the center sat High Chief Hiamovi's chair, the Phoenix throne. The feathers of the Phoenixes upon the chair burned fiercely. To the right of the Phoenix throne sat her grandmother, Holy Daughter, and head of the Office of Medicine. Her chair, the Dragon throne, was shaped with fierce golden dragons. Flames of crimson, chipped obsidian, sapphire, and emerald poured from their mouths. To the left of Chief Hiamovi sat Alo's chair, the Throne of Ravens. The throne was formed of ravens so black that the chair seemed to suck in all light around them, making the man in his radiant white robes who sat upon it shine all the brighter. Each throne was crafted from a form of magic that Jade did not understand. The creatures upon the thrones seemed to move as if alive and every once in a while Jade swore one of the dragons would turn its head and look at her. The thrones were truly magnificent works of art, and to Jade's eyes they radiated compelling magical auras. Auras she had never seen anywhere else. She didn't know what the auras meant and when she asked her grandmother about them she was always told that she wasn't ready for that knowledge yet.

So, Jade sat small, hoping that she wouldn't be noticed next to the three unquestionable figures of power sitting on their thrones.

Jade hoped in vain. After all, it was her party. A small table full of food sat before her, which she picked at without much appetite. She knew she should be eating all that she could because after this she was expected to fast throughout her entire spirit walk. This wouldn't have been that big of a deal for her except that her grandmother forbade her from taking any energy from, well, anything. That would be the true trial for Jade because as long as she could remember she had felt the ebb and flow of the energies of life around her—taking a little here, a little there. This was the reason she needed so little food and sleep compared to the other people of her tribe.

Jade wasn't allowed to speak at all and only Alo, as the Spirit Guide, was allowed to speak to her. From the moment Jade sat down in her chair and the feast began, she ceased to be a person in the eyes of the tribe. Instead she became a spirit and would remain so until she returned to her people with her totem, finally becoming a true member of their society. Still, everywhere Jade's eyes wandered, she was confronted with stares. Some were warm and friendly while others not so much. To Jade, those eyes said "Who is this girl that can spit upon our traditions and not be cast out from among us? Who is she to be so far above us?" Those eyes more than others made Jade sink within herself, wishing she could be truly invisible. Jade did admit to herself that she was enjoying watching the tribal members and their totems perform. Everyone was trying to outdo everyone else by using the physical gifts granted to them from their bonds to their totems.

Honaw and Honon, twin brothers each bonded to giant twin She Rock Bears, had drawn a large crowed as they wrestled. Their bears stood quietly by, each with what looked like amusement on their faces. And while Jade knew that this was a friendly bout, it looked and sounded ferocious. Honon connected with a punch that would have reduced a large stone to rubble, yet Honaw acted as if the punch had no effect at all upon him. Faster than a blink, Honaw was swooping in, grabbing his brother by his pants and shirt, picking him up then slamming him down with such force that the people around them could feel the ground shudder. Then Honon kicked up with both legs, hitting his twin in the stomach and sending him flying over fifteen feet away onto his back. Both brothers climbed to their feet, looking at the other then breaking into boisterous laughter; the people around them joined in. Jade always thought that if a person was strong enough to rip a tree from the ground and decided to break it on one of the brother's backs they would just laugh, thinking it was some grand game.

Chaska, High Chief Hiamovi's eldest son at age seventeen, and second son Menewa who was sixteen, had devised a game for themselves and a group of younger warriors. Both sons had Fire Eagle totems like their father. The Fire Eagles were little cousins to the Phoenix, a legendary creature of an Elder Race from the Second Kingdom. Chaska, future High Chief of the Areli people, and Menewa, future leader of all the tribal warriors, were furious competitors, and had proven themselves to be great warriors in battle.

Their totems had formed rings of fire by flying in circles in the air while jets of flame streamed out behind them. The rings started fairly low to the ground then climbed higher. The higher the rings climbed the smaller in size they grew. The goal of the game was for the brothers and the young group of warriors, each with some form of a bird for a totem, to jump through the rings, starting with the lowest. If a warrior was burned while going through a ring he was considered "out" and was forced to sit and watch in disgrace.

The game was now down to three contestants: Chaska, Menewa, and a female warrior from another village. The three soared higher and higher, making beautiful acrobatic twists and turns, threading the rings like a seamstress threads a needle. Suddenly, the unknown warrior misjudged her jump by a mere inch, burning her arm. When she landed she turned and shook her fist at the ring that burned her as if it were at fault. As she walked to the crowd of contestants that had fallen out of the competition before her, she was met with both jeers and hearty back slaps.

Now it was just Chaska and Menewa. Not that anyone was surprised. It looked as if the brothers had taken flight as they climbed higher and higher. Jade found that she had been holding her breath as each brother completed yet another ring; then finally at roughly forty feet in the air Chaska brushed the side of a ring nearly the same size and diameter as he was. Menewa smiled in triumph; as the smaller of the two, he had a definite advantage in making this jump. Menewa stood and studied the ring he was about to attempt, then scooted back a few feet to give himself a running start. With a few powerful strides Menewa took flight. It was breath-taking. He cleared the ring of fire then twisted and flipped, landing with slightly bent knees, a small puff of dirt rising up into the air. The dirt, usually damp during the rainy season, had been dried out by Chaska and Menewa earlier. They had poured out waves of flames from their hands to dry it, giving them surer footing for the game.

Chaska scowled at his brother but Jade could see bright colors flash through his emotional aura displaying, at least to her eyes, the pure joy and pride Chaska felt for his younger brother. As Menewa jumped high into the air, punching at the heavens, a large burst of flame exploded from his hand to momentarily add its brilliance to that of the bonfires, lighting up the night sky. The young warriors swarmed in around Chaska and Menewa, laughing and cheering, while pride and respect swirled throughout their auras for these two future leaders of the Areli Nation.

Jade felt herself blush as she gazed down at Menewa. *Man, he is beautiful*, she thought. While she was looking down at him, his gaze turned to catch her staring at him. Jade's cheeks blazed red in a deep blush. Quickly averting her eyes, she saw for the briefest of moments a rose-colored shade swirl around Menewa's aura. *Great, I've embarrassed him. This is the third time in two weeks that he has caught me staring at him. He's probably thinking 'Oh great! Chicken Girl is ogling me again!'* she thought sarcastically to herself. She knew he thought her a coward.

After she turned her gaze away from Menewa, pretending she hadn't been staring at him, she noticed Alo smiling at her. He was leaning back into his throne, leg thrown up over one of the arms, looking for all the world to be totally and completely relaxed. His totem, a raven named Catori, stood on his head as if it were a perfectly ordinary place for her to roost. Most of the time Jade felt like Alo was an affectionate uncle and she his favorite niece, but today she was quite mad at him, feeling that he was mostly to blame for her current predicament.

"What?!" she snapped despite the fact that she wasn't supposed to talk. She never was good at doing what she was supposed to.

"I think he likes you," he said with that insufferable smile on his face.

Jade blushed again. Alo often times could perceive people's innermost thoughts and feelings, and he wasn't shy about talking about them regardless of people's discomfort and embarrassment. He usually acted as if he didn't notice how it made people squirm. It didn't help that Alo was known to be a prankster. Jade had even heard her grandmother call him the most irreverent spirit guide she had ever known. And that was saying a lot because her grandmother had lived for so long and had known many spirit guides. She had said it with affection, however, so Jade new that she really did like him and felt he was a true friend.

"Ha, ha, real funny Alo."

Alo just shrugged as if to say, "Fine, don't believe me."

After that Jade just sat and continued to watch the games while trying very hard not to look at anyone too long. Especially Menewa—if he caught her staring at him again it would be disastrous. The feasting and games progressed throughout the night until the sky began to lighten and the new day approached. Alo stood and held out his hand to Jade's grandmother, Kendra.

"Are you ready, Kendra?" he asked with a rare expression of solemnity.

"I am," she answered with a faraway look in her eyes. Taking his hand, they stepped forward to the front of the stage.

# CHAPTER 3

“Oh remember, remember, brothers and sisters. Remember our elder parents and their sacrifices that reach through the ages to touch our lives even now. Remember our Holy Mother and the great chief Chikasha and the salvation of our people.” Kendra’s voice rang out, echoing in the ears of all who were there. Her memories combined with Alo’s vision magic pierced the people’s hearts and caused visions to open up within their minds…

*Jade saw herself as the Holy Mother flying on her Golden Dragon; seeing a world slowly blackening as a blanket of pure evil spread across the land. Then she saw them. A people brave enough to stand against the shadow. They fought bravely, but slowly and surely they gave ground before the horde of tainted men and demons as black as the Nethernight. They strove to turn back the darkness, but the Holy Mother could see the despair in their eyes, knowing that the end was drawing near. She knew if she did not help them the world would be lost. So from the heavens she came and landed amongst them. Her dragon sent wave after wave of magic flames into the darkness, and the shadows screamed in agony. She drew a sword of pure light that pushed back the darkness.*

*For three years they battled, and to strengthen her allies she granted unto them the magic of totems by writing upon their breast in Heavenly Script. She named them the Areli, meaning the Lions of God, for they fought like avenging angels.*

*As the Areli people fought beside her they found that their wounds would heal mere moments after receiving them. Their fatigue washed away when they grew too weary to continue. The totems that came and bonded to them gave them powers they barely could understand. With each bloody step they pushed back the darkness, forcing it back across the barren savannah of Zuya, and into the jungles that would be named "Megiddo" for the great and terrible battle that would take place at its heart. Chikasha was always by her side and she grew to love him, mortal though he was.*

*Whenever she found herself weakening she only had to look at Chikasha and see the love he had for her and she was strengthened, and in return the Areli people where strengthened. Then in the heart of the Megiddo Jungle a devil rode forth out of the darkness upon the back of a great dragon that had been twisted by the devil's dark arts turning its scales black. The devil trumpeted its challenge. Mounting her great Golden Dragon, the Holy Mother drew her sword and went to meet the devil on the field of battle.*

*She battled the devil and with each blow they exchanged, reality trembled and the world screamed. She slew the black dragon and destroyed the devil's mortal frame. Then in front of all, the devil was revealed for what it was. It seemed a creature of smoke and flame standing some fifteen feet tall; its form a mock parody of a man. It formed a sword as dark as her sword was light.*

*The Holy Mother stood before the devil, her Golden Dragon lying broken and bleeding upon the earth. The taint of the Nether coursed in his veins. The devil's eyes burned with eternal hatred and rage as they looked upon the Holy Mother. Then with a mighty cry that caused mortal ears to bleed, the devil charged her. Though it towered over her, she withstood its blows for a time. Then she felt herself give way before it as the devil drew strength from her. Just when she was about to fall, her sword broken at its hilt, Chikasha came to her aid. He fought with a strength and fierceness she had never before beheld in a mortal; he seemed driven beyond all reason. He met the devil stroke for stroke and forced it back away from her. Standing between her and the darkness, he took a blow that smote him to the earth. Rage like she had never felt before blossomed within her chest as she saw her love fall.*

*She stood and reached out to the life of the world, seizing it, drawing it to her, and with all the hate and rage she felt for the darkness she formed a Sword of Life, a Worldblade, and plunged it into the heart of the devil. Reality warped and twisted and the world trembled nigh unto death. The devil was slain but still disaster loomed, for in her rage she had taken too much life from the world and it was dying. Quickly and deftly she strove to give the life back to the world, stopping its death.*

*Tears of light flowed down her face as she turned to her love, fearing the worst, but Chikasha was still alive. His totem, a mighty Phoenix, held his death at bay though he was fading fast. With desperation she ran to him and kneeling, pulled him into her arms. Weeping her tears of light, she struggled to heal him just as mightily as she had tried to save the earth. His wound, filled with the nether from the sword of the devil, defied her attempts. But with each fall of her tears she was able to heal him a little more until she saw him smiling—looking up at her, meeting her eyes. Her tears turned from anger and sorrow to joy. Her love lived and the darkness had been driven back for now.*

*The years passed and she knew despair once more for*

*Chikasha, her beloved, slowly grew old and died. Still she found some solace in the children he had given her, especially their daughter who had green eyes just like her...*

The vision slowly faded from Jade's mind as the final words rang forth from her grandmother's mouth. "And so she left, giving us the charge to forever stand against the shadow so it would never again threaten this world and its people."

Jade's knees felt weak and her heart felt sick. *How was she ever going to live up to that? She couldn't; she was a coward.*

# CHAPTER 4

With the ending of her grandmother's words, the sun broke over the horizon, bringing in the new day. It was time for Jade to begin her Spirit Walk. One by one the people turned and walked away until all that remained was High Chief Hiamovi, her grandmother, and Alo. Breaking the custom of silence, her grandmother enveloped her in a big hug and whispered, "I love you."

With that, Grandmother and Hiamovi walked off the stage, leaving her with Alo. His raven cawed thrice, and while the sound of it was haunting and other-worldly, it did not unnerve her. Instead, it steadied her. Alo came to her and offered his arm, as if they were simply going for a walk. She took it, and he led her off of the stage toward a path that would take them to the jungle on the east side of the village.

They walked in silence, each second stretching into eternity, until Jade couldn't take it anymore. "Alo," she said, nerves evident in the sound of her voice.

"Hmm?" he said a little absently, while glancing up at Catori circling high overhead.

"Grandmother said that you had a vision about me."

"Among other things, yes," he said.

"Grandmother said that you saw me return from my Spirit Walk."

"She told you that, huh?" Alo rubbed his chin as if in deep thought.

"Yes... Is it true, did you see that?"

"Tell me this Jade, has your grandmother ever lied to you?"

"No."

"Then why do you need me to confirm or deny what she has said?"

"Well you don't. Not really. I'm just scared, that's all."

"I know," he said, his voice gentle as he reached down and patted her hand in a comforting way. "It's okay to be scared Jade."

"The Holy Mother was never scared."

"Ha, did you not just see the same vision that everyone else did?" This he said rhetorically.

"Well yes, I suppose," she replied anyway.

"Then you did not see."

"Wait, what do you mean? You know I saw the same vision as everyone else."

"Yes Jade, you saw the same vision, but you did not see. If you had truly seen, then you would have realized that the Holy Mother was often times terrified, but she did what she felt she had to despite her fear—just like you are doing now. I am proud of you," he said, smiling. With this they reached the edge of the village and the beginning of the jungle, for the eastside was not protected by a wall.

"You will come back to us," Alo said.

With that, he extracted his arm from Jade's and gave her back a gentle push, propelling her towards the waiting darkness of the jungle. Jade gulped, closed her eyes, and took a deep breath. Opening them, she stepped into the jungle and it swallowed her whole.

****

The Megiddo Jungle was dark and dank, it having poured five times in the past three days, and Jade was exhausted. Her throat burned for lack of water, and her stomach ached for want of food. Three days of not touching the life energies around her. Of not feeling it flow through her.

She was ready to scream, or at least she would if she had the energy. She had known that it would be hard but she had never imagined it would be like this. She had never been more aware of just how much of a reflexive action it was for her to draw on the energies around her. Here a little, there a little. Taking tiny amounts from everything around; amounts so small that the individual would never miss it, but it added up.

So now she found that she had to consciously force herself not to, and that, more than anything, wore at her. The thirstier and hungrier she became, the stronger the urge grew. *I have to resist. I can do this.* She knew that the fasting had a purpose. It wasn't just tradition or some cruelty the elders came up with. It was because as the body weakened the spirit grew stronger. And bonding with a totem was done spirit to spirit. If her body was too strong it would interfere with her bonding. And then she would fail.

On top of the hunger, thirst, and growing urge to draw life energies from around her was the constant and ever-increasing fear. She had thought that her fear couldn't get any worse when she had first entered the jungle, but she had been wrong. It did get worse, much worse. No matter how many times she told herself that both Alo and Grandmother had promised her that she would be successful and return safely; she just couldn't believe it. Well, a part of her did believe it, or she would have run back screaming an untold number of times. A part of her marveled that she hadn't.

As she stood trembling in the damp jungle, her fear reached a climax. Her wild, maniacally beating heart bruised itself against her ribcage as it pounded within her chest. She found herself bent over, clutching at her knees as the weight of some unseen doom pressed down upon her, stealing her breath away. Then with a strength she hadn't known she possessed, she forced her back to straighten, and her lungs to breathe. And though her knees shook, she took a step, and then another. With each step she took, the fear diminished until she slipped into a blessedly numb state. For hours she walked like this, wandering ever-deeper into the jungle's depths. Then she heard voices.

Jade's heart jumped into her throat as panic swept over her. All the blessed numbness was gone, replaced by stark, raving terror. She needed to run. She needed to get away from here, because the second Jade heard those voices she knew they were not Areli for they spoke in the language of the hated Belial. What were they doing behind the Great Wall, and how did they get here? Were they planning to attack a village from behind? Before panic completely overran her ability to think, Jade looked around, and noticed a small animal's den that had been dug down under the roots of a particularly huge tree. Jade ran for the den and snuggled down into it. She feared the Belial even more than she feared what could have made the den. The voices were coming closer.

Jade scooted down into the den a little more to make herself as small as possible while mashing her face down into the dirt, praying that they would pass her by. They were now standing not ten feet from her and she just knew that they would hear her heart. It roared within her chest, drowning out parts of the Belial's words.

"General Akecheta said that she would be here."

"Maybe she was until she heard you stomping around like a bloody Stone Bear."

"Hey, don't blame it on me. Besides, I don't know if I want to be the one to find her."

"What, are you scared of a little girl who doesn't even have her totem yet?"

"That's not fair! You know she is one of those witch women who have green eyes."

*Me! They are looking for me! Heavens above protect me,* she wailed silently, biting down on her arm to keep herself from screaming aloud. She tasted blood in her mouth. Her mind reeled at the import of their words. Tears rolled down her cheeks, leaving little streamers of mud.

Their voices became quieter as they moved further away. She was too scared to run. Too scared to move. Too scared to think. So she just stayed huddled in the small hole stolen from some poor animal. She wept silently, fearing that any sound would give her away and the Belial, the murderers, would find her. The day darkened and it rained again, hiding the fact that night had fallen.

Jade didn't notice the sun rising in the morning or setting yet again the next evening. Time blurred and everything became surreal, except her fear, which burned her and ate at her mind.

# CHAPTER 5

On the fifth day of her spirit walk she felt a warm blanket of peace wrapping about her. Her silent racking sobs slowly settled, then stilled, as her muscles unclenched, causing almost blinding pain with her first deliberate movements. Her eyes, having been crusted over from mud and salty tears, strained to open. Then she became aware of it. A presence; it was all around her. It was in her, and with it came peace.

*"Hush little one. Why do you cry?"* The words reverberated within Jade's mind. Words felt as well as heard. The voice was deep and rich, filled with confidence and power.

"They have come for me," she whispered out loud.

*"Who has come for you?"* The voice echoed again within Jade's mind.

"The Belial; they killed my parents and now they have come for me."

*"Belial?"* The voice said, accompanied by sounds of sniffing the air. *"No Belial. Too bad really; I am a little hungry, and they*

*sound tasty."*

Jade found herself smiling, despite her fears and the pain that was laced throughout her every muscle.

*"Well, out of the hole little one so I can get a good look at you."*

Jade rubbed at her eyes and forced them open for the first time in days. Then she looked up and her heart about stopped. Above her was a head of a truly massive midnight black cat, and it looked to be smiling at her. Her fear tried to come rushing back but it was blocked as if it had run headlong into a mountain. The face backed up from the opening. *"Come on little one, let me see you."*

Slowly, shakily, Jade climbed from the little animal's den to stand before this monstrous beast. Yet she did not fear it. In fact, she found herself feeling remarkably good. Her hunger and thirst felt distant and unimportant, and the stiffness and pain she had felt in her muscles was fading, being replaced with what could only be called strength. With a deep and quick breath, Jade steeled herself, and looked up, and up. Even standing at her full height she had to look up to meet the eyes of this glorious being—eyes a deep crystalline blue.

All fear forgotten, Jade just stood and marveled as she became more aware of him. It wasn't just that she could see him with her eyes. She could feel him inside of her, just as she knew he could feel her inside of him, and though his fur was as black onyx, his aura was an intense white that crackled with energy and radiated outward—pushing back the darkness, both in the world around them, and in Jade's heart and mind.

*"You are huge,"* she said telepathically, using the newly created bond between them to do so, and indeed he was by far the biggest cat she had ever seen.

*"And you are little, little one,"* he chuckled while sitting back on his haunches, his voice a rich bass.

*"What is your name?"* Jade thought in a rush, but even as she asked she knew that he was her courage. *"Courage, you're my courage."*

*"If that is what you wish to call me, then by all means, I shall be your Courage,"* he said, still chuckling.

Tentatively Jade reached up, standing on her tiptoes, and touched Courage lightly on the face. Then growing bolder, she moved forward, wrapping both arms as far as they would go around his neck, and buried her face in his shoulder. He smelled of earth and ozone. The way the world smells just after a violent storm, or maybe he was the storm. His muscles were like boulders —hard and unyielding. Yet his fur was soft and silky. He was a being of contradictions. She belonged to him, and he belonged to her. She felt whole for the first time since she lost her parents.

Courage purred in contentment and joy washed over her. Lightning flashed and sheets of water started to fall. Jade laughed. Stepping back away from Courage she noticed for the first time just how filthy she had become. Her clothing was ruined but she didn't care. Looking up into the sky she let the rain wash away the rest of the fear and grime that clung to her. She felt remade; still her, just a little better. Taking a deep breath, Jade let her mind relax. She reached out to the life all around her, allowing herself to connect with it again.

Courage perked up as if he felt the same jolt of energy. His purring became even louder, almost forceful. *"This thing you do. It is wonderful."*

Jade agreed with him. It was a part of her just like Courage was now a part of her. And it had been agonizing to go so long without it.

*"Courage, what kind of cat are you? You look like a giant cross between a tiger and a panther, or a lion and a lynx,"* Jade asked quizzically. He seemed to somehow change, yet stay the same, all at the same time.

*"A cross between a tiger and a panther?"* he huffed, sounding offended. But Jade was able to make out amusement in his aura, even though it was confusing, it being like no other aura she had ever seen. And she smelled amusement. Jade sniffed the air. *Yes,*

*that is definitely amusement,* she thought to herself. Jade didn't know how she knew. She just did, and while it was odd to her that she was now able to do this, she knew that the bonding imparted gifts to them. Often times the person would gain attributes that their totem had and vice versa. And sometimes whole new abilities would manifest. This usually took time. The longer a person was bonded to their totem the stronger the gifts became. Since their bonding was newly made it would take time before they would fully know the gifts they would receive from it.

*"I am not a cross between a tiger and a panther, nor a lion and a lynx. I am of an Elder Race. I am Therion,"* he said proudly. *"The races of your realm are nothing but weaker, younger descendants of me."*

Jade was stunned. Courage was of an Elder Race... but Phoenixes and Dragons were of the Elder Races. Elder Races were believed by some to be more elemental than physical. They were beings of pure magic that for some reason had chosen to take a physical form. Jade did not know if that was true, but looking at Courage she could believe it. What she did know for sure—what she had learned from her grandmother—was that creatures of the elder races existed in a higher realm or kingdom than they did. The only reason they knew anything about them at all was because of the Holy Mother—for she too came from such a place. *That probably explains his strange aura,* she thought.

*"Why? Why me?"* Jade said with wonder.

*"I.... felt it... the heavens felt it when you were born, and I could feel your need of me. It pulled at me, and so I have come."* Jade could feel his curiosity and confusion at this. Courage snorted, stood up, and shook his body from head to tail, flinging water everywhere though it was just swallowed up in the rain. *"Come little one, climb up on my back and I will carry you home."* Courage crouched down so that Jade would have an easier time climbing up on his back.

*"You want me to ride on your back?"*

*"Yes you are exhausted; I can feel your hunger and thirst."*

*"I don't feel tired, and I hardly feel hungry anymore. Well, I might be a little thirsty,"* she said, having taken some of her hair, sucking the water from it.

Courage growled.

*"Okay, I'm getting on,"* Jade said, grunting as she struggled to climb up onto his back. *"I've had easier times climbing boulders."*

Courage just laughed.

"Don't laugh at me," Jade huffed out loud. *"There, I'm on,"* she said, settling into place behind his broad shoulder blades. Jade clenched her knees tight as he stood in one fluid motion, his muscles rippling beneath. *"Uh, Courage?"*

*"Yes,"* Courage said, his voice rich with amusement.

*"I am completely lost,"* she admitted.

*"That is simple enough to fix. Which way have you been walking?"*

*"I... left the village on the east side,"* she said timidly.

*"Have you walked in a straight line?"*

*"I think so. I could be wrong; it is pretty easy to get turned around out here."*

*"That's okay, little one, I will find it."*

*"How?"* Jade asked curiously.

*"By heading west, for starters."* Courage said with a loud rumbling laugh that filled Jade's mind.

# CHAPTER 6

They flew through the jungle. Courage raced at impossible speeds, finding his way through the thick jungle foliage with ease. Jade knew that it should have been difficult to stay on Courage's back, especially at the break-neck pace he set. Yet it felt natural. It was as if they were one with each other—his movements where the essence of fluidity, grace, and raw power. But after only a few hours Courage stopped.

*"You need rest, little one."*

Jade, too tired to argue, slid off his back and stumbled to the ground. They were in a small clearing with a gently flowing stream running through it. During the rainy season the jungle was filled with thousands of streams such as this, though many were polluted with parasites and other things that could make a person sick. Jade crawled to the stream and used her second sight to check the water. It was clean. Cupping her hands together, Jade began scooping the water up to her mouth. She did this for a while, savoring the sweet taste of the pure water.

While the water felt good on her dry, burning throat, sharp painful cramps hit her stomach. Apparently it was angry with her for making it go so long without food or water. Drawing on some more energy from the life around her she was able to settle her stomach somewhat. And with that settling she realized she was ravenous.

*"You need to eat. Gather some wood for a fire and I'll be right back with something for you,"* Courage said to her, then bounded off into the jungle, disappearing from sight. Sighing, Jade forced herself to stand and began to gather wood, trying to find some that wasn't a soggy mess.

Jade was constantly pulling energies from around her to keep herself awake and moving. Dropping the sixth armload down on the pile, Jade grumbled, "Now what?" It wasn't like she had been allowed to bring anything with her as useful as a firestarter, and she seriously doubted that she could get a fire going with this waterlogged wood anyway.

She felt shame for not having learned to channel the essences. If she had bothered to learn even the simplest of firecraftings she could have had a fire going in no time.

*Maybe Courage will have an idea,* she thought as she laid the wood, getting it ready to light. When she finished she plopped down on the ground to wait for Courage to come back. She didn't have to wait very long before he walked back into the clearing carrying a rabbit in his mouth. He dropped it on the ground at her feet.

*"Why is there no fire going little one?"*

"Because I don't have anything to start a fire," Jade said out loud, crossly, her hunger and fatigue finally getting the better of her. Jade felt close to breaking. Courage looked at her a little curiously. He then stepped over to the wood Jade had laid for a fire, and simply breathed upon it. Steam started to rise off of the wood as it dried out. Then a small flame sprang to life. Courage breathed upon the wood once more and the small flame became a roaring fire.

"How did you do that?" Jade whispered.

*"You do not know?"* Courage asked in surprise.

"No! I do not know! If I did I would have already started it!" Her eyes welled up with tears that threatened to burst free.

Ignoring Jade's outburst he said patiently, *"Then I shall have to teach you, but not now. Now you must eat, and then you shall sleep."*

Jade took a deep breath and wiped at her eyes. She squelched the shame that had caused her outburst, knowing that it was not fair to Courage. "Sorry," she mumbled, then reached down and picked up the rabbit. "Thanks." With that she walked over to the stream and gutted and skinned the rabbit, getting it ready to cook.

Courage lay down by the fire and began cleaning his considerable fur, purring contentedly. Jade finished preparing the rabbit and skewered it with a thick green stick to roast it over the fire.

"Courage, there is something wrong. The world is getting darker the further we head west. It is as if we are heading directly into a storm." Goosebumps pebbled Jade's skin as she thought of this. Courage stood up, and walked over and laid down next to her, letting her lean up against him.

*"This thing I sense too,"* he replied solemnly. They sat quietly just enjoying each other's company. The rabbit finished cooking and Jade carefully pulled its flesh apart, trying not to burn her fingers and her mouth. She was too hungry to let it cool. As ravenous as she was, her stomach still wasn't very happy with her —it seeming to have forgotten how to work properly. Still Jade felt a little better getting the warm food into her. Then with grease still coating her hands and chin, Jade rested her head against Courage feeling his deep rumbling purr. Sleep stole her away. A deep yet troubled sleep.

She dreamed of a storm that raged all around her. It was a living thing that desired to crush her. Just as she was sure she would be consumed by it, Courage appeared beside her. He shined brighter than the sun casting back the storm. He stood in defiance of it, bathing Jade in his light, keeping the storm from her. The darker the storm grew the brighter Courage shined. Courage let out a mighty roar and the storm faltered. It trembled as if in fear then it redoubled its efforts to take them. But Courage stood immoveable before it, roaring his defiance.

Jade awoke with a start. Her head, resting up against Courage, vibrated gently as he purred slowly and rhythmically, though Jade could tell he was awake also.

The dream still fresh within her mind, "Was it real?" she asked, looking up at a cloudy sky that promised rain. Fear troubled her voice.

*"It was."*

"You were there inside my dream?"

*"Your dream, my dream, they are the same. We are one,"* he said matter-of-factly.

"The storm, it hates us," she whispered.

*"It fears us too."* Courage replied.

"It wants me."

*"It will not have you!"* Courage snarled. His voice thundered in her mind.

Jade remembered Courage in her dream somehow holding back the storm, light radiating out from him. Her fear quieted a little.

*"It is time to go,"* Courage said.

Jade stood up and washed in the stream, scraping the grease from her hands and face. After she finished, Courage crouched, letting her climb up on his back. Once she was settled, Courage stood, then bounded off into the jungle, once more heading towards her home—heading towards the storm.

# CHAPTER 7

Kendra paced. The light, yet elegant, sky blue dress she wore flared each time she turned. The fabric, woven from the hair of the Shytan goat, was soft and breathed well in the humid climate. And though the room's temperature was regulated, Kendra's forehead and arms glistened sweat. The darkness had been gathering for days. She first noticed it the day before Jade left for her spirit walk. The same day Alo had his vision. The same day that Hiamovi had his first reports that the Belial were gathering for war. It had been a long time since the Belial had attacked in force, and it was no coincidence that they were doing so now.

The Belial were an evil people who delighted in bloodshed and murder; they worshipped devils and demons, and to be possessed was a great honor that would make them Kaga. The Kaga had terrible powers; fortunately possessions were not that common, and they tended to be with only minor demons. The more powerful the demon the greater the power it granted to the possessed, but devils were altogether different. Devils ruled over demons and their powers where unfathomable.

It was a devil that the Holy Mother had battled—a battle that nearly destroyed the world. There had only been two other devils to appear over the ages and with each one the Areli were almost destroyed. And both times it had taken the ultimate sacrifice given by the Holy Daughter to banish the devils. Thankfully there had been another Holy Daughter already living to take their place. Now there was a third. She felt its presence in the darkness but she had hoped she was wrong. When Alo told her his vision, that hope died. A devil walked the land once more.

At first it was little effort to hold back the darkness from her people, but the rate with which it was growing alarmed her. Now it was like holding up a mountain. A mountain that grew heavier by the minute. She knew that eventually it would grow so heavy that it would crush her. As the eldest Holy Daughter she held the rights of the Dragon Throne and through it, a special connection to her people. She was not connected to the individual—although with effort she could be—but to the Areli as a whole. She sensed their overall fears, needs, hopes and dreams. It was a bond that the Holy Mother had forged—an inheritance passed on to her daughter. A bond that had been passed down through the ages until now it rested upon her shoulders, and when the time was right she would pass the rights of the Dragon Throne to Jade.

That is, if the gathering darkness did not crush them all. It was like the darkness was a living thing, and she could feel its hate, a hate for all living things, especially for her and her people. Already she could not hold all of it back and she could sense her people falling sick. So far it was only the very old, but she knew that as she weakened and the darkness grew stronger it would gain ground step-by-step until all were consumed by it.

The darkness was like an insidious poison that not only attacked the person but the bond between them and their totems, and as the person weakened so did their bond. Their totems would become more and more animal-like until they reverted back to their original state. By the end, right before death, the bond would be severed and the person would face death truly alone; leaving their totems nothing but rabid animals that rampaged through the Areli. It was the bond between the Areli and their totems that made the people strong enough to hold back the hordes of Belial, thus keeping the rest of the world safe. That was why the darkness was so dangerous. It not only attacked the people, it ate away at the very thing that gave the people their power.

And so Kendra fought it. She fought it with everything she was. She knew that in the end she would fail, but not today; today she would stand strong. Today she would not be defeated. If only she could last long enough; long enough for the possibility of Alo's vision to come true. But the future was not written in stone—instead it was like a river with a thousand diverging streams and it was man's decisions that determined the path that they would take.

Alo's vision had given hope, but that hope was like a candle in a storm. So very dim and so easily snuffed out, and ultimately it rested on the shoulders of her precious granddaughter. She would gladly sacrifice herself but could she sacrifice Jade? For a second the hopelessness of the situation threatened to overwhelm her. She felt her eyes sting from the tears she held back. She had to be strong, for her people, for Jade, for all the things she loved and held dear. Sinopa, pacing along beside her, whined and nudged her hand, expressing his concern for her. She paused long enough to scratch behind his ears than began pacing one more.

"Kendra, could you stop pacing please. You're giving me a headache, and you are making Sparks restless," Hiamovi grumbled while reaching up and stroking his totem's chest. Only Hiamovi would give a fierce Fire Eagle a nickname like Sparks. Sparks lifted her beak so Hiamovi could stroke the silk-soft feathers under it.

Kendra stopped and looked at Hiamovi, readying a wicked retort, but it died on her lips when she saw him smiling at her. For a very serious man he had a very disarming smile. *How can he possibly smile at a time like this?* she thought. Then she looked beyond his smile and studied his aura. Yes, he was smiling but she could see the bone deep worry written across his soul. She tried to return his smile to let him know that she could see through his facade but still appreciated his attempt to comfort her.

With a sigh she walked around her chair and sat down. They had been moved off the stage and back to the People's Hall after Jade's send-off. She leaned back, resting her head. Taking three long breaths, she composed herself as was fitting for her station. It wouldn't be good for morale if people thought she was worried, or even worse, scared.

"She's been gone for seven days; no one's Spirit Walk lasts that long." Kendra cast her mind out, looking for Jade's presence once again, using precious energy that she really should have been using to hold back the darkness. She sensed nothing. She often couldn't where Jade was concerned. The child was remarkably good at hiding her presence from others. She did so reflexively, not realizing what she was doing. Kendra's foot started tapping again. She looked over at Alo; he sat staring off into some faraway place and time. With Kendra so busy fighting off the devil's magic it fell to Alo to spy out their enemies' whereabouts; at least where they would be in the near future. That way they could set ambushes and traps to decimate the Belial's numbers, demoralizing them and disrupting their leader's strategies, there-by playing to the Areli's strengths.

Pitched battles were never a good idea with the Belial simply because they outnumbered the Areli vastly. They were prolific breeders, the Belial. The women among them would often have twins or even triplets. If it wasn't for the fact that most of the Belial didn't have powers like the Areli they would have been overrun a long time ago. But, demons tended to only possess the most evil among them; where all Areli had powers granted to them through their bonds with their totems.

Suddenly, Alo lost that faraway look and breathed a sigh of relief. "Found her. She should be arriving here at the village in a very short time. She is moving incredibly fast."

So Alo was being derelict in his duties also. Kendra wondered how long he had been looking for Jade instead of studying the Belial's future movements. She couldn't blame him though. She knew that he cared almost as deeply for Jade as she did. Alo had been best friends with Jade's father. Losing him had been devastating, and he vowed to look after and protect Jade as his friend should have. So Alo played the role of uncle and Jade his favorite niece.

"Praise the heavens," Kendra whispered. Alo had said that Jade would be successful and return to them, and she knew that if Jade hadn't left when she did they would all be lost. This Alo had foretold. He had said that every other path led to disaster. Still, if Alo had been as nervous as she was it could only mean that he hadn't told her the full truth. If she didn't know Alo as well as she did, she would be furious; instead she swallowed her anger. She knew it was often Alo's way to only tell people the things that would help lead them down the path that Alo saw would bring them the most success and happiness.

They all stood quickly, Kendra practically jumping out of her seat. Alo straightened his flowing white robe and picked up his wooden staff. It was carved with ravens in flight, and crowned with an obsidian raven perched with its wings spread as if it was about to take flight. Catori launched herself off the back of Alo's chair and swiftly flew out the door. Alo, able to see through her eyes, hoped to be the first to see Jade's return home.

Hiamovi held out his gloved hand and Sparks leapt from the back of the chair to land upon his wrist. They followed Kendra and Alo through their private council room doors and made their way outside. Sinopa trotted beside Kendra with his nose and tail held high as if too dignified to show the same level of excitement and relief. But Kendra could feel his desire to run ahead with the others. He would have if Kendra hadn't been practically jogging herself.

# CHAPTER 8

The food and brief rest rejuvenated Jade, putting her in a far better mood, and because of this she was finally able to truly enjoy riding upon Courage's back. It was exhilarating. Her hair streamed behind her, and she laughed for the joy of it, all her fears of the growing darkness temporarily forgotten. She lifted up her arms, pretending that at any moment they would take flight. Courage leaped over and flowed around obstacles, never slowing pace. A thirty foot wide ravine appeared before them and with a mighty leap they soared through the air, clearing the ravine easily. The landing was so smooth Jade barely felt it. Jade laughed again for the thrill of it, and she could sense that Courage was enjoying himself as much as she was.

Then to Jade's disappointment they started to slow down until they came to a walk. *"Why are we slowing down?"*

*"Because we are nearly there little one."* Pride was evident in his tone at how fast he was able to traverse the jungle terrain.

*"Wow, already?"*

*"Yep."*

*"We are fast,"* Jade said with a broad grin splitting her face.

*"Yes we are."*

*"I can't wait to introduce you to everyone, especially my grandmother. She is going to love you."*

*"I sense from you that your grandmother is an amazing person."*

*"Yes she is,"* Jade said seriously.

*"I'll try not to eat her then."*

"Courage, what a terrible thing to say," she exclaimed out loud in mock severity while slapping him on his back. "And besides, you really shouldn't eat people, it's bad manners. Well, unless they're Belial," Jade said more seriously. "They're not really people."

Amusement and mirth flowed from Courage through the bond, bathing Jade in its warm glow.

The sounds of the village reached Jade's ears before the sight of it, and it did not sound peaceful. The village was obviously in an uproar. Jade's heart sank. With the darkness she sensed all around her she shouldn't have been surprised. She had hoped to find everything normal. A part of her, however, had known what she would find when she got home. The Areli were preparing for war.

The Areli were always skirmishing with the Belial. There was never peace between them. How could there be? But from the sound of it this... this was different. There would be no feast tonight to welcome her home and celebrate her becoming the newest member of the tribe.

She and Courage stepped into the village, and were greeted with the sight of her grandmother striding towards her with a smile splitting her face. Sinopa hurried along beside her, as sleek as ever. Alo and High Chief Hiamovi were hot on her heels. Alo was waving with his free hand excitedly, and even the severe Chief Hiamovi had a small smile on his face. Catori and Sparks raced out before them all. Jade laughed and held out her right arm so that Sparks could land on it. Sparks beat out Catori by a few seconds, landing on her arm delicately, careful not to pierce her skin with her talons. She ruffled her feathers and tiny bright sparks shimmered off of her body, but they had no real heat so as to not burn Jade. Catori plopped down on Jade's head and started pulling lightly on Jades hair with his beak. Jade laughed; this was better than any feast. She had been missed. She was loved.

*"Welcome home, Jade,"* Catori's voice resounded in Jade's head, the alto a complete contradiction to the raven's screeching caw.

"Thank you." Jade responded with pleased surprise. Totems rarely spoke to anyone other than the individual they bonded with.

"Now shoo; as it is I'm never going to get all the snarls out of my hair."

Chuckling, she hopped off her head and flapped over to Alo to land on his broad shoulder.

"Yes, welcome home Stix," Sparks said, her voice beautiful and elegant. Jade had no idea why Sparks called her Stix, but apparently she was just as fond of giving people nicknames as Hiamovi; which had always seemed odd to her because Hiamovi seemed so serious.

She once said this to her grandmother who had then laughed and said, "Hiamovi, serious?" Her grandmother must have found that funny because for the next few hours she would periodically shake her head and laugh, muttering to herself "Hiamovi, serious."

Sparks let forth a powerful cry that made Jade's right ear ring then launched herself into the air, her talons lightly scrapping Jade's arm. With a few flaps of her wings she alighted upon Hiamovi's gloved arm. Hiamovi was in his full battle armor crafted from liquid steel with his mighty two-handed Cinderblade strapped to his back along with all sorts of weapons placed upon his personage.

They stopped a few feet in front of her, allowing Jade and Courage to approach them as was fitting to their stations. Jade, not able to wait any longer, slid off Courage's back and ran into her grandmother's out-stretched arms. They hugged fiercely, both laughing with tears clouding their eyes.

With her head still buried in her grandmother's shoulder, Jade said excitedly, "I did it grandmother, I did it!"

Her grandmother pulled back and cupped Jade's chin in her hand, lifting her head so that their eyes met. "I am so proud of you," she beamed, a tear rolling down her cheek. Yet there was sadness behind her eyes and streaked throughout her aura, along with a deep fatigue that Jade did not understand. Maybe the sadness was because Jade would not receive the kind of welcome home her grandmother thought she deserved with feasting and dancing after a much needed rest.

*No it's more than that,* Jade thought, *it is that our people march to war. It is this darkness that surrounds us. Maybe grandmother already knows what the darkness is. Maybe she knows how to get rid of it.* The darkness scared her; scared her even more then the jungle did before she had bonded with Courage. *Of course Grandmother will know how to get rid of the darkness—she knows everything,* Jade thought.

Jade's grandmother hugged her again before stepping back so the others could have their turn at welcoming her home. Alo wrapped his arms around her in a warm embrace, his staff bonking her on the back of her head. Catori let out a little squawk and shuffled around on Alo's shoulder, trying not to get knocked off.

"Way to go, kiddo!"

"Thanks Alo," she said, her voice slightly muffled against the fabric of his robe. Then pulling back a little, she freed an arm to rub the back of her head.

Alo grinned; then grinned even bigger when he looked at Courage. "You're even more impressive in person."

Despite the massive grin painted across Alo's face there was the same sadness in his aura. Circumspectly turning her head, she studied Chief Hiamovi. He too wore a big smile while his aura was streaked with sadness and even anger, though she could tell the anger wasn't directed towards her. Jade suddenly had the feeling that both emotions were for her. The happiness she could understand, but the sadness made her nervous. If the sadness wasn't because of the growing darkness, it must be for her. Her nervousness grew with this thought, but she could feel strength and comfort begin to flow through her bond with Courage, allowing her to push it aside for the time being.

Alo took a step back to allow Chief Hiamovi to step forward. Chief Hiamovi, a man of heroic proportions, had grey speckled throughout his hair. Jade knew that he could move like lightning despite his huge frame. Jade had to crane her neck to look him in the eye. Smiling a little broader now he reached over and placed his hand on her shoulder, nearly engulfing it. His touch was gentle, but she could still feel strength in his hand. It was solid, frightfully strong, but comforting all the same.

Looking up into his obsidian eyes, she could see warmth there that she had rarely seen before. "Jade, I would like to welcome you and... ah, where are our manners. Jade, you have yet to introduce us."

Jade blushed and turned a little shyly towards Courage. "Courage, this is High Chief Hiamovi, leader of the Areli nation and Alo, head of all spiritual matters for our people, and Keeper of the Lore. And this is my grandmother, Kendra, Holy Daughter, and head of the Office of Medicine."

Then turning back towards the three people she'd looked up to her entire life she said with profound pride and in a voice both breathy and giddy, "Grandmother, Alo, Chief Hiamovi; this is Courage. He is Therion, an Elder Race, and he has chosen me to bond with. We are now one." She looked back and forth between them and beamed.

The three leaders of the Areli nation bowed towards Courage reverently. Then Chief Hiamovi stepped up to Jade once more; this time placing a hand on each shoulder, looked into her eyes and said, "Let me be the first as it is both a duty and an honor to welcome Jade Abeque." Then meeting Courage's eyes he continued, "And Courage, bonded companion of Jade Abeque, as the newest members of the Areli nation. May you find strength in your union and through that strength bless the Areli Nation that all may prosper."

Then he gravely said, "Jade, Courage, we have much to discuss, for as you can see you have returned to us in troubling times."

Her grandmother stepped forward and interrupted Chief Hiamovi, placing her hand upon his arm. "Hiamovi, Jade is tired and hungry. She needs to get some food in her and get the much needed rest she has rightfully earned." This she said in a telling and not an asking tone of voice.

"Before you ask, I agree with Kendra in this," Alo stated.

"Yes, yes of course you are right as always, Kendra. Jade, I ask that you and Courage eat and rest, and when you have sufficiently recovered from your spirit walk you are to come to council with us. We have much of import to discuss."

"I will do as you ask, Chief Hiamovi." Nervousness laced Jade's words, for while she had sat in on many of their councils before she had only been allowed to observe and never comment or voice her opinion. The thought of discussing anything in council with them intimidated her greatly.

Kendra took Jade's hand and started leading her towards their home, leaving behind Alo and Chief Hiamovi who had turned towards each other and started talking. Jade's other hand rested upon Courage's shoulder.

"Um... Grandmother, how is Courage going to get into my room?"

"Alo saw that your totem would be quite large so the moment you left we had Honaw and Honon build onto your room, adding a space for Courage to sleep along with large double doors that even he can fit easily through."

"Thank you, Grandmother. Courage thanks you too."

"You're welcome, both of you. Now tell me all about your spirit walk."

Jade started at the moment she first entered the jungle; then went on to relate to her all the happenings. Kendra's lips pursed when she heard about the Belial but said nothing, letting Jade continue with her tale. And Jade saw her smile fondly down at Sinopa when she told her about how she and Courage first met and their swift journey home. The story lasted long enough for them to get home and for her grandmother to make her a large dinner, which Jade ate greedily. Kendra even placed a large roast of venison before Courage and commanded him to eat. To which he happily complied. Then as the story wound down and the food was all eaten, she and Courage retired to their room where she fell promptly asleep to Courage's quiet rumbling purrs.

# CHAPTER 9

Menewa chafed at his father's orders and sat fuming on their bastion's balcony. Chewing on the inside of his cheek until he tasted blood, he watched his brother Chaska. Chaska was downright livid as he paced back and forth in front of him. His face was red as he flung about nasty invectives. Menewa knew they should be out fighting with their brothers and sisters of war. He wasn't blind; he could see what was happening. News travelled lightning-fast among the Areli. The old were getting sick, and as they grew more ill their totems became more bestial. Some people had even died from the mysterious illness, and their totems became rabid, attacking all around them. The illness was striking hardest in the villages at the edges of the Areli Nation. But it was working its way towards the heart of the realm, and now at the edges some of the younger people were also getting sick.

Menewa knew it was the Belial behind it all. It was no coincidence that they massed in force to war against them now, and in numbers that hadn't been seen in his lifetime. He had always known that there were a lot more Belial than Areli, but from the reports he'd received from skilled Areli scouts, the Belial coming up against them were so numerous they didn't know how to count them. If only their father would let them into the War Room so he could see the map, and see with his own eyes what was being reported to him.

It was also no coincidence that the Belial were attacking the villages that had been hit the hardest by the illness. One on one, the average Belial was no match for an Areli, but throw enough Belial at an Areli and they would eventually wear them down and bury them under their massive numbers.

Kaga, possessed Belial, were an altogether different story.

A few months after he bonded with his totem, Menewa had been with a young group made up of a hundred warriors, his brothers and sisters in battle, when they had come upon a group of Belial. They numbered only ten so Menewa and his companions had set upon them with zeal and no real regard for tactics or stratagem; which was often the case with youth. Nine of the Belial fell quickly but the tenth struck back with a vengeance, slaughtering his companions.

The Kaga's powers had been terrible. Dark tendrils had flowed out of his body in all directions and every person they touched crumpled to the ground, their screams piercing the night sky. Their bodies had become bloated and grotesque, decomposing while still alive. Blood streamed from their ears, mouths, and noses. As they lay dying, the monster formed black Netherflames so cold, they had burned the flesh of any nearby warrior. Anyone touched by the icy flames were frozen solid, their bodies shattering as they hit the ground.

Menewa was one of only three who had survived the encounter. He had encased himself in a cocoon of fire that protected him from the wicked black flames. Clever, his totem, defying his orders to fly safely above the fray had swooped down, attacking the Kaga. Her claws had raked the Belial's face, leaving burning crevices of fire that refused to be quenched, distracting him just long enough for Menewa to dodge and twist through the ropes of black tendrils to get close enough to plunge both his Cinderblades into the Kaga's chest, killing the body instantly.

The demon spirit purged from the Belial's body rose up in front of Menewa, enraged that his host had been killed, and battered up against the flames protecting Menewa's body. The young warrior fell back before the relentless onslaught of the demon, but Clever let forth a mighty screech that had caused the demon to pause, then the totem burst into brilliant white flames that radiated off his body, making the dark night as bright as day.

The demon had cried out in pain and tried to flee, but Menewa attacked, wrapping ropes of flame and air around the demon's shadowy form that caused it to writhe in agony. Then with a hoarse shout, Menewa pointed his right Cinderblade at the demon and poured out wave after wave of the most powerful flames he had ever conjured, draining all of his body's energy but destroying the demon spirit.

He and Clever had collapsed to the earth. The other two survivors had sent their totems for help. Chaska had been the first to respond and when he had seen his brother lying amongst all the carnage, he feared his brother had perished. He greatly rejoiced when he found that his brother still lived. With a gentleness that few would have been able to credit to Chaska, he had picked up his brother and swiftly ran to the Holy Daughter while his totem Feather, who was delicately carrying Clever in her talons, struggled to follow behind. The people had mourned for all those who had died but they exalted at the death of such a powerful Kaga. Their respect for Menewa grew tenfold, hailing him as a great warrior even though he was barely old enough to be called a man by Areli's standards.

He should be out there with his fellow warriors removing the Belial scum from the earth. After all, he was twice--no, three times--the warrior he had been when he slew his first Kaga. His powers growing as his bond with Clever continued to mature, and they would only grow stronger the longer they were bonded. He had killed twelve more Kaga over the past three years, only being trumped by his brother who had slain seventeen.

Chaska believed the high kill count was Alo's doing; he being able to foretell where the groups with Kaga would be. He had a theory that they were being trained for something big. That was Chaska for you, Menewa had thought. He just figured that if it was Alo's doing it was because they were already considered to be the finest warriors of their generation; much like their father before them. They were the future leaders of their people. It was expected of them.

Menewa wanted to be storming around like his brother because their father wouldn't let them go up to battle, but one of them had to keep a cool head.

Even though they were angry with their father they would never openly defy him; the truth was that both he and Chaska held their father in awe. Whenever they would spar with him, the older warrior would soundly trounce them. It didn't matter if they fought him individually or together, and Menewa was very much aware of the older tribal warrior's whispers about their father's prowess in battle before he had to step back and lead the battles from the rear as Chiefs were supposed to.

It was this and this only that kept the brothers from sneaking off to battle the Belial. Their father forbade them to go and commanded them to stay close. They were not even being allowed to leave the village to hunt, which would have helped them relieve some of their pent-up frustration at basically having their wings clipped. He had said that if they did leave, he would track them down and drag them back by their heels as if they were a couple of unruly children. Menewa's heart had sunk a little when his father had said this, because he knew that their father really could do it if he wanted.

"That's it; I am going to talk to father again!" Chaska said, then turned and hopped over the railing of the balcony, falling thirty feet to the ground below.

Menewa sighed, then stood up from his chair and walked over to the rail to look down at where Chaska had landed. *Guess I better go try to talk some sense into him,* he thought. Jumping up onto the railing, he stood for a second, watching his brother walk purposely away from him and towards the People's Hall. Instead of simply jumping straight down like his brother, Menewa leaped from his perch and sailed gracefully through the air to land lightly next to Chaska, picking up their conversation right where they had left off. "And what good will that do, Chaska?"

"He'll listen this time. He has to."

Menewa sighed, quietly shaking his head. "If he hasn't changed his mind by now he's not going to, Chaska."

"We should be out there, Menewa. This is the biggest threat to our people in generations and Father has us sitting on our butts while our friends are out there fighting. They're out there dying!" he raged.

Menewa reached up from behind and grabbed his brother's shoulder, "Blazes! Chaska, you're as stubborn as Father is and if you two keep banging heads, yours is the one that's going to get cracked. You're not going to change his mind by arguing with him."

Chaska stopped and looked at his brother, taking a calming breath, "Trying to talk sense into your older brother, Menewa? Isn't it supposed to be the other way around?"

"You've talked sense into me plenty of times, Chaska, and you know it."

"Then how are we going to get him to listen to us?" he said with a slight pleading in his voice.

"We don't. We just have to wait. He can't keep us here forever."

"Wait! Flames and ashes Menewa, we are the best. Both of us are worth at least a dozen other warriors."

"Well I don't know if we are the best. Honaw and Honon are seriously good, not to mention many of the elder warriors."

"You know what I mean. And besides, just because their magic is more powerful right now doesn't mean we aren't better warriors."

"Well, like I was saying, Honaw and Honon are pretty freaking good and they aren't really that much older than we are."

"Yeah, and that's just it—Honaw and Honon are still here too. What's going on Menewa? First this weird sickness and now the Belial coming at us in numbers I would have never believed possible. It can't be coincidence. They have to be linked somehow." Chaska balled up his fists and let a growl escape his clenched teeth.

"I don't know Chaska, but I do know that Father knows a flaming lot more about what is going on than we do. What if the idea to keep us here isn't Fathers, but Alo's or Kendra's? Maybe Alo has had a vision, or Kendra has something planned for us. You yourself have said before that you believe they have been training us; putting us into situations to force us to become better warriors. What if you are right? You know that we will never be able to convince Father to go against their wishes."

"That's it, Menewa; you're a genius."

"How's that?" he asked wryly.

"We try to get Alo or Kendra to tell Father to let us go. He won't listen to us, but he almost always listens to them. So if one of them will talk to Father for us, we are as good as gold."

"I must admit that is a better idea than trying to argue with Father again. One problem, though," Menewa said, looking down for a second while chewing on his bottom lip. "I don't see how we are going to convince them to change their mind any better than we have convinced Father to change his. Plus, they've been in council for days now talking strategy and tactics for the war, and who the blazes knows what else," he said matter-of-factly, looking up to meet his brothers eyes.

"I know," Chaska said, clearly frustrated while kicking a small rock hard, sending it careening down a narrow passage between two houses. "But we have to try anyway."

"I guess then we wait outside the People's Hall until they take a break," Menewa sighed.

Chaska turned back around and started walking towards the People's Hall again. His pace was slower, and he was in a much calmer state of mind, for which Menewa was grateful.

Menewa studied his brother from behind. Chaska was both taller and broader through the shoulders like their father; while Menewa took after their mother—being shorter and leaner of build. A dark shadow passed over his soul at the thought of his mother.

He was faster than Chaska, though, and he had learned through experience how to use that speed against bigger and stronger opponents. Of course, their father was both stronger and faster. Sometimes their father moved so fast when he was training them they would find themselves laying prone in the dust before they realized that he had even moved.

His father claimed that both his sons had the same fighting and magical ability at their age as he had had; maybe even a little more. It was possible for them to one day even surpass him. Still, he and Chaska constantly measured themselves against each other and against their father, pushing themselves to always do better. On training days they would usually keep training long after the others had quit, refusing to stop while the other brother still practiced.

It had always been that way between them. Some thought that there must be a strong animosity between the two of them, because when they trained together they would fight each other with an almost feral intensity, attacking with a brutality that was bordering on the insane. That couldn't be farther from the truth, for they had a deep and abiding love for one another; each valuing the others life above their own. Each had faced Kaga. Both knew the truth. Kaga gave no quarter, showed no mercy, and if you made a mistake you were dead. It was that simple. The brutality when they fought didn't come from enmity at all; it came from love. Each doing what was needed to make sure the other was prepared, and if that meant bashing the other's head in while trying to burn each other to cinders, then that is exactly what they would do. Their father knew this and approved.

Menewa also believed that these were the same reasons their father pulled no punches when he sparred with them. He let them know in no uncertain terms that though they were good they needed to be better. If he could beat them then it was likely that one day they would come up against an opponent that could do the same.

Menewa and Chaska made their way in as much of a straight line through the village as possible. The Areli called them villages, though by the standards of the nations in the east they would have been considered nothing less than full scale cities. All Areli villages were built in what would have appeared to an outsider to be a haphazard way. This couldn't be further from the truth. The villages were carefully planned to slow any enemy who managed to get past the Great Wall. This would allow time for the very young and the extremely old to escape into the jungle while at the same time providing perfect killing zones by which the Areli could slaughter their enemies. All buildings were tall with flat roofs so that the Areli warriors could stand upon them and rain death down upon the foolish Belial.

The Great Wall was the first defense. It stretched a hundred miles from north to south only ending at the impassable mountains said to climb into the very heavens where the air was so thin that it meant death for anyone foolish enough to try to climb them. The Great Wall stood a hundred feet high and fifty feet wide, allowing thousands of warriors to stand upon its battlements. The Great Wall had been built with powerful earth magic, making it strong enough to withstand even the mightiest of demons and the dark forces they controlled. The Areli, however, did not hide behind their wall for protection, for their enmity for the Belial was as eternal as the Belial's enmity towards them. So the Belial would continually send groups of warriors out to probe for weaknesses in the Areli's defenses while the proud Areli warriors would seek out and slaughter all such groups. Honor and prestige was to be found beyond the Wall, and was where Menewa and Chaska had proven they were worthy to be their father's successors.

This was yet another thorn in the brothers' sides. Every day they were stuck in the village while their fellow warriors were out fighting, they lost a little prestige in their people's eyes, and this could only undermine their father's rule. It didn't matter if their line was ordained to rule by the Holy Mother herself because without respect, the people were not as likely to follow orders, regardless of the position held. The Areli people had to be united. It was one of their greatest strengths, unlike the Belial, who were said to fight between themselves as much as they fought the Areli.

What else could be expected of demon worshipers?

These thoughts weighed upon Menewa's mind as they approached the People's Hall, just in time to see their father, Alo, and Kendra rush out of the front doors and down the long marble steps. He called to them but they didn't pause as they headed towards the east side of the village.

"Well, either we are being attacked from behind or Jade is back," Chaska said.

"Jade is back."

"What makes you say that?"

"If we were being attacked, the alarms would have been sounded."

Chaska's fist slammed into Menewa's arm causing it to cramp painfully.

"Ouch, what in the world was that for?" Menewa said while rubbing his arm.

"For stating the obvious," Chaska quipped, "Come on, let's go see what kind of totem Jade's got."

Still rubbing his arm Menewa smiled. "She probably has a cute, fluffy little bunny."

"Cute like Jade?" Chaska said slyly.

"What? Wait, no... I mean..."

"Hah, I see how you look at her sometimes."

"I don't know what you are talking about." A slight blush tinged Menewa's cheeks while he pointedly stared straight ahead, trying to ignore his brother's knowing smirk. "I... I don't know how I feel about her. Do you know that father once told me I was supposed to marry her when she comes of age? Now that she has her totem...."

"Wow," Chaska said at the same time he slammed his fist into Menewa's arm again.

"Will you stop doing that?!" Menewa howled.

"Be a man, don't rub it," Chaska laughed, then punched him in the arm yet again. "And that is for not telling me."

"You're right, I should have told you. Sorry," Menewa said while consciously trying not to rub his arm again.

"Blazes right, you should have told me." A mild look of hurt painted Chaska's face. "She is kind of cute, though."

"Yeah, she's cute, but she's a coward."

"You're right, she is a coward, but a cute coward," Chaska said, smirking.

Menewa was the one this time to take a swipe at his brother, connecting solidly in his arm's muscle tissue, knocking him to the side a step or two.

"Ha! What, did a fly land on me?"

"You're a butt."

"True, true," Chaska chortled.

The Elders had come to a stop ahead of them in the cleared field separating the village from the jungle. Menewa and Chaska stopped back among the buildings, giving the Elders room and privacy to welcome the newest member of the Areli Nation home.

Menewa would show this respect to Jade even though he thought her a coward, and if she really was going to be his future wife it would look ill of him if he didn't always show her the proper respect. Plus she was a Holy Daughter and she would one day hold a powerful position amongst the Areli. But most important of all if his father didn't skin him alive for showing disrespect, Kendra would.

Then Menewa saw her materialize out of the jungle. She seemed surer of herself. Probably because she wasn't slouching like she usually did. He could see that she was thinner, having gone without food for so long, and where she should have looked weak from the trials of her spirit walk she somehow looked stronger than he had ever seen her.

Chaska grabbed his arm. "Holy crap, that is definitely not a fluffy bunny."

Menewa was so hyper-focused on Jade, his brain completely failed to register that she road upon what had to be her new totem's back. *She really is beautiful.* Then the pain from his brother's grip and the words he had just spoken sunk into his mind. "Holy crap, that is definitely not a fluffy bunny."

Chaska looked at his brother with a strange look on his face. "That is what I just said."

"Oh," Menewa said a little sheepishly as he stood stunned at what he was seeing. Jade road upon the back of the largest cat Menewa had ever beheld. It had to weigh more than a thousand pounds easily. It also somehow looked like a mix of every cat he had ever seen, or maybe all the other cats he had seen were poor copies of the one that Jade now rode upon. It was perfect. Menewa, who had always been sensitive to things like this, could feel the power radiating out from this magnificent creature. "Definitely not a bunny," he muttered.

"You can say that again."

"What does this mean, Chaska?"

"I don't know, Brother, but I think I have greatly underestimated Jade. I think we all have."

"That is probably the wisest thing I have ever heard you say."

"Hardly," Chaska rolled his eyes and pulled Menewa back the way they had come. "Let's head back to the People's Hall and wait there for the Elders. There is no use talking to them right now.

Menewa allowed himself to be pulled along with his brother, his head spinning from all the emotions and thoughts running through

Lloyd D. Frazier

it.

# CHAPTER 10

Jade slept all through the afternoon and night, enjoying what would be the last good night's sleep for a very long time. She awoke to the sound of rain and wind pounding against the house and this caused her to want to snuggle up even more within her covers. Courage, however, had something else in mind. Jade could feel Courage standing next to her bed, his breath warm against her cheek.

*"Time to get up, little one."* Jade, keeping her eyes closed, pretended not to hear his voice rumble gently in her head.

This time instead of talking to her Courage put his wet nose softly against her cheek. She swatted at him and grumbled, "Mm."

Courage chuckled. *"You leave me no choice."* Then he licked her; his wet rough tongue scraping across her face.

"Arrrrrrrggghh! Courage, that nearly took my whole face off!" Jade scowled, sitting up while gingerly touching her face to make sure everything was still there.

*"Hahahahaha."*

"What!"

*"You look funny when you first wake up."*

"Gee, thanks," Jade said with sarcasm thick in her voice.

*"And the look on your face is priceless."*

Jade bared her teeth at him with a look that said, *careful I bite.* Courage backed up, allowing Jade to swing her feet out of bed and down onto the plush carpet that covered her floor. Standing, Jade raised her arms high above her head while arching her back, her heels lifting up off the floor. A sound of contentment escaped through her lips. The stretch felt good after being asleep in one position for so long, increasing her blood circulation and waking her up some more. Her bowels had woken up too and were now demanding her immediate attention. "Excuse me," she said while hurrying over to her water closet, shutting the door behind her. A few minutes later Jade stepped back into her room feeling much relieved. Her room had been big before she had left for her spirit walk but the renovations had made it simply huge. The room held all the modern comforts created from the Arts of Science and Magic taught to them by the Holy Mother.

Jade moved over to her bathtub and turned on the faucet. Hot, steamy water poured into the tub, splashing off of the pearl-colored tiles and quickly filling it. Jade turned and looked at Courage who sat quietly watching her. "Umm, Courage..."

*"Yes."*

"Could you turn around?"

*"Why?"*

"Because I am going to get into the tub."

*"So?"*

"I don't bath in my clothes. So I will be naked."

Courage tilted his head a little to the right, a questioning look on his face.

"I'm a girl," Jade said.

*"And I am a cat."*

"Yeah, a boy cat..." A blush spread across her face.

*"Yes, I am a male cat and you are a female human."*

"Well turn around." Courage stood up and turned completely around then sat right back down in the same position he had been in originally.

"Now you are just playing dumb," Jade said accusingly.

Courage sat looking proud and regal, but Jade could hear his laughter in her mind. *"You're right, little one, but you are just being silly; we are bonded."*

Face crimson, Jade said, "Fine, I was just trying to be modest." With a huff, Jade pulled off her nightdress and quickly stepped down into the tub, submerging her body up to her neck in the water with a small splash. As she turned the faucet off, she mischievously splashed water into Courage's face.

*"Hey!"* Courage said as he backed up out of easy splash range, *"I already gave myself a bath."*

"Serves you right, embarrassing me like this," she murmured.

*"It's worth it, and there is no reason for you to be embarrassed."*

"Well, I am just not used to people seeing me naked."

*"Yes, I figured that, but I am not a person. And I am your bonded."*

"There is going to be a lot for me to get used to, that's all."

*"For me, as well, little one,"* Courage said, his words gentle within her mind.

"Courage?"

*"Yes."*

"Where are you from; I thought that all the Elder Races left with the Holy Mother?"

*"This Holy Mother you speak of, is she like you?"*

"Yes, I am her great, great, great, great, great, great granddaughter. Well, probably more 'greats' than that but you get the idea, why?"

*"What do you know of the order of Heaven?"*

"Well, the Holy Mother taught that there are three realms and each individual realm is divided into three degrees. She taught that we live in the first degree of the third realm."

*"What realm did the Holy Mother come from?"* Courage asked, though Jade figured he probably already knew.

"She came from the first degree of the second realm."

*"This too is where I am from."*

Jade sat up in the tub and looked at Courage incredulously. "Really?"

*"You doubt me, little one?"* A little hint of laughter colored his words.

"No! No... I do not doubt you, it's just incredible—that's all." Awe filled Jade as she studied Courage, her Courage. The enormity of it all crashed down upon her shoulders, causing her to feel both fear and amazement. "Why? Why me?" she said as she gazed into his eyes; thinking that they looked to be deep wells of crystalline blue water that morning's light danced upon; eyes deep and ancient. She knew the thought was a little romanticized but true nonetheless.

*"Remember the words I spoke to you when we first met?"* Courage asked.

"Yes you said you felt me be born. You said you felt my need."

*"Indeed I did. Your birth roared like thunder deep within my soul and from that day forth it was as if a fisherman's hook had been placed within my heart. It gently but persistently pulled at*

*me. At first I tried to resist it, but each time I did, the pressure would build until it became unbearable and the only way I could find relief was to follow where it wished me to go. I could not rest nor turn aside. In the beginning it was enough to merely walk; for as long as I was heading in the right direction it pulled but gently. But as time went on I found that walking wasn't enough. I had to run. It was your need of me that pulled me onward, and as your need grew for me the pressure I felt grew too. In the end, before I found you, I was passing through worlds so swiftly that the earth barely felt the kiss of my feet. I felt great anger in me for who would dare summon me thus. In the height of my anger I found you. In the height of my anger I would destroy you; the being that dared torment me so. But there you were huddled and hiding in that little den, shivering from fear and sorrow. My heart broke and my anger fled from me, and I knew that from then on I would do anything to protect you, anything to ease your fear and sorrow. I knew that from that time forth if I was to ever feel joy it would only be because you felt joy."*

As Courage spoke Jade felt what he had felt, and in her mind's eye she could see his travels through worlds she could scarcely imagine. She felt the pull of her need as it had pulled him. She felt his anger; no, his rage at being ripped from his rightful place and forced to travel from the second realm into the third where the light of heaven was the darkest. She saw her death stand before her as she lay huddled in the ground. She felt his heart break and his anger drain away, leaving his body weak and trembling. She felt the moment their bond formed. His soul connecting to her soul; but that was not quite right for in a way their souls had always been connected, though it had been a weak and tenuous thing. Jade felt his heart mend as love and compassion for her filled him until he nearly wept.

Jade leaned against the back of the tub, tears streaming down her face. Her mind reeled with all the emotions and images she had just experienced. Stillness filled the room as the storm outside lessened, leaving only the sounds of Jade's quiet sobs caused from sorrow and joy. Love and concern flowed from the bond between Courage and her. There was a gentleness to it that seemed to engulf her and cradle her in its warmth.

"I'm so sorry Courage," Jade whispered.

*"Don't be little one. Half of my heart was missing though I did not know it until I found you. I am whole. I am complete."*

Jade bowed her head and took three deep breaths. A conviction formed within her that she would be worthy of her bond to Courage though she didn't know how this could ever be. Jade heaved herself up out of the water and reached over to the side of the tub and took up a small cloth to dry her eyes. Once that was done she used the cloth to blow her nose which somehow settled her, ceasing the fall of more tears. She wadded up the cloth and aimed for her dirty clothes hamper. For once she made it. There was a straightness—a trueness that had never before been in her aim. "How about that. I made it."

Courage snorted though he made no other comment. Jade picked up the soap along with another cloth and began to work up a good lather. After washing she let the water out while using the overhead shower to rinse and scrub her hair. As it rinsed under the falling water, she just stood there letting it stream down around her body, enjoying the heat of the water and the warmness that filled her heart. Sighing, she turned off the water and got out, taking up a large towel that she vigorously used to dry her body. It felt wonderful to be truly clean again. Jade knew that her grandmother would not be pleased with her for taking so long to get ready. Jade was a little surprised that she hadn't already heard from her grandmother, telling her to get a move on.

"Courage, have you seen my grandmother this morning?" Jade asked as she got dressed in a loose fitting green shirt trimmed in gold that would bring out the color of her eyes and some black doe hide pants.

*"She poked her head into the room early this morning but when she saw you still sleeping she quietly closed the door and I haven't*

*heard a thing since."* Courage was quiet for a second then said, *"There are a couple of people in the house but your grandmother is not one of them."*

"Those would be this week's volunteers who wish to serve the Holy Daughter so she has time to better serve the tribe." All Areli gave one tenth of their increase; whether that might be personal wealth or time. Jade was especially thankful for the volunteers who chose to serve her grandmother, because her grandmother was notorious for loading Jade down with studies, leaving Jade very little free time. It was a good thing that Jade needed less sleep than normal people because otherwise there would be no way she could possibly keep up with everything her grandmother demanded of her.

"She must be at the People's Hall with Chief Hiamovi and Alo," Jade said while walking over to her vanity. She sat and looked at herself in the round framed mirror. The framed mirror and the vanity were like all of her furniture, simple yet elegant. The kind of furniture her grandmother preferred. But though the furniture was beautiful even in its simplicity, it was dead devoid of the spirit that had once possessed it. No life remained in the grain of the wood. No spirit dwelled within. They were just objects or things. Tools to be used; no tears would be shed if they were lost or destroyed. To Jade, true beauty was life in all its forms. So when

Jade picked up an intricately carved ivory comb she thought little of it, or its value, as she carefully combed out her hair and pulled it back simply so it would be out of the way. Courage lay patiently watching her get ready, letting her talk and answer her own questions.

With a small knock on the door, a girl not much older than Jade poked in her head. "Oh good, you're up. I brought you and Courage some breakfast." With that the girl opened up one half of the double doors to pull a cart into Jade's room.

"Good morning, Ahyoka. Did my grandmother really tell you to bring Courage and I breakfast or did you just want to meet Courage?" Jade asked wryly.

"Um, both Miss Jade," Ahyoka squeaked. Having turned around, Ahyoka found herself standing directly in front of Courage, who now stood, his tail swishing back and forth.

Jade could see a slight tremor in Ahyoka's hand as she slowly stretched her hand forward to timidly touch Courage's face inches away from his fangs. Fear filled Ahyoka's eyes, but Jade could see that underneath the fear was a steel resolve to be brave; something that Jade related to whole-heartedly. Courage closed his eyes and leaned his cheek a little against Ahyoka's hand, which started to vibrate gently from Courage's soft purrs. Jade could see some of the tension leave her; her shoulders slumping a little in relief as if she had just seen her own death and narrowly escaped it. Her totem, a small dove that always sat on her shoulder, also relaxed; though not as much as Ahyoka did. The dove still seemed to hold Courage a little in reserve, being very much aware of the fact that it would only take a little nip for Courage to reduce him to nothing.

*"I choose not to eat this one,"* Courage communicated silently to Jade, his contentment apparent.

"Ahyoka, you will be glad to know that Courage has decided not to eat you."

"Um... Thanks Courage." The dove on Ahyoka's shoulder ruffled his feathers, puffing himself out to look bigger than he really was. "I'm not going to say that to him, Cheerful!" she said, her cheeks stained scarlet.

*"Peace, fierce one,"* Courage's voice rumbled in all their minds. *"You and your bonded are safe in my presence."*

Jade smiled as Cheerful, in defiance of his earlier fear, hopped from Ahyoka's shoulder and flapped once to alight upon Courage's head. Jade couldn't help but laugh at the sight. Courage, clearly annoyed, still patiently allowed Cheerful to perch on his head.

*"Maybe I spoke in haste,"* Courage whispered in Jade's mind. *"He would make a tasty little snack."* Jade laughed again, knowing Courage was just jesting with her.

Ahyoka looked between Jade and Courage "Come on, Cheerful, these guys must be hungry. I will be back in a while to clean up."

"Thanks Ahyoka."

Cheerful hopped off Courage and landed back on Ahyoka's shoulder as she walked out of the room. As Ahyoka was shutting the door she laughed and said, "Oh yeah, I forgot, the Holy Daughter said for me to tell you to hurry and meet her at the People's Hall." She shut the door and Jade could hear her whistling to Cheerful's lilting chirps.

"Great! Now she tells us," Jade growled.

*"I think that one is a prankster. Now let us see what she thinks is appropriate food for me."*

"Courage, we need to go. Grandmother expected us to be at the People's Hall a long time ago and she does not like it when I keep her waiting."

*"Kendra can wait; I am hungry."*

"Okay, but it is on your head not mine."

*"I think my head will be just fine. Besides, I smell pork, and little pigs are good eating."*

"Are you drooling?"

*"Only a little,"* Courage said defensively.

Jade walked over to the cart and sure enough a giant slab of pork roast sat on the top shelf. With an obvious effort Jade picked up the platter that held the pork roast and started carrying it over to Courage, grumbling, "At least you could get your own food."

Courage laughed. *"Here little one, let me get that,"* and with that the platter lifted up out of Jade's hands and floated over to Courage, coming to rest at his front paws. Then smacking his kitty lips he began to eat with gusto taking only a few seconds to devour the whole thing.

"Wow... apparently you are what you eat. Maybe you should breathe next time between mouthfuls," Jade said as she picked up her plate which had a slice of the pork roast that Courage had devoured and two eggs.

*"I could go for about four more of those,"* Courage said as he started to bath himself by licking his front leg and rubbing it against his face over and over.

Amused, Jade sat back down at her vanity and quickly ate her meal. She really was worried about keeping her grandmother waiting. That done, she washed her hands and face. "Come on, let's go and see what Grandmother wants."

# CHAPTER 11

Jade and Courage walked through the village. Jade was not used to keeping Grandmother waiting and wished to jog, but Courage seemed to be in no hurry so she moderated her pace to match his. The village was strangely deserted; however, the few people they did see all stopped to gawk in amazement at Courage. Pride swelled in Jade's chest. She had done it. She had gone into the jungle on her spirit walk and had been successful. She had her totem, and not just any totem, she had Courage who was of an Elder Race. She was a full member of the Areli Nation.

For the first time since she had refused to go on her spirit walk when she was twelve she felt like she belonged. She felt that she could hold her head up high. People would still judge her. She was to become the next Holy Daughter and as one of the future leaders of her people, she would be judged. She knew this, but with Courage at her side she believed that those judgments would lead to respect instead of embarrassment. With Courage by her side she could finally become the person she always dreamed she could be.

She could be brave. She could face the world without the overwhelming sense of doom that always plagued her. Her thoughts turned dark as this reminded her of the dream she had had again.

*"Courage I had that dream again,"* Jade said telepathically.

*"I know."*

*"What is it?"* Jade asked.

Courage was quiet for a minute and Jade was just about to ask him again when he answered, *"Your need drew me, but I fear I am not enough."* A shadow seemed to pass over Jade at his words. *"There is much I do not know yet, though I fear the worst,"* Courage said; then picked up his pace just a little. *"Come, Kendra may know more than I and I believe it would be best for us to hear it from her instead of me speculating."* Courage stomped a small puddle of water, splashing Jade's clean pants in an attempt to lighten the mood.

"Hey!"

*"Just paying you back for earlier."*

Jade's mind remained on Courage's words. A cold seeped into her soul even though the day was warm and humid.

*"Oh little one, remember even in the darkest of times there is much to find joy in."*

Jade placed her hand up on Courage's shoulder. "Thank you."

She tried to return to her earlier mood, when the world seemed bright and sunny in spite of the dark clouds moving across the sky, threatening to send rain down upon them again. Jade knew that even though she had gained Courage of an Elder Race for a totem she would have a relatively small role to play in whatever the darkness brought to her people, but she dreaded whatever that small part might be. She could be brave; she just wasn't brave yet.

She was still trying to find her earlier resolve to be brave and to live up to the bond she now had with Courage when they arrived at the People's Hall. The People's Hall was a large spacious building that was the center of the Areli's government. In the heart of the building lay a large cavernous chamber where the three chairs of leadership generally rested. This was where chief dignitaries met; however, the chairs would be moved for important functions, or when one of the three leaders were fulfilling other governmental functions they presided over. The People's Hall also consisted of the Office of Court where Chief Hiamovi, Alo, or her grandmother would sit in judgment for minor cases or issues the lesser Judges were unable to resolve. Whenever there was a major case or issue, all three had to sit in judgment and only a unanimous decision could settle the matter. Except when her grandmother chose to issue a decree as the Holy Daughter—then none could gainsay her. Her grandmother had never done this in Jade's lifetime.

The People's Hall also held the War Room where the three leaders along with their generals would plan and debate over the eternal state of war with the Belial and the demons they worshiped. Along with the Office of Court and the War Room it held the Offices of Trading and Finance. The three Areli leaders ruled over this also, but the day-to-day management was run by the heads of the Artisans' League, made up of various masters of craft.

The Areli had to become masters at the art of trade in order to support themselves because of the constant drain warfare had upon their people and resources. The Areli were known throughout the Kingdoms of the east for their masterful works in magic arms and armor. This alone would make them a wealthy nation, for the nations to the east were known for their diplomacy with the sword more than the word. Jade had wondered before if the whole world was at war. All the nations to the east, however, treated the Areli people with great respect mostly born out of fear, for the Areli nation had much technology that they kept from the outside world. And while other nations had magic, none could compare to the might an Areli warrior could wield.

The Areli people were known not just for their marvelous works in arms and armor but for their art and craftsmanship in all other areas as well. The Areli were a passionate people in all aspects of their lives, and as a result all things they created tended to not just be functional but elegant and beautiful as well. So all nations sent traders to the Areli despite the dangers found in the Megiddo Jungle.

Jade did not think of this as she walked up the sweeping stairs into the People's Hall, nor did she stop to appreciate the beauty of the building itself. Instead the dream and the words of Courage weighed on her mind, and while the village seemed empty of inhabitants, the People's Hall was filled with people. All of whom moved from task to task with a fevered frenzy. This could only mean one thing. The Belial were coming in force. It was the only thing that made sense to Jade. There was even a small group of traders standing unattended in the foyer who had obviously been kept waiting for some time judging from the looks on their faces and the low angry words they were trading amongst themselves.

When Jade walked past them they quieted, their eyes going round and their pale skin becoming whiter. They huddled closer together. Jade knew that it was Courage and not her who caused such a strong reaction from the traders. However when she made eye contact with one of the apprentices, for he was considerably younger than the rest of the group, he made a curious gesture by kissing the fingernail on the back of his thumb then ducking his head. All this took place in the manner of moments it took Jade to sweep past them on her way to the War Room where she believed, judging by the look of things, she would be most likely to find her grandmother.

Since Jade was destined to become one of the future leaders of the Areli Nation she was often forced to attend cases in the Office of Court. She was expected to pay close attention so that afterwards she would be able to recite back to her grandmother the ruling of the case. She was also expected to know what laws and reasoning were used to come to the court's decision.

The same thing was expected of her when it came to trading and war. She was forced to sit for hours of boring trade negotiations as well as large amounts of time spent studying war tactics and strategies.

Jade moved swiftly through the halls designed to accommodate even the largest of totems. Courage was able to walk beside her while still leaving plenty of room for others to pass. Her steps faltered as she drew close to the doors leading into the War Room. The earlier feeling of dread gripped her heart for she could not shake the sensation that the moment she walked into the room her life would be forever changed; that it would be set on a course from which there would be no going back. She knew that this was irrational but the feeling remained all the same. With a deep breath she composed herself, then opened the doors and marched into the room with Courage by her side, resolved to face her destiny whatever that might entail.

The feeling in the room was intense, as if she had interrupted an argument that had been taking place. The War Room was a large square room with an equally large round Ironwood table that sat in its middle. On the table was a conjured map. The map could be manipulated in countless ways, revealing the surrounding areas. Jade could see all the placements of the Areli warriors and the Belial hoards, or at least where they were predicted to be in the near future. *Tooth and claw, Alo's magic is powerful,* she thought. She often marveled at Alo's power. Her grandmother had told her once that even compared to the spirit guides of the past Alo was a rarity. His ability to see and read the possible futures of so many, all at once, was mind-numbing. She didn't really understand Alo's powers, not really. She understood the theory, but the reality of it... that was something else. It wasn't like a person's future was a direct course from point A to point B. No, a person's future was filled with thousands of possibilities which shifted and changed with each decision they made. Yet here Alo was keeping track of all those possible futures which he then projected onto the war table for everyone to see.

Jade felt herself become entranced by the map and without really realizing it, she had walked up to the edge, her eyes drawn to the Belial horde. That was the only way to describe it. Their numbers seemed endless.

*Where are all of these Belial coming from, and how in the world are they feeding themselves?* It was almost as if their numbers had doubled overnight. There were too many of them; that was plain even to her. There was also something wrong with the map, usually the land and everything in it appeared crystal clear. Instead there looked to be a smoky haze that covered the whole of it. The smoke was the thinnest over the land nearest to the Areli. The further west one travelled the thicker the black tar-like smoke became until everything was obscured beneath it.

*It is like the darkness in my dream,* she thought. *How many more Belial are hiding beneath that smoky darkness? And how would I fight them?*

The last was a new thought for Jade because though she had been trained in military tactics for years she never once went to the training fields to practice fighting, or studied under one of the martial masters. She never even went down to watch the people training. Fighting scared her and her grandmother knew that forcing the issue would only make it worse. So she had never really thought about how she would defeat someone in a physical fight.

*I guess I would just suck all the life force out of them.* This was such a terrible thought to her that she quickly put it out of her mind.

Jade looked up and found her eyes locking with Chief Hiamovi's; the same dread she felt was reflected in his eyes. Jade broke eye contact with the Chief, looking around the room; purposely trying not to make eye contact with him again. The first thing she noticed was that her grandmother was slumped in her chair. Her eyes, half lidded, made her appear as if she were in a stupor. Her aura however was churning and swirling, with brilliant light shining through every few seconds. Whatever magic her grandmother was working it was far more potent than anything Jade had ever seen before. The dragons upon the Dragon Throne were moving faster than they usually did, as if agitated.

Jade had never seen her grandmother look so weary. She had appeared tired the night before, which had been weird. Seeing her grandmother like this scared her more than anything- more than the dream, more than the map, more than the look in Chief Hiamovi's eyes. Jade felt herself grow faint, her knees threatening to buckle under her. She plopped down onto one of the chairs that were placed around the table.

She felt Courage reach out to her through the bond, strengthening her. The sensation of this was much like when she pulled energies from living things around her. She would have done that here except that the only living things in the room which had any significant energy were the other people and she was forbidden to do this by her grandmother because she could unintentionally harm them. Jade wasn't supposed to use her powers on anything except simple plants and small animals, because the more intelligent and complex the life form, the easier it was to harm and the more difficult it was to heal.

Along with the energy he sent to strengthen her body he also projected a sense of peace into her mind. Between the energy and the peace that Courage sent to Jade she found her breathing calm and her pulse steady. Closing her eyes for a second she gave Courage a mental hug and whispered in his mind, *"Thank you."*

"She's here Father, now will you tell us why you have us sitting here on our butts while others are out fighting?" Jade jumped at the sound of Chaska's voice. She hadn't even noticed Chaska and Menewa sitting in the chairs that ringed the walls of the War Chamber; their totems resting on the chairs' backs.

An annoyed look passed across Chief Hiamovi's face as he said, "Patience Chaska, we still need to wait for Honaw and Honon." It didn't take more than a few minutes before the doors opened again and Honaw and Honon strode into the room with their giant Rock Bears following behind them. With the twins' entrance Jade also noticed that the usual number of War Generals were absent.

"Finally!" Chaska growled.

Placing his hand on his brother's shoulder and leaning over, Jade noticed Menewa whispering into his brother's ear. Whatever he said, it caused Chaska to calm down a little. Jade thought that having Menewa in the room was almost a welcome distraction— almost. Trying to pretend that Menewa wasn't sitting just a few feet from her was difficult especially because she could feel Courage's amusement at the emotional turmoil she always felt when Menewa was near.

Honaw and Honon took seats, placing an empty chair between them to accommodate for their large size. Their bears each turned in a circle twice and then plopped down in front of them, looking completely carefree. The twins, like their totems, both looked calm and unflappable as usual.

Alo tenderly placed his hand on Kendra's arm. "Kendra, it is time." Slowly, as if coming out of a deep trance, Kendra blinked her eyes a few times and looked around the room. Then her eyes focused on Jade and a look of profound sorrow and regret flashed across her face so quickly that if Jade hadn't been watching her grandmother closely she would have missed it—for because as soon as the look passed it was replaced by a stone mask. With what looked like great effort that only the truly old could understand, Kendra gripped the arms of the Dragon Throne and raised herself up out of it. She swayed a little but then her back straightened and she looked proud and strong once again.

"Yes, now that all of us are here it is time to get started; Hiamovi, would you like to give a brief summation of the situation we are in?"

"Yes, I would," Hiamovi said grimly. "It's simple. Within two weeks' time every man, woman, and child of the Areli Nation will be dead. Within two weeks' time we will cease to be."

A stunned silence filled the room. Then Chaska and Menewa jumped angrily to their feet and began to shout denials at what their father had just said.

"Impossible, Father; we are too powerful to be overcome by the Belial scum," Menewa said venomously, while almost incoherent invectives flowed out of Chaska's mouth.

If Jade hadn't already been shocked down to her very core she would have been appalled at the language Chaska was using. In fact, Jade thought detachedly, she had never heard anyone cram so much profanity into a single sentence in her life.

"Enough!" Hiamovi roared, slamming his fist down onto the table. Only the powerful enchantments that had gone into making it prevented it from being ruined. Jade felt the blow in the ground beneath her feet.

Chief Hiamovi's sons looked stricken, their protests cut off by the sight of their father losing his temper, something they had never seen before. They had seen their father angry many times, but nothing like this. Chief Hiamovi's eyes seemed to have a fire burning in their depths. His breath was short and ragged. Then with an extreme effort Jade saw him slowly rein in his anger, so it boiled just beneath the surface—threatening to burst free again at any moment.

Chaska and Menewa both choked down their bruised pride at being called to task by their father in front of the others, and slowly sat back down in their chairs. Then in contradiction to his vicious outburst just seconds before, Chaska said softly, even reasonably, "Father, how can this be? There are at least two hundred thousand Areli warriors and each one of them is worth ten of the Belial. And judging by the map, the Belial do not number more than two million."

"You're right son, I would easily wager one of our warriors against ten of theirs, but let me ask you a question: How many Areli warriors does it usually take to kill one of the Kaga?"

"It depends; they vary a lot in power."

"True, so how many does it take to destroy a weaker one?"

"I've destroyed one by myself."

"Not all are as mighty in battle as you are son," Hiamovi said sagely.

"Two or three of our more powerful and experienced warriors, or maybe as many as five or six of the less powerful and experienced ones," Menewa stated.

"Again I would agree with both of your assessments. Alo, Kendra; between the both of you, how many Kaga have you sensed?" There was steel in his voice and his shoulders were tensed as if he were preparing for a blow he knew he couldn't avoid.

"Alo and I agree; we have sensed at least fifty thousand Kaga scattered amongst the Belial warriors," Kendra said wearily.

"How can this be?" Honon said, "There have never been more than a few hundred at any given time, as far as I know."

"No Honon," Kendra said. "There have been a few times in our history when they have come at us in numbers as great as this. From the memory visions, I believe there were a few hundred thousand of them during the time the Holy Mother did battle with them."

"Then all is not as lost as you say," Honaw said calmly. "You say our ancestors have done battle with numbers such as these, yet we are still here. Surely we will defeat them this time as well."

"Always the optimist, Honaw," Alo said with a wan smile upon his face.

"No, this speak of doom does not become you, our leaders. I agree with Menewa and Chaska, we are great warriors and we will not allow ourselves to fall," Honaw said confidently.

"There's more, isn't there Grandmother?" A sudden flash of insight caught hold in Jade's mind. "It isn't the number of Belial warriors, or the number of Kaga. It is the darkness. The darkness pressing down upon us even now; it hates us. It wants to destroy us... I can feel it." Jade's voice trembled with fear and apprehension.

The three leaders of the Areli Nation shared a look. "Yes," Hiamovi said, "if it were just the Kaga and the Belial warriors we had to deal with I believe that victory would be possible."

"What?! This darkness that covers the map? This is what has everyone so worked up?" Chaska said while waving casually towards the map as if it were of no consequence.

"No, it is not the shroud of darkness that clouds my vision that Jade speaks of, though it is a part of it. It is another darkness. Though I will tell you this now, Chaska, I fear both kinds of darkness equally, for both are equally deserving of our terror."

"I did not take you for a coward, Alo."

For the first time in Jade's life she saw Alo truly angry. "A coward, Chaska?" Alo said as he rose ponderously from the Raven Throne. His milky white eyes locked onto Chaska's, pinning him in place. Whatever Chaska saw within Alo's eyes caused him to turn pale. Pointing a finger at Chaska, Alo said in a calm and terrible voice, "Let me tell you of that which clouds my vision, boy." With that his eyes swept over all five of them, sending a shiver down Jade's spine. "There is only one thing powerful enough to cloud my vision, Chaska, and that is a Devil, a demon lord. You, Chaska, who have slain demons and have accounted yourself a masterful warrior even at such a young age would be nothing before the might of this being, this Devil, which clouds my vision."

"Sorry Alo... I spoke without thinking."

"Yes you did, and if you are ever going to be worthy of taking your father's place as leader of the Areli you are going to have to master your tongue." Alo said, his tongue a razor's edge. He held Chaska's gaze for a moment more then sighed in resignation and slumped back down into the Raven Throne, saying quietly, "I only pray that there will be a people left for you to lead."

The room fell quiet once again and all within sat and pondered Alo's words. Then after what seemed to be an eternity to Jade, Menewa asked, "Alo, you spoke of two kinds of darkness; if one is the Devil, and I agree it is worthy of our fear, what is the other? Please tell me so that I might know all the enemies we face."

Alo looked to Kendra to answer. "The Devil Alo speaks of has cast a curse upon our people."

"Is this why people are growing sick?" Honon asked.

"It is," Kendra answered. "And I fear this Devil may be more cunning than we are. It knows that we draw our strength from our bonds to our totems, and it is this strength that has allowed us to defeat all sent before us. The curse the Devil has placed upon us is therefore both brilliant and insidious in its nature, for it attacks the bond between us and our totems, eroding it, poisoning our bodies and our minds."

"You are the Holy Daughter; surely you are strong enough to defeat this curse." Honaw stated.

"Thank you for your confidence in me Honaw, but no, I fear I am not equal to the task. I grow weaker by the minute; at best I will only last another seven days."

"No!" Jade wailed in denial of her grandmother's words. "No! You are wrong; you have to be wrong." Tears streamed freely down her checks.

"Oh Jade..." Kendra said as she moved around the table to get to her beloved granddaughter.

Jade rushed out of her chair and ran to her grandmother's arms, sobbing into her shoulder. They were loud wracking sobs that spoke of loss, anger at the world, and pain words cannot describe. It tore at the hearts of all present, though each reacted differently. Both Chaska and Menewa found themselves embarrassed at the raw outpouring of Jade's grief, for it was one thing to show anger, but grief was a weakness that a warrior could not afford to show.

Honon and Honaw shared emotions; that of compassion and a strong desire to protect like a mother bear would protect her cubs. Indeed it was the same powerful emotions that poured into them from their twin She Rock Bear totems.

Hiamovi remained stoic, his face a mask of stone hiding the torrent of sorrow and burning rage. Sorrow for the pain Kendra and Jade were feeling, sorrow for all the pain and suffering that was falling upon his people, and beneath that sorrow the rage burned and seethed at all who would dare bring harm to his beloved people.

Alo sat and wept silently along with Kendra and Jade, a daughter of his heart. Alo was not the kind of person who found shame in tears; his own, or others.

Then in the depths of Jade's despair, her desolation, Courage entered her mind, filling her with light—pushing away the darkness that threatened to drag her down into oblivion. She felt him take upon himself her pain; lifting the burden a little from her soul to keep it from crushing her.

Then Courage whispered almost delicately into Jade's mind and heart, *"We can save her. We can save them all."*

*"How? How can we save her Courage?"* Jade wailed back silently.

*"They know of a way. I can sense it in them, but you will have to put aside your fear if there is to be any hope."*

*"I can't, Courage, I don't know enough; I'm not strong enough."*

*"You are not alone little one. I have knowledge. I have strength, and these things I give unto you. Together the task will not be too much; this I promise you."*

Jade trembled in her grandmother's arms from the maelstrom of emotions that battled for supremacy within her mind. Her fear was like lead weights tied about her ankles; pulling her down into the deepest, darkest recesses of her mind. Yet she stubbornly clung to the hope Courage offered her; refusing for at least this moment to give in to her despair.

"Grandmother, Courage says that you know of a way that you can be saved."

Jade heard her grandmother sigh then felt her pull away from their embrace. Stepping back, her grandmother placed her hands upon Jade's shoulders and looked regretfully down into her eyes. Then with a sad, twisted smile she leaned forward and placed a gentle kiss upon her granddaughter's brow. Her lips felt hot and dry on Jade's skin as if her grandmother burned with fever. The kiss, lasting but a moment, ended all too soon.

"I am sorry," Kendra whispered to her granddaughter, "for not being strong enough."

"Grandmother, how can you not be strong enough? You're the strongest person I know."

Grief marred her grandmother's face as she turned her head to look at Alo. "Alo, take Jade to the Hall of Visions. It is time for her to learn the role she is to play in all of this."

"Are you sure, Kendra?"

"Is there any other way Alo?"

"None... none that I have been able to foresee," he said sadly.

"Then I am sure. Courage, take care of her, and please bring her back to me."

Courage bowed his head to her. Kendra turned her back to Jade so she would not have to see her tears.

Alo placed his hand lovingly on Jade's shoulder. "Come."

With false bravado, Jade wiped the tears from her eyes and followed Alo out of the War Room, Courage walking silently beside her.

# CHAPTER 12

The world around her seemed surreal as Alo's visions unfolded before her. As the last of the vision faded away, Jade felt as if she were trapped within a dream, a living nightmare from which she couldn't awaken.

Alo stood before her, holding one of her hands, and spoke gentle words to her; words that floated and swirled around in the air yet failed to ever reach Jade's ears. There was a pounding in her skull that coincided with each hammering beat of her heart. Her lungs felt made of iron; iron that was slowly being crushed in a vice, making each breath feel more difficult than the last. Her vision narrowed, with little dancing lights zigzagging before her eyes, leaving her feeling as if she were looking at the world through a deep tunnel.

All of this was caused by the deep raging panic and sense of impending doom that gripped her soul, and the only thing that kept her from being swept away completely down her own personal river of hell was the fistful of Courage's hair clenched tightly within her trembling hand. He was her anchor.

*"Jade. . . Jade... JADE! Come back to me, Jade,"* Courage said.

Jade could feel herself move closer to Courage, not physically, but spiritually. It was as if he were pulling her towards him, into him.

*"Jade, feel my heart. Feel it beating."*

And she could; she could feel his heart in direct counterpoint to hers. Hers like the fluttering wings of a humming bird. His like a slow rhythmic beat played upon a massive drum, thump . . . thump . . . thump . . . thump. Each beat slow and powerful. Slowly, ever so slowly, Jade's heart quieted until it beat in time with his. As this happened, she could feel the vice squeezing her lungs loosen, allowing her to take deep calming breaths. She could feel Courage gently push her spirit back into her own body and the sense of being physically one with him lessened and became more distant. She was she and he was he, linked together yet two separate beings. Then, as if a bubble had burst, she was back in the world of the living.

Though she was much calmer, tears still streamed down her face. "Why Alo, why did you have to show me such terrible things?"

Alo stood before her, his hand holding tight to hers. As she looked into his eyes, she saw pain; pain kindred to that which she felt. "Sorry Jade, you had to know; you had to see for yourself the price of failure in this thing with which you and Courage must do."

Jade shuddered; it was one thing to be told that people were going to die. People she loved and cared about. It was something altogether different to watch it happen over and over again in dozens of different ways.

When they had first entered the Hall of Visions, Jade found it to be exactly the way it had been the few times previous she had been allowed in it. There really wasn't much to it. The room was large and square in shape with no furnishings except the Raven Chair occasionally placed in the center of the room. What made this room different was that every surface was covered in mirrors. The mirrors weren't made of glass but something infinitely stronger, infinitely clearer. When one looked into the mirrors it wasn't like seeing a reflection of something, but the very thing itself. Standing in the center of the room was like standing in the center of eternity. Jade could see forever in every direction, and within that space existed a million Jade's; no, a million times a million, and each one seemed as real to her as she did to herself. It created a strange sense of vertigo and left her with the sensation that maybe she wasn't the real one and that it was one of the other Jade's that was real and she the reflection.

When they had entered the room, Alo had taken her hand and

led her into the center of the room where he explained what was going to happen.

"What you are going to see is a lot like the vision stories your grandmother and I share with you," Alo had said.

Jade had relaxed a little. *This shouldn't be too bad then,* she had thought, remembering the vision story Alo and her grandmother had shared with her and all the people at the feast before her spirit walk. She also knew that someday she would be trained to help Alo perform them.

"There are a few differences, however; a few very big differences, and I am afraid that there is very little I can do to prepare you for what you are about to experience, and for that I am sorry.

*"I'm not familiar with what you are saying. What are these vision stories and how is this going to be different?"* Courage had asked while he sat back on his haunches; his tail lazily swishing back and forth.

"The vision stories are memories that have been preserved through time. The bearer of the memories and I work together to allow a person to experience those memories as if they were their own. What I am about to do is the same in that I will open up your minds to what I see; however, what you will see are not memories but my visions. There is one difference, a very dangerous difference. You see, memories are removed from the event that formed them. They are shared after time has passed, allowing the person to form natural protections to guard against the difficult or traumatic events they experienced. This does have an effect upon the quality of the memories that are eventually shared but our ancestors learned that memories taken and saved at or close to the moment of their inception were too real, too potent, and too dangerous for others to experience. What I am about to show you are not memories but visions of the future. There are no buffers, no protections, for what you will see and experience. It will seem to you that what you are experiencing is happening right now instead of looking back on it after time has passed. This will leave you open to the full brutality of it. I am sorry Jade for what I am about to do is neither fair, nor kind, in any way, but I swear upon my bond to Catori that it must be done. I just hope that one day you will be able to forgive me."

The visions began and Jade saw with horror the consequences of her decisions to the choices she would be forced to make—choices in her near future. She must go on a quest into the heart of the Belial nation and find and destroy the source of the curse. The same darkness that had blanketed the map in the War Room also tainted the view of the visions, keeping her from ever being able to see just what the source of the curse was. The visions came hard and fast and in every one she had to watch as her friends and loved ones were destroyed—many even succumbing to demon possession. Whether she refused to go, or went and failed, all paths led to her death and everyone else's, but it got even worse for she saw that when the Areli fell the Kaga went on to destroy and enslave the entire world.

*"Is there no hope?"* Jade wailed in the chambers of her own mind.

Then came a singular vision. One in which she chose to go on the quest. She and Courage walked into the darkness and though she couldn't see the source of the curse she somehow knew that they had found it and she had somehow managed to stop it. She couldn't see past this for the vision went completely dark, but it left her with a vague sense of hope. She wept for that hope; a hope so small, so tenuous that it was as delicate as a butterfly's wings.

"Will you, Jade and Courage, do that which must be done?"

Jade trembled before him; eyes squeezed shut; tears streaming down her cheeks. With a quick jerk of her head she nodded, then turned and flung herself into Courage's shoulder. Clinging tight to him, she wept.

\*\*\*\*

All was quiet in the War Room as everyone looked at the door

Alo and Jade had just left through. *There goes the hope of our people,* Menewa thought disbelieving. *If she is our hope then we are doomed.*

Menewa had to admit he may have feelings for Jade. He may have feelings for her but it was more confusion then anything and he refused to believe that she could play a vital role in all of this, despite her new totem. She wasn't a warrior and it would take a warrior- no, *warriors*- to save them, for the task was obviously too big for any one person. Warriors like Chaska and himself, and Honaw and Honon. *This is why Father has held us back. He has been saving us for a truly vital mission.*

Echoing Menewa's thoughts, Honon spoke up, "It is requisite that Jade should be doing something to help, but she is no warrior, and it is going to take a warrior to dig us out of this pit we find ourselves in."

"Don't discount the role Jade will play," Hiamovi said flatly, "for it is more important than all of ours, and if she fails there is nothing that we can do to save our people."

"Impossible, Father!" Chaska exclaimed.

"He's right, Father," Menewa said "She's weak and cowardly, but we are strong and fierce. Tell us how to save our people and we will do it."

Kendra mouthed the words "weak and cowardly." She stood

slowly, eyes staring down at the map that now stood static without Alo in the room; her hands resting on the side of the table. Snapping her head up, her eyes focused on Menewa as a hawk focuses on its prey. "Weak and cowardly," Her words cut through the room like a knife.

Menewa felt his feet leave the ground as he was slammed back up high against the wall by some unimaginably powerful force. His head made a resounding crack, causing his vision to go white then dark as he struggled to remain conscious. He struggled and strained against the force that held him, though he found that he could not even move a finger. All air had been forced from his lungs. He was being crushed. Terror like none he had ever felt before washed over him causing his thoughts to become wailing gibberish. *I am going to die.* Then the pressure on his chest lessened a fraction, allowing him to suck some air into his lungs. It was the sweetest he had ever tasted.

"Weak and cowardly," Kendra said again, "You are a fool."

Menewa watched Kendra move around the table and cross the room to stand before him—no strain or effort apparent upon her face, her head tilting up to look him in his eyes. As she approached, it was all he could do to pull in one ragged breath at a time. His eyes darted to his brother and Honon and Honaw, pleading for help, only to find them rooted in place—shock bleaching their faces a ghostly pale. Then he looked to his father who stood with arms across his chest. He could see anger flashing in his father's eyes yet his face remained as impassive as if it were carved from marble.

"Look at me," Kendra snapped.

Then a force seemed to reach inside him and seize control of his body; forcing his eyes to move back to Kendra; forcing him to look her in her eyes.

"If she is weak, then I am weak, and if I am weak then you, Menewa, are nothing." Kendra stated.

Menewa had never seen her like this before; so cold, so hard. He had always been told his whole life that a Holy Daughter was powerful; far more powerful than the strongest warrior, but until now he had never truly understood. Looking into Kendra's eyes, he knew deep in his bones that she could snuff his life force out with nothing but a thought.

"As to her being cowardly; is it cowardice to know fear? I think not. For only a foolish man could feel no fear and account himself brave. No, doing what must be done despite fear, that . . . that is courage. There will come a time in your life when you shall know fear, and then Menewa, then we shall see if you are truly brave."

The force that had reached inside him and seized control of his body let go and Menewa found himself in control once more, though he was still held tight against the wall. "Please, please let me down. I am sorry. I shouldn't have spoken so." he said, his voice coming out in a choked whisper.

He watched the hard lines of her face soften a little and she stepped back away from him. The pressure that held him fast against the wall released and he fell hard to the cold marble floor where he lay for a few seconds, panting as if he had just run the full length of the Great Wall. Every muscle in his body burned as he struggled to rise to his feet, though he kept his eyes cast down upon the floor, fearing to make eye contact with Kendra. He sought his seat and resolved to keep his mouth shut the rest of the meeting.

"Kendra, was that really necessary?" Hiamovi asked.

"Yes, I think it was. These boys need to know what it is they face. What it is we all face," Kendra said.

"And they are going to learn this by you tossing my boy around, Kendra?"

"Ask Menewa what he has just learned."

Menewa heard his father grunt, "Are you alright, boy?"

"Yes Father," he said, though his whole body felt bruised and he could feel his face flushing from embarrassment.

"What lesson have you taken from this, son?" His father asked.

Menewa took a moment to compose himself. "I learned that I

am not nearly as strong as I thought I was; I mean, she handled me like I was an infant Father. I couldn't do anything. I was completely under her power, and she wasn't even really trying. You have told me that Holy Daughters were powerful but I never really understood. I think I understand better now. I said that Jade was weak but she is a Holy Daughter too and if she is as powerful as Kendra then I am a fool and I spoke rashly," he admitted miserably. "I also understand now that if Kendra believes this Devil to be at least as powerful as she is then Chaska, Honaw, Honon, and I would stand no chance against it. The only person besides Kendra who could hope to fight it and win would be Jade." Menewa turned his head, though not really looking directly at Kendra whispered "Is she really as powerful as you?"

"Yes," Kendra said simply, "Though she is young and inexperienced, her powers are equal to mine, and if she survives long enough to learn how to use her powers to their greatest abilities she will eventually become far more powerful than I could ever hope to be."

Menewa shuddered to think that just moments before he had been so naive, so sure of his own strength.

Chaska cleared his throat, "I'm a little confused," he said, addressing both his father, and Kendra. "If we four are no match for this Devil, then you cannot be sending us to kill it; so since you are busy fighting off this curse the Devil has set upon us, that leaves only Jade to track down and kill this Devil. I know that Jade is a Holy Daughter and as such has great power, but like you said, she is young and inexperienced and knows next to nothing about hunting down and killing these types of beings. I guess what I am asking is; do you want the four of us to go with her and act as guides so that she can find this thing and destroy it?"

"No, Jade is not ready to have a direct confrontation with a being such as this. If she did it would only end in her death. Jade's task is to find the source of this curse and destroy it without directly confronting the Devil. Once the curse has been lifted from our people I will be able to quickly regain my strength and then I will go and confront this Devil, and if I can, I will end its miserable existence," Kendra said.

"Before you ask any more questions I think it is time for us to share with you what Alo has seen in his visions," Hiamovi said, raising his hand up to forestall the questions the four boys were about to ask. "Alo has foreseen that Jade must search out the source of the curse on her own with only her totem by her side. If any go with her they will die and she will fail. This does not mean that Jade does not need our help nor does it mean that we will not give it.

"As you all know by now, Alo's vision is being clouded by the

Devil; however, Alo has been able to see one possible pathway to success. Both Jade and you boys will be heading towards Talberic —the largest of the Belials' strongholds, though you are to take different paths. We don't know what kind of help Jade will need or how you are to give it but we do know that once you have reached Talberic you are to sneak into the heart of the stronghold to the foot of one of their Temples they have built there.

"We also know that if you are not there by the dawn of the sixth day from today all will be lost. Once you have discovered what it is you need to do there, you are to do it as fast as possible then flee." Hiamovi raised his hand again to forestall the questions he knew they were dying to ask. "Before you ask; no we do not know why you must flee, nor from what, but Alo has said if you fail to do this you will all die. He says that in the visions where he has seen you flee, in almost all of them you still perish. Alo also says that you must find a cave. Honaw and Honon, with your strong earth magic you should be able to find a cave, and once you do you must delve deep. Alo is sorry for he cannot tell you more," Hiamovi sighed. "He doesn't even really know why it is you need to do this; he just knows that if you don't you will die."

Menewa swallowed the lump in his throat and looked to his brother and the twins, already knowing what he would see; each one had a look of sheer determination on their faces. They would go, even knowing it was likely they would die. Nothing less could be expected of an Areli warrior. "When do we leave Father?" he said, proud that his voice was strong and steady.

"You leave within the hour, and may the Light of Heaven forever shine down upon you, my sons," Hiamovi said, his eyes taking in all four of the boys that sat before him.

"May the Light of Heaven forever shine down upon you," the four boys said in unison as they hopped to their feet, preparing to leave.

"Oh, and boys, one more thing before you leave," Kendra said, "The Devil and its minions will be looking for Jade. I want you to try to draw as much attention away from her as possible without getting yourselves killed. You will need to take these for protection."

The boys watched as she reached into a little leather pouch and pulled out four small clear crystals attached to sliver chains so that they could be worn around the neck, and handed one to each of the boys. Menewa accepted his gratefully and slipped it over his head while trying not to look her in the eye; his embarrassment at his own rash words and the sharp lesson the Holy Daughter had taught him was etched firmly in his mind and he knew it would be for a very long time.

Honaw and Honon had also slipped theirs on without comment,

and while Menewa's crystal hung loosely around his neck the twins' fit snugly. They were just simply built on a much larger scale than he, and if Menewa could be honest with himself, he would have to admit that he felt rather small standing next to them. Even his brother who had a couple of inches on them and a healthy dose of muscle somehow looked slighter than he really was.

Menewa watched his brother weigh the crystal in his hand and ask the question Menewa had been going to ask but held back due to his earlier embarrassment; which only sent yet another wave of embarrassment through him. *Maybe I'm the coward,* he thought, a little ashamed of himself.

"So," Chaska asked, "you said these are to protect us; will they protect us from demon fire?"

"No, they are to protect you from the curse. You are all young and strong and so the curse should take longer to affect you; however, the further you go into enemy territory and the further you get from me the more susceptible you will become and eventually my protection will fail completely. When that happens you will feel yourselves begin to weaken and grow sick rapidly. What you need to do is prick your finger and smear a drop of your blood upon the crystal. This will link the crystal to you and it will begin to draw the curse away from you and into the crystal. But be warned, the crystal will only work for a short time before it will become saturated with the curse's taint and shatter. If you activate the crystal too early, you will not have the strength to make it to Talberic and then escape again before Jade is able to lift the curse. If that happens you will die, and if you die before you reach Talberic, so shall we all."

"Thank you," Chaska said, and then he too placed the crystal around his neck. "We will not fail you."

****

Hiamovi watched his boys walk out of the room, praying that it would not be the last time in this life that he saw them. His shoulders slumped a little and he looked at Kendra, who was back sitting in the Dragon Throne doing whatever she could to stem the curse.

"Kendra," Hiamovi said, and then repeated her name twice more before her eyes came back from some far off distance.

"Yes, Hiamovi?"

"Tell me I will see my boys again, and that I did not just send them to their deaths."

"My friend, you have sent your boys out to face death countless times; this is no different."

"Is it? It doesn't feel the same way. It feels as if we are sending lambs to the slaughter."

"I know, I feel the same way about Jade," Kendra said, a slight catch in her voice.

"If they die I don't know that I will be able to forgive myself."

"If what Alo has said is true, if they die, we will not have to live with our sorrow for long," Kendra whispered softly.

Hiamovi could feel love and concern flow through his bond with Sparks, giving him some comfort and helping him feel not so alone.

# CHAPTER 13

Jade stood staring at the Great Wall separating her from the jungle she was about to enter. This time when she entered the jungle she would be heading west into the heart of the Belial territory. If anyone, even a few days ago, had said that she would be doing this she would have called them crazy.

Her hand absently played with a small pearlescent stone that now hung around her neck. When Jade looked closely, she could see movement from within this stone, as if milky white clouds swirled lazily around and around. The stone's surface, though solid, had a feeling of liquidity; yet her fingers came away dry after touching it.

The stone was a gift from Alo, though not for sentimental reasons. He had told her that the stone was linked to his vision, and her carrying it with her would allow him to better see into the darkness that had been created by the Devil. He could then better coordinate their warrior's movements, seeking advantage against the overwhelming odds the enemy was bringing against them. It would also allow him, "in theory," he had stated, to guide her to the exact location of the curse that lay somewhere in the heart of Talberic.

Talberic was the largest of the Belial strongholds. Though she had never seen it, she had heard many stories from warriors who had dared to journey so deep into enemy territory; stories that had given her nightmares. The nightmares didn't live up to the reality of it; the reality of it shown to her in the visions was much, much worse than anything her mind could have created on its own.

She could feel a gentle tug on her thoughts, directing her out towards some vague location in the west; out beyond the wall she had hid behind her entire life; out where vicious battles between her people and Belial and their Kaga masters were even now taking place. And she was going out there; out into the killing grounds. Passing through the killing grounds was terrifying but it paled in comparison to her end destination; Talberic itself.

The reality of it all made her feel like weeping, and though her eyes were filled with tears none fell—for which she was proud of herself. Maybe she was getting a better handle on her fears and emotions, or maybe she had just simply cried herself out upon Alo's shoulder earlier after he had shown her the visions. Still, she couldn't make herself take another step towards the Great Wall and what awaited her on the other side of it; her feet felt as if they had become roots that had sunk deep down into the soil, holding her fast.

Jade had been standing there like an idiot when Menewa, Chaska and the twins passed through the wall a little while ago. Jade could still feel the hot, tingly sensation on her arm where Menewa had touched her. In an incredibly awkward and embarrassing moment when their small group had passed by her, Menewa had stopped in front of her and placed his hand upon her arm, sending those electric tingles throughout her body.

Menewa had looked searchingly into her eyes, though she didn't know for what. "I . . . am sorry," he said.

"For what?" she had asked faintly, confused at Menewa's unprecedented behavior towards her.

"For . . . for everything." Menewa had shook his head as if frustrated. "Just be careful. I don't want this to be the last time I see you."

"Um, okay," she had said, not quite knowing how to respond to him.

Menewa had dropped his hand and stepped back, looking as embarrassed as Jade felt. She had watched him adjust the light travel pack on his back before turning away from her and moving swiftly to the Great Wall. Jade's eyes had followed him until he disappeared from her sight all the while trying to ignore the thick, almost syrupy sensation of amusement she could feel radiating at her from Courage.

"What?" she had snapped.

*"Cubs,"* he chuckled.

So she stood, trying to ignore the bubbling mass of terror she had chained inside of her with strands of gossamer silk. Terror that threatened to burst its bonds and come flooding back to crash against her soul, burying her in despair. She wanted to hide; to turn and seek safety in Grandmother's arms, but her grandmother fought for her own life and the life of their people. There was no safety there. A small part of her that had somehow remained rational knew that. The rest of her didn't care. The knowledge brought to her by the visions drove her forward. Her fear; her own cowardice drove her back so here she stood rooted in place putting off the inevitable as long as possible; her hand sliding the guidestone back and forth along the simple gold chain that hung around her neck.

*"Jade."*

"Yes, Courage?"

*"Time flows but one way for beings such as us and it is quickly slipping away. We must be going."*

"I know. I keep telling my legs that but they won't listen to me."

Courage crouched down until his belly rested upon the ground, *"Then come little one, climb up on my back and let me be your legs."*

Jade climbed up on Courage's back and sat just behind his front shoulders, grabbing fistfuls of his hair in her hands. In one smooth motion Courage stood up and started trotting towards the Great Wall—his pace not slacking in the least as they approached what looked to be solid stone. At the last moment the magical sensors on the wall registered their approach, causing the wall before them to liquefy and flow apart to form a tunnel through which they could pass. Courage roared as they passed through the tunnel, the sound of it echoing in the small space, causing Jade's ears to ring. Then like an arrow leaving its bow, they shot out of the tunnel; it sealing behind them as they sped across the open ground beyond the Great Wall.

Jade couldn't help it; she smiled despite the fear that was her constant companion. Then she found herself laughing. Riding on Courage's back was intoxicating. The raw power with which he moved; it was like... well it was like riding on the back of a thunderstorm, Jade imagined. Letting go of Courage's fur, Jade lifted up her arms and held them out while imagining she was the thunderstorm as it marched across the sky. In her mind's eye she pictured herself hurling lightning bolts down upon her enemies, and for now, at this very moment, she felt free—Courage having somehow outrun her fears.

A few seconds later they had passed over the half mile of cleared ground and hit the jungle wall, causing Courage to slow in the dense jungle foliage.

Like Courage through the jungle, time flew by; night had descended down upon them yet they ran on until the early hours right before dawn. The pathway through the jungle they were taking zigzagged back and forth as much as it moved them forward; the guidestone tugging on her one way then the other, their course changing direction with each tug of the stone. While the indirect route slowed them down, it had its benefits, for they had not seen a single Belial yet; which in Jade's mind was a miracle. She vividly remembered the map in the War Room filled with hordes of Belial and Kaga. Though they hadn't seen any Belial, they had passed several groups of Areli warriors. These groups tended to be small, kept to numbers that could move swiftly and hide easily, attacking the Belial in deadly raids and ambushes, leaving the enemy confused and disoriented. Each of these groups had been amazed to see them pass, some even forgetting themselves by calling after them, though Courage never slowed nor acknowledged their existence.

"Courage," Jade said.

*"Yes little one."*

"I know that you can run forever but I am getting hungry and my backside is killing me."

Courage slowed down to a trot. *"You are right, a little rest and some food would be welcome."*

"Great, keep an eye out for a good place to stop and rest," Jade said.

*"No need, I can sense a small group of Areli warriors just up ahead and it smells like they have cooked us some breakfast."*

"I don't know…" Jade said nervously.

*"Are you afraid of your own people little one?"* Courage said with a sense of mild confusion.

"It's not that; it's that they think I am a coward and they all look down on me."

*"Why would they look down on you? Are you not going to be one of their future leaders?"*

"I am, but it is only because I was born a Holy Daughter, not because they respect me. Most of them don't even like me, or even worse they are ashamed of me," Jade said dejectedly.

*"Again, why do you think they don't respect you, and how can you be so sure they do not like you?"*

"Oh they respect the office of the Holy Daughter, and so they show me proper respect to my face, but they can't hide their true feelings towards me. No one can—except my grandmother, but it is something she has to be doing deliberately; which she seldom does."

*"It is also difficult for any being to hide their emotions from me."*

"You can smell them, can't you? I mean, you can smell people's emotions."

Courage stopped and looked back at her by tilting his head to the side; his giant blue eyes gazing at her. *"Yes this is how I do it."*

"I knew it," Jade said. "Almost immediately after we bonded I started to be able to smell emotions like you."

*"What a wondrous thing this bond is, I wonder what other changes will come about because of it,"* Courage said. *"Yet this is a new thing and the way you talk, you have been able to tell what people are feeling for a long time."*

"I have almost my entire life. I can see it in a person's emotional aura."

*"Emotional aura?"* Courage questioned.

"Wait! You can't see people's auras?"

*"No, why would I be able to?"* Courage said while turning his head away from Jade and started walking again.

"But you are from the second realm like the Holy Mother."

*"I am a cat, not a person,"* Courage said as if this explained

everything.

"It's just that you seem to know so much and I just thought that because you were from the second realm you could see auras too."

*"Jade, I may be very old by your people's standards, but I am still young by the standards of my race. There is much that I know that you do not but I am neither omnipotent nor am I all-knowing. I am sure these are things my elders have tried to teach me in the past but I was never one to sit still and listen to my lessons; not when I could be out hunting. I will tell you much the same things I told them. I am a hunter not a philosopher,"* Courage concluded proudly.

"Well Mr. Hunter-Not-Philosopher, if I am going to be able to answer the question you asked me I am going to have to tell you a little bit about auras and what I can do or what I will be able to do once I am fully trained." Jade paused for a moment, collecting her thoughts. "First, there are at least four parts to any living soul, a soul being the physical self and spiritual self combined as one. Are you following me so far?" Jade asked.

*"Yes I am following you, go on,"* Courage said with a little exasperation and annoyance in his voice.

"Okay, great, now the four parts of a living being's soul are: the physical, the spiritual, the emotional, and the intellectual. Each individual part creates its own energy or aura. I have the ability to see these energies or auras and manipulate them. Well, I can manipulate the physical and emotional auras; truthfully, I have a hard time even seeing the spiritual and mental auras, unless they are really powerful like yours. But this has been true with every Holy Daughter."

*"So you can see people's emotions by looking at their emotional aura,"* Courage stated as if it made perfect sense to him.

"Well yes, and no," Jade said.

*"That's a straightforward answer if I have ever heard one,"* Courage said, chuckling.

Jade could feel her face flush. "It is the most straight-forward answer I can give you. People's emotions are extremely difficult to read because everyone feels multiple things all at once and they usually get all jumbled together. On top of that auras reveal themselves as colors and every color means something different. But what makes reading the emotional aura so difficult is that sometimes I see red and it invokes a feeling in me of love, but other times that same color of red invokes feelings of anger, or lust, or perhaps it means both at the same time."

*"So when you say you can manipulate the auras does that mean you can change them by taking things out and putting things in?"* Courage asked, his genuine interest and curiosity coming through the bond.

"Yes, that is exactly what it means."

*"So couldn't you just take away the bad feelings people have towards you and replace them with positive ones?"*

Jade chuckled faintly. "I don't think that would be such a good idea."

*"Why?"*

"First off, my grandmother would skin me alive, and then she'd put my skin back on and skin me alive again. Messing with people's emotions like that is forbidden. My grandmother will do mild emotional aura manipulation on people but she would never just simply take something completely out and put something else entirely in. I'm not really sure how that would affect someone. I'm not even allowed to do any form of emotional or physical aura manipulation on anything more complex than a plant. My grandmother says that the more complex the life form is the easier it is to do serious damage or even kill it by changing anything in their auras.

"Oh, sure," Jade continued, "a large number of our people can alter emotions and the medicine men and women can heal using one or more of the four essences: earth, air, water, and fire."

*"Yes, the four essences I know well,"* Courage said, *"I am extremely proficient in their uses in the art of the hunt. My question is: Why are you not proficient in them?"*

"Because I'm not a cat of an Elder Race!"

*"Ha, little one, using the same excuse I just used. Clever, but it doesn't work; not with this. I know full well that as a daughter of the second realm you have the ability to harness the power of the four essences."*

"Courage, can we please just let this go for now." Jade knew that Courage could feel the hurt welling up inside her just talking about this subject, just as she could feel the annoyance her response had triggered in him; annoyance that was quickly replaced with a feeling of love and patience.

*"I will drop it for now, but we are going to have to talk about it sometime."* Courage said, *"Now please continue what you were saying."*

"What our people can do with the four essences isn't the same thing my grandmother and I can do by aura manipulation. Well, what Grandmother can do. Doing something with the four essences is completely different than aura manipulation even though they can often accomplish similar things. In the end, even the few rare medicine men and women who can use all four essences cannot even come close to accomplishing the things Grandmother can do through aura manipulation alone, let alone the things she is able to do by mixing the two abilities."

*"You do take little bits of energy from the things around you all*

*the time—don't you?"* Courage asked, though it wasn't really a question.

"I do. How did you know?" Jade asked.

*"I can feel it every time you do. It is like a little jolt of electricity is injected directly into my veins. It feels . . . invigorating."*

"Like if I pull energy from that tree?" Jade asked, pulling more energy from the tree then she normally would.

*"Yes, that feels incredible."* Courage said, shivering under her. *"It makes me feel more powerful. So with that power, why do you fear the Belial? It's irrational."*

"What do you mean, irrational?" Jade snapped angrily. "They worship demons that possess them and grant them terrible powers. They delight in killing and suffering. My mother was gentle and kind and they murdered her. My father was a powerful warrior and they murdered him too! So answer me; is it irrational to fear beings of such pure evil?"

*"Yes, anger is the more appropriate response; not fear. From everything I have seen and sensed about you, you could crush any number of Belial set before you. You are a full grown lion who thinks itself a cub."* His answer matched her intensity.

"And just how would I crush these Belial?"

*"Well that's simple enough; instead of taking a little bit of their*

*life energy, take it all."*

Jade shuddered at the thought. It wasn't that she had never thought about it before; it was just that the thought repulsed her. Her abilities should be used for healing, not killing. Then a strange notion struck her, like a bell rung by a Cold Iron Maul. Didn't she kill weeds in the garden all the time? She sucked the life force out of the weeds' physical aura only to turn around and give that same energy back to the plants she and her grandmother had planted. If she didn't kill those weeds, they would grow and spread until they had choked out and killed all the plants they had sowed. They would grow and spread just like the Belial would grow and spread until they had choked out and killed all good things. Yes, yes she could do it. Next time she wouldn't run and hide but instead she would do to the Belial what she had been doing to those weeds all these years. Jade's back straightened a little, her resolve growing firmer; the thought of killing was not so repulsive now that she had thought of it in this way.

"Courage," Jade said.

*"Yes Jade?"*

"I think I can do it. The next time I see a Belial I will treat it no different than I would treat a weed."

*"That's my little one."*

"So Courage, where's that group of warriors you sensed?"

*"You don't know?"* Courage said a little exasperated. *"We have had three of them following us for the past ten minutes."*

"Really?" Jade said while looking around trying to spot one of them. "I don't see anyone."

Courage laughed. *"They are there little one. There were four of them but I believe the fourth one ran ahead to tell the rest of the group that we would be arriving shortly."* Courage stopped. *"You might as well tell them to come on out so that they can give you a proper escort."*

Jade cleared her throat loudly, then addressed the air in front of her, "We know you are there, so why don't you guys come on out and give us a proper escort to the rest of your group."

*"Nicely put,"* Courage said.

*"I thought so,"* Jade thought back sheepishly.

A tall Areli warrior stepped out in front of them. His clothing was mixed colors of green, brown, and black designed to blend into the jungle underbrush. It worked, too; Jade would have sworn up and down that no one stood there until the man had moved. Jade was now able to see the tell-tale signs of a thin mesh of liquid steel armor under his clothing. He carried a shadow-bolt bow made from the finest black-steel in his hands; he carried no quiver upon his person for he needed none. A shadow-bolt bow was designed to shoot powerful energy bolts that would form when the bow was drawn. A person had to be careful with that kind of bow because the energy bolts it shot would explode upon impact and collateral damage from friendly fire was always a very real possibility. However, when used correctly, one bolt could vaporize a good dozen Belial. Jade was just glad it wasn't drawn and pointed at her. He also wore two Cinderblades upon his hips and twin knives strapped to each forearm. Both of which Jade would bet were coated in poison taken from the back of a Skullbelly tree frog. The man's totem, a sleek spotted Jaguar, prowled at his side.

Looking behind her, Jade saw that two other similarly attired warriors had stepped out behind her; one, a giant brute of a man, and the other a diminutive woman. Both looked deadly despite their size and gender differences. Neither of their totems were visible, yet Jade knew they would be close by. Jade also knew that she had most likely met all three of these warriors before but for the life of her she couldn't quite place when and where, let alone their names. So she decided to let them speak first, hoping to avoid that awkward moment when a person expects you to know their name and then it becomes obvious that you don't.

The man in front addressed her formally by placing his right hand over his heart in a fist and bowing slightly towards her at the waist. "Holy Daughter, it is an honor to welcome you this day, but I must say it is an honor not expected. If I may be bold, Holy

Daughter; what brings you out here and seemingly alone as well?"

Though the warrior addressed her with respect, doubt and confusion swirled around his aura. Jade could feel herself growing angry. If it had been her grandmother whom they had come upon, there would be no doubt and confusion in their auras, only excitement at being in the presence of the Holy Daughter who would heal their wounds, then crush their enemies. Instead these warriors were worrying about how she would complicate their battle plans. They would feel they needed to protect her—that she couldn't be trusted to such an important task by herself.

So she started wracking her brain to come up with a plausible lie that would allow her to somehow get the food and rest she needed without revealing her true purpose at being there, but she could feel disapproval from Courage. Courage couldn't read her mind without merging themselves through the bond, but he could sense her emotions and he was getting very good at discerning her thoughts from her feelings.

*"You are right, Courage. A lie would only add to the confusion, and they deserve to know the truth. Besides, they would never believe a lie. The truth is hard enough to believe as it is. I just hope they don't decide that I'm not to be trusted with such an important mission and take the guidestone to seek out the source of the curse and destroy it themselves. I have to admit that part of*

*me would be relieved if they did, regardless of what Alo showed us in the visions. I am having a hard time believing that I am the best choice for this mission and that someone other than me wouldn't be better able to save us."*

*"Have faith in us, Jade,"* Courage thought back with a quiet strength.

Sitting up straight on Courage's back, Jade looked the warrior scout in the eyes, and tried to imitate the dignified authority her grandmother always used when she addressed someone. "I have been sent on a most vital mission by my grandmother, Alo, and Chief Hiamovi. The Belial have managed to cast a curse upon our people. The Holy Daughter Kendra, my grandmother, battles this curse even now. It is a powerful curse and it is taking all her strength to combat it, leaving her with no strength to seek out and destroy the source of this wickedness towards our people. The nature of this threat—this curse—is such that only a Holy Daughter may overcome it. Therefore it falls to me as a Holy Daughter to take my grandmother's place and seek out this curse and destroy it for our people."

"If what you say is true," the warrior scout said, "and I have no reason to disbelieve you, then should you not also be accompanied by a group of the finest warriors to help secure the success of this mission?"

"Good Warrior," Jade said, "I would take every warrior in our beloved Areli nation if I could, but it has been forbidden. Alo, our Chief Spirit Guide, has had a vision in which he has seen that if any go with me they will die and our mission will fail. I must go, and I must go alone," Jade gulped as the last words left her mouth in a squeak, wishing she hadn't sounded so weak and pathetic towards the end. If the warriors noticed the fear in her voice, they did not react to it. And while their auras still swirled with confusion and doubt, she swore she saw a shadow of respect, and that was something she hadn't seen in a very long time. That hint of respect meant more to her than she would have ever thought possible, and she found herself craving more of it.

The small warrior woman walked forward to stand before them also. "If Alo has said you must travel alone, then you must travel alone, but I did not hear you say anything about receiving help along the way. There is a small group of us just ahead. Let us lead you there that we might feed you and watch over you as you take a rest so that your strength won't fail you when you need it most," she said.

Jade's eyes became misty. "Thank you. Courage and I would be most grateful for any help that doesn't violate the rules for this quest Alo has given us."

The three warriors walked off into the jungle while Courage and

Jade followed behind them silently. Jade's stomach rumbled at the thought of food.

# CHAPTER 14

The Devil Raum sat within the Heart of Darkness; darkness as deep and black as Raum herself. It was a darkness that flowed out from her, slowly devouring the light of the land, casting the world into perpetual night. A smoky vapor filled the air, bringing with it the stench of sulphur and of rotting things. Belial not yet blessed with spirits of the divine Nethernight cringed away from the black oily vapors for their touch caused great pain and left behind festering boils and blistered skin that seared as if touched by an Areli's Cinderblade.

The pain and suffering of the Belial people did not bring her joy, for joy was an emotion beyond her capacity to feel; yet it did bring her pleasure. This pleasure was greatly intensified by possession of the flesh, weak though it may be. She was beautiful again, young and voluptuous, having taken a new body. She drew a dagger across the top of her thigh, feeling the fine steel bite into her flesh. She shuddered and moaned, her eyes half-lidded. The pain was bliss.

The throne she sat upon rested within the bowels of the Belial temple, holy for the fact that no light had ever burned within its walls. The pitch blackness was a balm to Raum's eyes, for even the light of the night sky was enough to scorch her eyes. Unlike the gash upon her thigh, the pain that light brought was not euphoric. For the briefest of moments the thought that one source of pain could induce such sensations of pleasure while the other only agony, was both amusing and frustrating at the same time. She took comfort in the knowledge that her darkness spread, and with it, her ability to move about this world grew. The demons who served her did not suffer the same way she did from the light, though they too preferred the night.

Raum cast her mind out yet again looking for that cursed girl. She couldn't quite pin her location down. She had set the twelve Demon Huntsmasters under her command to find the girl. Each Demon Huntsmaster had a pack of at least twenty four Hell Hounds. A few of them even had packs as large as a hundred Hounds with which to conduct their search, though it was rare for packs to grow so large. Few Huntsmasters possessed the required strength and mastery over the Nether to control such a large number of Hell Hounds. But they knew the price of failing her. Many would prefer to die and have their soul return to the Nether than to face her wrath. No, they would not fail her.

A part of Raum knew that if she was patient enough, the girl would eventually come to her on her own; however, time was growing short. The one that had sent her was growing suspicious. Maybe suspicious enough to come himself and if that happened, then all her careful plans would be undone. He would take the girl's body for himself and probably destroy Raum for daring to challenge him. Without that girl's body, she would be no match for his might.

The sound of footsteps echoing within the chamber disrupted her concentration, causing her to lose focus, thus making it impossible for her to continue her search. With a feral rage she lashed out at the source of those steps. She heard a grunt as a body slammed against the far wall. She opened her eyes, expecting to see a broken and bleeding body. Instead she saw Akecheta picking himself up off the floor and dusting himself off. Raum frowned; the force with which she had lashed out should have been enough to render even one such as Akecheta crippled. He was far stronger than she had thought and that annoyed her.

She did not like underestimating potential enemies.

Still, she smiled when she saw the heat of his blood running from his ears, mouth, and nose. A small feline growl rumbled lightly in Raum's chest as she watched Akecheta lick the blood off his lips while flashing his most wicked grin. Raum gathered up dark energies, preparing to punish Akecheta further; her body quivered with the anticipation of it.

Akecheta reached the center of the room, bowing down to the floor. "Master, you sent for me?"

Raum sat staring down at Akecheta's prostrated form, trying to decide if her need for him outweighed her desire to punish him. In the end her need for him won out and she slowly released the dark energy. She smiled down at him, knowing that one day his usefulness would be over and then she would have the pleasure of inflicting him with pain and suffering unimaginable even for his kind.

"How goes the war, Akecheta?" she asked, while signaling him to rise.

"Very well," he said, rising up to a kneeling position. "I have sent the bulk of our armies to the far edges of the Areli nations where the curse has taken the most effect. It is my plan that if we can overrun those villages it will allow us to flank our enemies and attack them from all sides, leaving them with no pathway to safety. By the time we have them encircled, the curse will have rendered them too weak to fight back. We should be able to take our time and enjoy the slaughter."

"Won't that leave us vulnerable, if we split our forces, to an attack up the middle?"

Akecheta's smile broadened even more. "They won't, and if they did we would just simply turn our forces and crush them between us." Akecheta held up his hands and slammed his palms together like a steel trap; then chuckled. "Besides, if we leave a clear pathway open for the girl, she will come straight to us, and it will be easier for the hunters to find her. This is your desire, is it not?"

"It is. If this is what you have been doing, why haven't the hunters already found the girl?"

Akecheta looked somewhat less confident. "I don't know! It is as if she is able to see where the hunters are and somehow slip between them."

"What else are you not telling me, Akecheta?"

"There are also small groups of Areli warriors attacking the hunters. They never stand and fight; instead they attack swiftly then retreat only to attack again later, disrupting the hunters' search patterns, creating the holes in which the girl has been slipping through." Akecheta hesitated for a second. "May I make a suggestion?"

"Make it!"

"Bring in flyers to help the hunters. If you do this there will be no more holes in which the girl might slip through, and when she is caught, one of the flyers could bring her back here in hours instead of the days it would take the hunters alone."

Raum drummed her fingers on the arms of her throne; she had thought of this days before herself but was hesitant because she had no flyers under her command. She would have to send a request to the one who sent her; possibly arousing his suspicion even more. She made her decision. "The hunters shall have their flyers within a one day cycle."

She dismissed Akecheta and watched him leave, arrogance in his every step, thinking of several different ways she would make him scream when she had her new body and his usefulness was done.

**** 

Her grandmother had said a week; a week to live, a week to die. That had been three days ago. That left just four more days until the end of everything. The worst part was that Jade had no real idea how far they had actually travelled in those three days, or how much further they needed to travel before they reached the source of the curse.

There was also a dark dread that ate at her, telling her she had less time than that. Jade ground her teeth in frustration; for every step they took towards their destination they were forced to take three or four away from it. The guidestone pulled them in one direction only to pull them back in the very direction from which they had come. Jade knew that Alo was trying to lead them safely through what could only be described as a maze of Belial; a maze that was becoming even more difficult to traverse the further they travelled into the heart of Belial territory.

The group of Areli warriors she had met up with earlier fed her and watched over her as she rested for a few hours. She had awakened even more tired than when she had gone to sleep. The same nightmarish darkness filled her dreams; the only comfort was the presence of Courage fighting back the dark. It seemed that the darker the dream became the brighter Courage shined, and no matter how hard the darkness tried to crush her, Courage simply would not let it. She had awakened weeping, however, for Courage's light protected her and her alone. She could sense her people being consumed by the darkness, and this made her fear greatly for her grandmother for she knew that it could only mean her grandmother's strength was failing. She was also able to see the effects in the warriors that had watched over her as she rested. They seemed to be moving a little slower; a little less graceful.

With a wave and a word goodbye she had left them. The guidestone pulled her in a different direction than the group was heading. She had since met up with two other small groups of warriors, though the urgency that plagued her would not allow her to stop and rest with them.

What if her grandmother had been wrong in her estimate and she really didn't have a week? Jade could not risk it. She had to keep pushing forward, and so she ground her teeth and wept in frustration every time she had to turn aside from the direction leading to Talberic. It wasn't just the guidestone or the visions Alo had shown her that guided them towards Talberic; it was the darkness that had been in her dreams. The darkness she could feel in her gut; in her bones. It wasn't just the feel of darkness growing anymore, but the world itself that grew darker with each step she took towards her journey's end, and the auras of all living things began showing signs of blight and disease. Each time the stone told her to turn aside and head in a different direction, she wanted to scream; her fear slowly giving away to a cold burning rage.

So when the guidestone again started pulling her aside from the course she could feel would take her directly to the source of the curse, she ignored it and told Courage to keep heading in the direction they were going. It wasn't long before she could hear the sounds of battle ringing in the air ahead of her. Courage slowed and then stopped, even though she urged him onward.

*"Keep going Courage,"* She urged, her rage giving her the strength to keep moving forward.

*"There is battle ahead little one."*

"I know! I don't care!"

*"What is the guidestone telling you?"*

"It is telling me to head north."

*"Then we should head north."*

"No! We don't have time, Courage; can't you feel it? We are running out of time. We must go forward even. . . . Even if it means we have to fight."

*"Finally,"* Courage growled, *"I am tired of this game of hide and seek. Let us bring terror to our enemies."*

Now that the decision had been made, doubt crept into Jade's mind. "Um, Courage?" she said. "I have never actually fought before."

*"Never?"*

"Never," she said. "My grandmother always planned on teaching me after I bonded and had progressed further in my studies."

*"Have you ever seen your grandmother fight?"*

"No," Jade said, "My grandmother rarely went with our warriors, and when she did I never went with her, and I never saw her practice either. She's always focused on teaching me healing, saying that it was much harder to heal something than it is to kill something."

*"So, Jade, how would go about killing something?"*

"Well... Like you suggested earlier, instead of only taking a little of something's energy I can just take it all."

*"How much control do you have over your ability to manipulate auras and take energy from things?"*

"I do it instinctively; if my body feels like it needs energy, it just draws energy from other living things and adds it to mine," she said. "I can keep myself from doing it, or I am able to exclude things or draw from something specific."

*"Okay, I have a few ideas, but first I need you to relax your mind."*

Jade tried to relax her mind and immediately started to feel Courage's mind begin to merge with hers. Reflexively she started to resist it, but then she felt a calming reassurance from Courage flowing through the bond and she could feel herself relaxing once again. This was a little different from the other times. Before there had been more of a mutual sharing or Courage projected his memories into Jade's mind. This time, however, Jade could feel Courage prowling through her memories; examining them quickly then moving on to others. He stopped for what seemed like ages when he came to some of her memories of the visions Alo and her grandmother had shown her of the Holy Mother and her battles with the demon hordes.

Jade felt Courage's mind separate from hers and they became

two distinct beings once again, though the natural barrier that existed between them seemed to be getting thinner with each merging. Jade briefly wondered what it would be like when that barrier was completely gone.

*"All right,"* Courage said, *"this is what I want you to do; take one of these trees and I want you to take all of its energy. Just draw it all into yourself as fast as you can."*

Jade shuddered at the thought of killing any of these magnificent trees, but her desire to do as Courage asked was greater than her aversion to such an act, and if she was honest with herself, she wanted to see what it would feel like. Jade reached out with her mind to the tree in front of her and seized its aura in her minds grip—then she just yanked; pulling it all into herself at once.

The tree's life energy slammed into her, setting her blood ablaze and causing every hair on her body to stand on its end. Intense pleasure blossomed within her chest and quickly spread throughout her entire body from the crown of her head to the tips of her toes. A moan escaped her lips as she struggled to adjust to her body's extreme euphoric reaction to the raw life energy coursing through her veins.

She now understood her grandmother's caution to doing something like this. She could easily become addicted. Lifting her hand up in front of her face, she could see tiny sparks of greenish white energies dancing back and forth between her fingers. She felt…powerful.

Courage's body trembled beneath her, a loud purr rumbling deep in his chest. Some of the energy that Jade had pulled into herself had bled into his body through the bond, and Jade could feel his blood buzzing with it. They both sat for a few seconds, lost in the sensation of it. The tree was slowly crumbling into a fine powder that drifted off upon the wind; wind that was promising a new storm.

The sound of battle seemed to be moving closer to them; the time for experimenting was running out. "Okay," Jade said, "now what?"

*"Try forming the energy into a physical weapon."*

Jade nodded her head then focused on the new energy in her body and tried pulling some of the energy into a concentrated form in the palm of her hand. The euphoric sensation dimmed just a little as a greenish white light began to coalesce into a spherical globe that pulsed and throbbed to some unknown rhythm in her hand. Then, not really knowing or understanding how, she shaped that small globe of energy into a small glowing spear. Gripping the small spear in her hand she spotted a giant boulder a good fifty paces off, partially obscured by the jungle foliage.

Normally she wouldn't believe herself capable of throwing

anything that far but she was still filled with the potent life energy she had stolen from the tree, and it coursed and surged throughout her body, granting an almost feral strength to her limbs. In a whip-like action Jade raised herself up upon Courage's back and hurled the spear towards the boulder. The air keened as the spear streaked towards its target. Jade's eyes burned from the blinding flash of light that ignited the air when the spear met boulder, followed by a deafening roar.

Ears ringing, Jade blinked the tears from her eyes only to behold terrible destruction. The boulder was completely gone, leaving a crater in the ground ten paces in diameter. Fortunately the force of the blast had moved away from Jade along the same pathway the spear had been moving. Everything that was not destroyed had been reduced to rubble, clearing a large swath of land before her.

Jade sat stunned, staring at what she had just done. Not even an Energy Cannon caused such destruction, and she had done it with nothing but a small amount of the energy she had taken from that tree. She was suddenly glad that she had not used more of the energy still coursing through her.

Courage, seeming to have read Jade's mind said, *"Don't be afraid, and don't hold back; I can shield us from your blasts."*

The sounds of battle had died down following the blast but it was quickly picking up again. Jade gulped, then steeled herself to the unknown; letting anger boil and churn within her—stilling her trembling limbs.

"Courage," she said, "I am ready."

# CHAPTER 15

"Good, because the fighting has come to us," Courage said.

It was true. Jade could see Areli and their totems moving swiftly in retreat through the jungle's foliage and what followed behind them could only be described as nightmarish beasts. Jade knew they must be Hell Hounds. She had seen Areli warriors bring in dead Hell Hounds as trophies. The killing of just one was considered an impressive feat. A single dead Hell Hound scared Jade. Over twenty living Hell Hounds crashing through the jungle heading directly towards her made her want to wet herself.

A Hell Hound could look Courage in the eyes and weighed a good half ton. Their muscles bunched and rippled under leathery flesh. Their flesh was marked by burning symbols believed to be used by the demons to create such monstrosities. Jade had watched her grandmother dissect a beast similar to the ones she now saw bearing down upon her, although it was believed that no two pacts of Hell Hounds were identical, but were more of a reflection of their Huntsmaster's demented mind. These had thick barbed spines that started at the base of the skull and ran down their necks, forming a narrow mane. Their tales ended in a wasp-like stinger that injected a vicious neurotoxin into their victim's body. Their deadly power was enhanced by razor claws, jaws that could crush rocks, and saliva that burned like acid.

Their auras were dark and murky, streaked throughout with violent reds, muddy yellows, and pus-colored greens. The thought of pulling anything from those auras made her want to vomit. *"I lied, Courage. I'm not ready. Courage. Courage!"*

*"It is too late to run little one. We fight."* With a mighty roar that caused the earth to tremble and set Jade's ears ringing, Courage charged into the heart of the pack of Hell Hounds.

Panicking, Jade hastily formed another energy spear and hurled it at the Hell Hound directly in front of them. The world flashed white and green as the life-energy spear detonated upon impact with one of the Hounds that was swiftly moving towards Jade and Courage. Though the ground shook, the blast did not touch Courage or Jade. Instead, a clear pearlescent shield deflected the impact's blast, and for the briefest of moments Jade could see themselves cocooned within the blast's raw energies.

Her vision cleared. The Hell Hound that had been descending upon them was no more, and two more standing next to it had been hurled away, their bodies broken and bleeding a black, smoky substance. A good portion of the jungle that lay before her had been wiped clear; leaving an open pathway before her with trees burning along the edges. The blast and the destruction on one of their own had caused the Hell Hounds to pause briefly in their attacks against the fleeing Areli. However, the pause was brief and as one being, they all turned away from those they pursued and were now swiftly moving towards Courage and Jade.

The sight of all the Hell Hounds swarming towards her scared her so badly she could hardly breathe. But a small part of her was reveling in the fact that she, Jade, had slain a Hell Hound all by herself, and had hurt two others. Jade could feel the energy she had taken from the tree had lessened considerably; having put more energy into the second blast than she had intended too.

Jade reached out with her mind and seized the life force contained within the auras of the four closest trees, yanking all the life energy from them into her own body, some of it flowing into Courage. Jade yelled and Courage roared at the pure pleasure of it.

*"It's my turn now little one; let me show you how it is done."* With that, brilliant white tendrils flowed out of Courage's body to snake around the four closest Hell Hounds that were descending upon them. At the touch of the tendrils, the Hell Hounds screamed in agony; their cries a thousand tiny needles piercing Jade's ears

and burrowing deep into her mind. Without really understanding how, she managed to block the sound from her ears and the energy that she had taken from the trees began to heal her now-ruptured ear drums.

The brilliant white tendrils continued to wrap about the Hell Hounds as they writhed and screamed. The one closest to them opened its maw and liquid fire poured forth from its jaws only to be reflected by that clear pearlescent shield, cocooning Jade and Courage. The tendrils swiftly tightened around the Hell Hounds and they burst into ash and cinders; their screams silenced. Courage had dispatched the four Hell Hounds in seconds.

Still more came—their snarling growls and howls rending the air. In those seconds they had killed five and crippled two more, bringing the number of Hell Hounds below twenty.

Out of the corner of Jade's eyes she could see the once-fleeing Areli begin to turn and engage the Hounds closest to them. They moved back behind the remaining Hounds and were attacking them from the flanks, acting as the hammer against the anvil Jade and Courage had created, crushing the Hell Hounds between them. With little regard to all around her, Jade started creating one energy spear after another; hurling them as fast as possible into the mass of the now confused and panicky Hell Hounds.

They were not used to being the targets of such great

destruction. Jade laughed hysterically as she flung energy spears. Then she felt a wave of fatigue wash over Courage as he expended more and more energy, protecting them from the continuous blasts of the energy spears.

Jade ceased her attack immediately. She quickly transferred energy from herself to Courage and felt him strengthen. As the smoke began to clear, Jade realized that her wanton destruction had forced the Areli warriors to cease their attack against the Hell Hounds from the rear, leaving a pathway open for the few remaining Hell Hounds to escape.

She had done it! Her first battle and she had won! For the first time in Jade's life she felt . . . confident. The dead Hell Hounds lay scattered before her while the jungle burned. A light mist of rain began to drizzle down from the heavens, dampening Jade's hair into a mess of dark chocolate curls.

The jungle was simply too wet in the rainy season and the fire quickly burned itself out, leaving behind smoldering embers that fitfully tried to flare back to life before they too succumbed to the jungle's wet environment.

Though the brilliance of the explosions caused by her energy spears blinded her first sight it did not affect her second sight, and it was through her second sight that she knew where to strike at her enemies. It was through her second sight that she had seen the remaining Hell Hounds escape beyond her reach. As her first sight slowly returned she could see how ancient trees had been ripped from the earth, leaving behind massive craters where their roots had been; large boulders had been reduced to sand that had then melted and was now rapidly cooling from the wet drizzling rain into what looked to be glass.

The Hell Hounds' burnt and torn bodies decayed at an unnatural rate; far swifter than any she had ever seen before. They already looked as if they had been decaying under a hot sun for a week; the stench of them causing Jade to gag, but it was her second sight that showed her the true devastation her energy spears had caused. Before her lay darkness so total, so complete, that it created a heaviness that weighed down upon her soul.

Jade knew that the darkness was not caused from a lack of light; for through her first sight she beheld a world that had been thrown into early twilight by the thick churning clouds above her; no, the darkness was caused by the absence of the light of life.

Jade quickly slid off of Courage's back, took two steps, and then promptly threw-up the contents of her stomach which consisted mainly of stomach acid due to the fact that she had eaten little over the last few days. Jade wiped off the vomit that clung to her chin with her hand while spitting a couple of times, trying to get the foul taste from her mouth. Grimacing, she looked at the hand she had used to wipe the vomit form her chin and held it palm up, letting the rain wash it clean. Steeling herself, she turned to face the darkness once more.

For the first time in her life, she had stood fast in the face of her fears and she had fought back. She had fought back and she had won, but now looking into that void she wondered if the price of her victory had been worth it.

All her life, she had been taught to heal, even though she had just a little earlier come to the conclusion that the Belial were like weeds that needed to be killed so that the rest of life could flourish —so that her people could flourish and no more children would have to lose their parents to the constant war that existed between them and the demon worshipers. There could be no truce between them; the only possibility for peace had to come by way of total victory over their enemies. But what good would a victory be if she left the land broken and devoid of life, and what kind of effect would that have upon her knowing that she was responsible for it?

*Look at me,* Jade thought, *one small victory and I am already getting full of myself. It's not like I have even faced a full demon yet or,* Jade shuddered as she thought, *the Devil.* Still, there had to be a better way to fight them. She could just seize their life force like she did from the trees but the thought of having the Hell Hounds polluted life force coursing through her body made her insides quiver. The energy spear was Courage's idea; maybe he would have some more.

The sound of cheers intruded upon her thoughts, and with great effort she tore her eyes away from the dead zone before her and noticed that the Areli were cheering her. Jade should have felt elated, but instead she turned and looked back at the pit of darkness she had created before her. They could not see the dead zone the way she could. *If they could,* Jade thought, *they would not be cheering.* Jade placed her face into Courage's shoulder, fingers gripping a fist full of his fur, and breathed deep, taking in the scent of him, earth and ozone, the way the world smelled after a powerful storm. Courage's mood was subdued as well, though he could not see the darkness the same way she could, she could feel his emotions and that helped settle her stomach. He understood at least.

Courage knelt down and she climbed up on his back and they started off in the direction the guidestone was pulling them, not waiting for her people to come congratulate her on their perceived victory; not trusting herself to keep from crying in front of them.

Thankfully the guide stone was leading them away from the dead zone. Jade pretended the wetness upon her cheeks was all from the rain.

They didn't notice the flyer circling high overhead, hidden

amongst the clouds. Or the Huntsmaster who had somehow cloaked himself from both Courage's and Jade's sight, its smell hidden amongst the reek of decaying Hell Hounds, eyes burning with hate and rage.

# CHAPTER 16

Menewa laughed for the joy of it. He danced and flowed amongst his enemies. It was a beautiful dance, a sacred dance; it was a dance of death. Flame, ash, and wind were his to command. Flame to scorch and burn. Ash to choke and blind, and wind that cut like razors and howled as fierce as a mighty gale bringing death to all who stood before him. Menewa, Chaska, and the twins decimated the Belials' rank and file, slaughtering indiscriminately. The blood of his enemies misted the air. The stink of burnt flesh and opened bowels assaulted his nose.

He saw real terror in their eyes and he laughed again. This is how it should be; how dare they think they could attack his people and bring corruption into the world. He would rather see the world burn than for the Belial to have possession of it. He would die to see that it did not happen. The Areli, his brothers and sisters, would fight until every last one of their bodies littered the ground before they would let that come to pass.

They had their orders, to cut their way through any enemies that might get between them and the heart of the Belial territory—the city of Talberic. The place of unholy temples where the Belial offered up sacrifices to their dark gods; huge pyramids made of black and silver-veined marble, stained even blacker from the rivers of blood that flowed from their altars and down along their steps. Menewa planned on making them pay tenfold for each drop of Areli blood spilt upon those altars.

Still, for all the Belial they had killed, they had had little real resistance to their incursion into the heart of the Belials' realm. True, they had killed a pack of Hell Hounds and their Huntsmaster. But Menewa knew that something wasn't right; they should have faced a horde of Kaga by now but instead they had only encountered a handful. The Huntsmaster they had killed had been challenging, at least.

This was but a brief flutter in the back of Menewa's mind as he swept low, cutting the legs out from under the Belial warrior in front of him. Chaska slid in from the side and took his head before his body began to even fall. Then Chaska was off racing to engage another warrior. Their brief exchange ended in a rather spectacular conclusion as Chaska spun a thin rope of liquid fire and air, white in its intensity, which wrapped around the waist of the Belial. Chaska pulled it taut, cutting the Belial in half only to turn around and plunge his Cinderblade into the chest of another, causing flames to burst from the warrior's mouth and eyes, then exploding outward to consume several of the Belial that surrounded him, leaving behind charred corpses in his wake.

If Menewa and Chaska and their totems were twin twisters of fiery death, then Honaw and Honon and their She Rock Bears were two massive avalanches. Their flesh was covered by living rock that had flowed up from the ground, cocooning them in impenetrable armor; each wielding two massive Cold-Iron Mauls. The hammers were double-headed and each intricately carved with imagines of their totems. The Mauls burned cold and their touch was baneful to all Netherspawn. Though Honaw and Honon looked to be two boulders in human form, they moved with a kind of fluidity and grace that one would not expect. Each hammer they wielded weighed as much as a good-sized man, yet they handled them effortlessly and precisely, and to devastating effect. With broad sweeping movements their hammers cleared the field before them, flinging Belial bodies right and left leaving them broken and bleeding; frost crusting their flesh.

The onslaught of the four broke the Belial and they began to flee before them. As the Belial retreated, a Kaga moved forward from the back of their ranks. The body of the Belial that it had possessed had been reshaped and molded to better fit the demon's spiritual form. It stood over eight feet tall and had horns like a bull.

Large ebony spikes protruded out and swept back from its elbows, and large barbed claws adorned its fingers meant to hook flesh and hold its victims fast while it fed upon them. It stood only in a loin cloth to cover its nakedness, revealing powerful rippling muscles, and skin tattooed from the crown of its head to the soles of its feet with Netherscript that looked to have been branded into its flesh. In its hands, the Netherspawn held, almost delicately, a long two-handed blade the color of burnt ivory.

Menewa admitted to himself that this was one of the more impressive Kaga that he had ever seen, and he wondered if its powers were as impressive as its appearance. Still, it mattered little between the four of them, eight if you counted their totems; the Kaga would fall before them in quick order.

"Kneel before me, mortals, and I might let you live to serve me."

"Do you hear that, guys?" Menewa said, "If we kneel to this thing we'll get to serve it."

"Tempting," Chaska said sarcastically as he circled slowly to the right.

"Yes, tempting," Honon and Honaw said in unison, chuckling as they circled to the left, completing a half moon formation that placed the Kaga in its center. The two rock bears growled and the earth trembled and quaked in response. The twins' chuckles grew to full laughs. The Kaga just sneered in response, seeming to be completely at ease.

"I have a better idea," Menewa said, "Why don't you kneel to us and we will kill you quickly instead."

They all moved at once. Chaos reigned.

Clever and Feather, Menewa's and Chaska's Fire Eagles, burst into brilliant white flames as they circled above the Netherspawn's head, lighting up the jungle with their radiant light. The Kaga screamed in pain, its attack towards Menewa faltering for the briefest of moments as it raised one of its hands to cover its eyes from the despised light-piercing rays.

Menewa and Chaska struck at once, both casting out a rope of fiery essence made from the elements of air and fire. Menewa's rope wrapped around the Kaga's hand that it had cast up to protect its eyes while Chaska's snaked around the wrist of the hand that held its fatal blade. Both boys flung themselves back and away from the Kaga, summoning the essence of air to drive them away, pulling at its arms to pin it down for the twins to get in close to attack it with their Cold-Iron hammers. Menewa pulled aggressively towards Chaska, trying to force the Netherspawn to present its back towards the twins and their totems.

Menewa knew that every Kaga encounter was different. Just like people, they possessed their own unique skills and abilities.

Menewa was strong, especially for his size. His air and fire magic often lent greater strength to his movement. If this had been a regular Belial or even a weaker Kaga, he probably would have just ripped its arm off with the force with which he pulled. However, it seemed that this Kaga was strong like Honon and Honaw were strong; strength that could crush boulders with bare fists, or uproot a tree with a causal shove—as strong as their She Rock Bears.

Menewa realized that this Kaga was probably even stronger than the twins. Instead of Chaska and Menewa sending the Netherspawn sprawling, they were the ones pulled up short. It felt as if Menewa had just pulled every muscle in his body.

What made Menewa's gut sink even further was the fact that this Kaga seemed to be somewhat fire resistant. The ropes of fiery essence should have been searing the flesh from its bones. Instead, only a few wisps of smoke rose up from its forearms. Still Menewa, and his brother, were not one trick ponies. They had been devising all sorts of nasty tricks they could use to slay Netherspawn for years. This was not the first time they had run into a Kaga that was fire resistant.

The Kaga hadn't even begun to fight back yet, and the first thing it did was grab their fiery cords and yank on them, doing to them the very thing they just tried to do. Menewa was quite annoyed when he found himself sailing towards it.

Menewa let the cord dissolve, freeing up his hand for his next attack. Gripping his Cinderblade with both hands, Menewa channeled his body's energies into manipulating the elements of fire and air. Instead of using them to halt his approach towards the Kaga, Menewa hurled himself even faster towards the Netherspawn. Soaring gracefully fifty feet through the air, whipping past trees, he approached the demon with the deadly velocity of an arrow released from a bow. Menewa was fast but the Netherspawn was even faster. Its form blurred into motion. So instead of cleaving the Netherspawn from crown to crotch, Menewa's blade merely lopped off one of the horns from its head, causing it to scream in rage and indignation.

Its response, instant and vicious, slammed Menewa to his knees as the demon's blade hammered into the thin layer of condensed air Menewa had hurriedly summoned around himself. It always amazed Menewa how something as ethereal as air could, when condensed, protect him from such deadly blows. The force of the blow required Menewa to expend a massive amount of energy in order to hold his now tenuous shield in place. The blow to the crown of his head caused his vision to blur, then dim, as if he was staring down a long narrow tunnel. It was all he could do to remain conscious, leaving himself completely vulnerable to the next blow that was already descending down upon him.

Menewa was going to die. He did the only thing left and looked his death in its rage-filled eyes. It was then that a large fireball smashed into the Kaga's chest, causing it to stagger several paces away from Menewa's dazed form. The intensity of the fireball's white and blue flames flashed brilliantly in his eyes, blinding him —filling his world with a white haze. His skin flashed red as if burned from prolonged exposer to the sun, and only his own fire-resistance and the thick shield of air kept him from being severely burned. The fireball his brother had summoned was powerful in its intensity.

Blinded, head spinning, Menewa thrust his hand out in front of him, channeling a powerful blast of air. He flung himself up and away from where he believed the Kaga to be and didn't stop until his back cracked against the trunk of a tree, his head rebounding from its surface. The spin and tilt of the world caused his stomach to heave and strain to expel the contents of the small breakfast he had consumed earlier that morning. Menewa swallowed it back down, causing his throat to burn from the acids of his stomach.

Blinking rapidly, he struggled to make his stinging, tear-filled eyes focus on the white-washed world around him, but his vision was creeping back slower than Chaska getting out of bed in the morning. With the sounds of battle still ringing in his ears,

Menewa merged with Clever, allowing him to see the world through Clever's eyes. The world snapped into intense focus. Clever's eyes were far sharper than Menewa's own, allowing him a clear view of the battle raging below. Menewa and Clever had practiced sharing each other's senses countless times, so the process caused little disorientation, though Menewa was completely unable to do anything but watch the fight unfold before him.

After that first initial fireball Chaska had hurled at the demon, allowing Menewa to escape, he had quickly changed tactics. With Clever's sharp eyes, Menewa was able to make out the warped air around the demon's head; that could only mean that Chaska had formed a vacuum, thus depriving it of all oxygen. Menewa smiled despite his throbbing headache. He didn't know too many beings that could fight for very long when they couldn't breathe. One of the twins had manipulated earth, causing it to flow up and around the Kaga's legs, cocooning it from the waist down in solid rock— rooting it firmly in place. It was only a matter of time now. But the Kaga didn't seem willing to accept its defeat just yet.

The Kaga had dropped its sword and was now raising its hands as if in supplication to Chaska, then with a crack that split the air, black bolts of lightning struck in rapid succession, pummeling Chaska into the ground. Its black energies radiated around the shield of air Chaska had formed around his body, drawing a cry of pure anguish from his throat. The vacuum that surrounded the Kaga's head wavered then dissipated. It roared in triumph as it sent bolt after bolt into Chaska's writhing body.

The Kaga never saw what Menewa believed to be Honon's swift approach; even with Clever's sharp eyes he had a hard time telling the twins apart. The demon's head burst like an overripe melon as the Cold-Iron Maul came crashing down upon the back of its skull; the Kaga's body crumpled beneath it, releasing the spirit within.

A being of smoke and cinders arose from the corpse that lay upon the ground in a vague rendition of the physical form it now vacated. The demon lashed out at Honon but with a dancer's grace he flowed out beyond the Netherspawn's deadly reach. He then flowed forward again to connect a mighty blow with the hammer in his hand. Though the creature was spirit, the hammer connected solidly, flinging it to the earth, only to be followed by blow after blow. The Cold-Iron of the Mauls stole away the demon's strength, bleeding away its dark energies.

The demon's form grew more ethereal with each blow until not even a shadow remained. Honaw approached his brother gently so as to not interfere with Honon's mad swings and placed his hand on his brother's shoulder. Honon's chest heaved mightily, sucking in life-giving air after such intense exertion.

Menewa watched as the rock that surrounded the twins turned to dust and fell from their bodies, leaving little trails of muddy sweat that clung to their faces. Menewa withdrew from Clever, returning his vision to his own body to find sight slowly returning to his burning, watery eyes. With an exaggerated groan Menewa climbed to his feet, his bruised muscles aching fiercely. But he was young and he knew that they would recover swiftly, though he decided that it would be okay if it was a little while before they had some more fun like this. Blinking his eyes, Menewa made his way over to his brother, a little concerned that he hadn't gotten up yet.

Menewa looked down at Chaska, who was laying on the ground, rubbing his chest with his eyes closed, a pained expression upon his face. So Menewa did what brothers tend to do when concerned about the other's physical well being. He kicked Chaska in the foot and told him to get his lazy butt up. Chaska cracked his eyes and glared up at his brother and politely told him where he could go stick his head. A laugh escaped Menewa's lips, though it was mainly due to relief because if Chaska felt good enough to engage him in insults then he was going to be alright, and Feather, his brother's totem, wasn't acting worried.

The two radiant birds quieted their flames, returning their feathers to a rich golden brown.

*"Clever, do you see any more Belial close by?"*

*"None close, boss, though the jungle gets a lot thicker in about another mile or so, and there could be some hiding over there. It's my opinion that they are all still fleeing from the good spanking we just gave them."*

*"Well, keep scouting above us and let me know the second you see something."*

*"Will do, boss,"* she said.

"Come on, get your butt up, lazy bones," Menewa said while kicking Chaska in the foot again.

"All right, all right, I'm getting up," Chaska said, bringing himself into a sitting position, wincing in pain.

Menewa gave his brother a hand, pulling him to his feet. "You know, you could have distracted him with something other than a giant fireball in my face."

"Yeah, well, you're welcome. Next time I will just let you get that ugly little head of yours lopped off, you big cry-baby. All you got was a little rap on the head; it wasn't like you got hit with that black lightning crap he started flinging at me," Chaska growled.

Honon laughed while walking over to Chaska and Menewa, Honaw strolling along beside him. "What are you two yacking about? That thing was nothing; at least nothing that a good thumping of one of my hammers couldn't take care of."

"I won't deny the effectiveness of your hammers," Chaska said, "but holy light you sure took your sweet flaming time about it."

"My brother's attack was neither early nor late, but came at the exact moment of perfection with which to strike," Honaw said, coming to his brother's defense.

"Easy, Brother," Honon said, "I think he's just cranky because that Kaga spanked his scrawny hind-end."

Chaska, glaring at the twins, said through clenched teeth, "You wouldn't be so cocky if one of those blazing bolts had struck you."

"This is probably true," Honon said peacefully, trying to sooth Chaska's ire, "and besides, you killed more Belial than I did."

He said this as if it settled everything. Of course, Menewa thought, for Honon it probably did. Menewa wouldn't be surprised if Honon knew exactly how many more Belial Chaska had killed. Though how in the devil Honon could keep track of all that in the heat of battle was beyond him.

"Hey guys," Menewa said, "doesn't this bother you?"

"Does what bother us?" Chaska asked.

"This," Menewa exclaimed while gesturing around them. "All of this. Shouldn't we be hip deep in Belial and Kaga and other Netherspawn? You guys saw the map in the war room."

Chaska and the twins shared a troubled look; Menewa knew they did not like what he was saying, but he was flaming right;

they should have had to fight every step of the way. Instead, they often went hours between fights and even then the Belial seemed more intent on fleeing than fighting. It was as if they were being let through the Belial lines. Why would they do that?

"Look, Brother," Chaska said, "I know what you mean, but this is a good thing if we are going to get to Talberic by the time Alo said we would have to be there."

"I know, I know, but doesn't it bother you guys even just a little? It is as if they are letting us by them."

"I am thinking that you are making this into a bigger deal than it really is," Honaw said.

"Yes," Honon chimed in, "I am thinking that this is because your brother has killed more Belial than you so far this trip, but don't worry, there will be plenty more Belial to kill before we get to Talberic."

"That's not it, I swear."

"Look Menewa," Chaska said, "we know what you mean but what can we do about it—nothing. So we keep doing what we are doing and hope that we accomplish whatever we are supposed to accomplish."

"That's another thing," Menewa said, "we were told we had to make it to Talberic but no one told us what we are supposed to do once we get there."

"Of course they told us what we are supposed to do. When we get to Talberic we are to sneak into the heart of the city. This is what we are supposed to do," Honon stated.

"Yes but why?" Menewa asked them.

"Look, Menewa," Chaska said holding up his hand, "you are forgetting what we were told. We are to meet Jade at Talberic so we can help her somehow, and Father wouldn't have us doing it this way if he didn't have a good reason—so just trust him, alright?"

"But…"

Honon clapped Menewa on the shoulder, almost causing his knees to buckle, "Menewa, you know I like you but all your questions are giving me a headache, and we are not getting any closer to Talberic by sitting around discussing them. Come on, we have a long way to go and hopefully many more Belial to kill."

Menewa just shook his head and sighed. They were right. He was probably overthinking things like he usually did, so he let the subject drop. Besides, he grinned to himself, he really was having fun, despite his fatigue and throbbing head. Killing Belial was just too much blazing good fun to allow his mood to sour over whys and what-ifs.

# CHAPTER 17

Alo's heart clenched in pain; never in his life had the visions caused him so much anguish. The visions, a sweet juxtaposition between blessing and curse, shaped his life just as much as those he used his visions to help. His visions were neither perfect nor infinite in their nature, and it was the limitations, his limitations, his weaknesses, that haunted him so. The fear that he may have led them all to destruction pressed down upon his chest —crushing the breath from his lungs. He tried to tell himself that the path he had sent them all down had been the only one that presented even the possibility for success—the best possibility for survival. But was it, or was he simply too weak to see the better path? In his youth he had been so proud, so arrogant, about his skills.

Spirit, the rarest of essences found within the Areli, and any who possessed it, were guaranteed an honored place within their society, often acting as the village's spirit guide—a member of the Trinity of Leadership. Almost without exception the ability to manipulate the essence of spirit resided in men, and for that reason the Office of Spirit Guide was held by men, and it was both Alo's skill and raw power that had raised him to the Office of High Spirit Guide over the Areli nation.

The Office of Medicine was similar to the Office of Spirit Guide in many ways except that the Office of Medicine was held by both men and women, and this in general was determined by both strength in the necessary essences and the skill and knowledge with which they were able to apply them to the complex art of healing. The High Office of Medicine was always retained by the eldest Holy Daughter though never in history had there been more than two living among the Areli. The offices of Chief and High Chief were hereditary. The position always passed to the Chief's or High Chief's eldest living son and if the Chief had no sons the position would go to the closest male relative who had the greatest skill and raw power over their essences.

The low offices of the three, while fulfilling different functions within their society, were considered equal in authority, and it was only through unanimity that major decisions could be made. If a decision had to be made that would affect more than one village or if unanimity could not be reached among the three lower offices, then they would request council from the High Trinity of Offices who would then work with the lower offices until a unanimous decision was reached.

Only the High Trinity of Offices could make policy that would affect the entire Areli Nation. However, if the lower Trinities believed the policies set forth by the High Trinity were wrong then they could veto the policy if they could get the majority of lower Trinities who ruled their individual villages to vote it down.

A veto by majority vote by the lower Trinities could still be overruled for while the High Office of Medicine held equal power with the other High Offices, and therefore subject to the majority ruling of the lower Trinities, the Holy Daughter who retained that position was not regarded as equal for she was considered sacred; held apart and above all others. She was an entity unto herself while at the same time the embodiment of the very heart and soul of the Areli. Her word was law for she was the law, and none could contest her while she invoked her right to speak as the Holy Daughter.

Kendra was the heart and soul of the Areli, and Alo's heart and soul, for he desperately loved her. He knew that she was aware of his love for her, but she did not return it. At least not in the way he desired. In this he cursed his vision, for though he had looked he could never see a future pathway that could lead them together. He could not hate her for this, though, for his supreme strength in spirit allowed him to see what no others could or had ever been recorded by other spirit guides. He could see the cavernous wound in her spirit, a wound both ancient and profound, just as he could see the spirit that resided in all living things. He had learned from Kendra that in a few ways this was similar to what she could do; however, in others it was vastly different. For one, Kendra saw the physical and emotional auras of a living being, but was almost completely unable to see the spiritual being within; while Alo had no power to change what he saw, or at least he lacked the knowledge of how to do so in the way that Kendra could, and since his ability was unique, there was none to guide him in all of its uses.

To see the spirit of a living being was to know its true nature. And no being was as complex and varied as that of man. For within the essence of every man resided the potential for true nobility, and within that same man, great depravity. It was only in man that Alo had found this duality to exist. A leopard was a leopard. A deer was a deer. A fox was a fox, but man... man was paradox.

Alo knew this ability to see men for what they truly were would have bred contempt and hardheartedness in many. But for Alo it bred compassion and empathy. Yes, there was darkness in man. But, despite this darkness, many elected to take the better path, to choose nobility. And he loved them for it. For Alo knew that true nobility found in man could exist only because within that same man resided both weakness and the potential for evil. Nobility existed because evil existed, and it was man's duality and the ability to choose between their two natures that made him truly unique among all of God's creations.

When Alo looked at Kendra, he saw her for all that she was: strength, compassion, love, virtue, pride, a hint of arrogance, and a streak of stubbornness that could fill the world, and woven throughout all her being was a sorrow so rich, so deep, that it must be buried in her very marrow.

For all of this and more, he loved her. She was his heart, his world, and there she sat, dying before his eyes, and he was powerless to stop it. Already he may have committed an unpardonable sin by sending Jade to an almost certain death or worse along with Hiamovi's boys and the twins Honon and Honaw, but blazing hells it was their only chance.

*Was it?* he thought. He had wept in fear and frustration when the visions of what was coming came crashing down upon his consciousness. For days after the first vision he had searched the streams of the future, praying to find a glimmer of hope, and it almost broke him when he did. He turned his mind away from the sacrifice that Jade would have to make before it could maim him even more. His eyes stung from unshed tears; for his people, for

Hiamovi, for Kendra, and yes, even for himself.

He shrugged his shoulders in an attempt to somehow lessen the burden bearing down upon them. It didn't work.

"Show me my sons," Hiamovi said, his face a mask of stone.

Alo closed his eyes and focused on the two familiar spirits of Hiamovi's boys, then indicated on the map where they were located.

Hiamovi sighed. "They still live." Then for what must have been the hundredth time he said, "Tell me Alo, tell me my boys are going to live through this." Pain and pride only a father could feel for his sons laced his words.

Alo gathered his courage. "There is hope, I have seen them live."

"Oh, my friend, your words are meant to comfort, but I know how your visions work. You say you have seen them live, but how many times did you see them die? You refuse to show me; no... don't... don't show me." Hiamovi's body shook with strong emotion, his knuckles cracking as he clenched his hands into fists. "You say there is hope, but dammit Alo, I see the map. I hear the reports; my people are dying. Even here in the heart of the realm I see people starting to weaken from this curse. Look at her! She is killing herself."

Alo looked to where Hiamovi pointed at Kendra, and his heart was pierced anew. He touched his chest expecting to find blood. *Dear Almighty in Heaven, there is grey in her hair.*

"Look Alo, she is aging! How is this possible? She is a Holy Daughter! She has lived for more than three hundred years and up until a few days ago she didn't look to be more than twenty. Now... now she looks to be in her forties maybe fifties. Tell me Alo. Tell me true—is there hope?"

Not daring to look his friend in the eyes, Alo stared down at the map; stared into oblivion, his voice rasping as he said, "There is hope." Forcing himself, he turned his head to look at his friend, praying he didn't see the lie in his eyes. Hiamovi's shoulders were slumped but Alo could see that his spirit within was shining a little brighter. He believed him and in a strange way that gave Alo a little hope too.

Maybe... maybe that singular pathway to success and safety seen in his vision would come to pass, and maybe he just didn't lie to his best friend after all. If only Jade didn't have to die. Alo turned to look back at the map, his mind turning inward, seeing the vision play back in his mind once more. The Heavenstorm would fall upon this world and even if they did survive he was damned.

Silence stretched, while Alo and Hiamovi studied the map laid out before them upon the War Table. Alo had studied for years, pushing himself sometimes beyond physical endurance to maintain the vision map so that they would be able to more effectively maneuver their warriors against the Belial. They took the battle beyond the wall to keep them off balance; never letting their enemy's population and resources grow too great in fear that they would be able to come at the Areli en masse. Now, despite all they had done, that was exactly what was happening.

Maybe it had always been a foolish belief; for as long as the Dark Portal remained open, the Belial could summon more reinforcements and supplies. The Areli had to make do with what they could grow, make, or trade, and because of the constant war their population had never grown great. And if the Holy Mother had been unable to close the Dark Portal, what chance did mere mortals have? Still, year after year, decade after decade, century after century, millennium after millennium, the Areli had kept the Belial in check. That was all at an end, and in their hour of greatest need Alo's vision was swiftly failing him. It was getting harder and harder to predict the movements of the Belial from their interactions with Areli warriors. The pall of darkness the Devil was casting out before it was like a toxic cloud that blinded Alo's foresight, blocking his vision of the Belial. At the same time, Alo could feel the Devil struggling to stretch its tendrils into the Areli's time streams so that it could read them the way Alo was able to read the Belials. The two waged a personal war for visions of the future. So far Alo had been able to block much of what the Devil could see of the Areli just as now the Devil was blocking more and more of his vision of the Belial. Soon the Map before them would be nothing but a black shroud, and then their warriors would be left blind to all Belial movements. Alo reached a decision that had been plaguing him since he realized he would be unable to maintain his vision of the Belial.

Alo had barely noticed the man that entered the War Room and engaged Hiamovi in quiet conversation, both of them pointing at the map. He waited for the man to leave before speaking.

"Hiamovi, we need to pull our warriors back to the wall. We will have to hold them there—I am no longer able to effectively see their movements." Alo slammed his fist down upon the table. "Three days, three blasted days and already the Devil has almost blinded my vision completely. Soon we will be operating completely blind."

"Are you sure you are not a mind reader, friend?" Hiamovi said while still studying the map.

"I am glad you still have kept a semblance of your sense of humor," Alo retorted.

"Peace friend, you said there was hope so let us act as if there is hope."

"You are right, as usual," Alo said. "So what was the message just brought to you?"

"It was a report that more and more of our warriors in the field are getting sick, and so I was just contemplating that it was probably time to move them back to the wall so we could better conserve our strength. Maybe that was what we should have been doing from the start."

"No," Alo said. "We needed the warriors out there to give Jade and the boys a better chance at getting through to Talberic, but I fear we have given them all the help we are going to be able to give them. Our fate truly resides in their young hands now."

"Hope." Alo said with forced cheerfulness.

"Hope." Hiamovi agreed.

Hiamovi signaled the guard at the door and told him to get a runner. Moments later a runner entered the room. The runner would relay the news to the communications center which would then contact the generals in the field so that the new orders could be disseminated to all under their command—thus changing from an offensive to a defensive war. What the runner thought of this information never reached his face, remaining impassive, taking the news like a true Areli warrior. With a salute he left. Within hours every Areli out fighting the Belial would be retreating to the wall.

Every Areli except for Jade and the boys. *May peace find their souls,* Alo thought.

# CHAPTER 18

A part of Kendra's consciousness floated along the streams of energy that connected all the Areli people, while another part of her was anchored firmly to her body that sat slumped in the Dragon Throne. She knew her body was failing her but she was powerless to prevent it. Well, she knew that wasn't true but she was not yet ready to pay the price that would be required to preserve her life. The life of others was just too precious to her; whether plant, animal, or person, it didn't matter. She who held all life in the palm of her hands; to give or take as she pleased. It was such a simple thing for her to reach out and steal life from others and make that life her own, but life was the ultimate beauty and she cherished that beauty above all else. And so she bled out her own life instead of others. So as the curse ate away the life force of her beloved people she replaced it with her own. Faster and faster the curse grew, building momentum with each passing second, stripping that precious life force away faster than she could replace it, and in the end she knew she wasn't sufficient for the task.

It was a well-kept secret that with each new generation of Holy Daughters the abilities they possessed were becoming less and less. The first Holy Daughter had been a little weaker than her mother and the trend had continued with each new Holy Daughter born.

Until Jade was born. For the first time in millennia, a Holy Daughter had been born with more potential than her predecessor. When Jade eventually came into her full powers, her strength would dwarf that of Kendra's, but still no matter how much future potential Jade had, for now she was still just a frightened young teenage girl, and that had been why Kendra had been taking Jade's training so slowly.

That and fear.

Kendra believed she had to heal the wounds in Jade's soul before Jade would be able to truly cope with her true abilities, and the responsibilities that would come with them. So it was easy not to push Jade when she refused to progress, and now—now Jade would never have the opportunity to reach her full potential. Maybe if she had been less sparing with Jade's feelings she would have had a chance. Maybe they all would have had a chance. Then again maybe if she had pushed Jade harder she would have shut down completely and no progress would have been made at all. In the end, though, sacrifices had to be made no matter how high and terrible the price.

Kendra had been taught when she was young, not much older than Jade was now, that the Holy Daughter was the ultimate authority among the Areli. What that really meant was that she was the first servant of her people, and if it meant that her life was required to fulfill that service, then it was a price that was expected to be paid willingly, and in full, without regret or hesitation. To lead was to serve. It could be no other way. She just wished that price hadn't fallen upon Jade's shoulders at such a tender age and that she would have had a chance to truly live her life; or at least as much of a life that a servant of the people could ever live.

Still, Kendra had enjoyed a time in her life before the full responsibilities of her position fell upon her shoulders. Before her predecessor left to seek out the Holy Mother, Kendra had loved and had been loved. Her husband hadn't been a leader among their people, nor had he been powerful in wielding magics. There were even some who had said that he was beneath her and she should have sought out a more appropriate match for a Holy Daughter, but he was sweet and possessed a child-like innocence unchanged by time or circumstance. He was gentle, yet passionate, and above all he saw her not as the Holy Daughter to be held in awe but as a woman. A woman who needed to be held in the quiet of the night, and reassured that everything was going to be all right when the pressures of her position grew past her ability to endure.

He gave her six blessed sons, but no daughters who might have carried on her legacy. He died in a senseless accident, his life bleeding away before she could get to him. Only two out of her six sons lived long enough to give her grandchildren, the rest stolen away from her by the cruel Belial.

In the end she buried them too. Each death cut at her soul. Then she started to bury her grandchildren, then their children, yet she remained ever youthful. The wounds to her soul eventually became scars and she found it harder and harder to allow herself to grow close to anyone. She cherished life, yet resented her own. Then Jade was born and she had held her legacy in her arms and felt hope for the first time in over a century. Hope that she would be able to finally put down her mantle of leadership and leave behind all this death. And with that hope she carefully let her heart open up once more, letting herself love a little, to be vulnerable.

Her heart was breaking again, but at least she wouldn't have to live with the pain for long; a flash of scarlet pain followed by burning shame pierced her consciousness at such an unworthy thought. The end of things for not just her people but the entire world lay before them with untold pain and suffering for millions upon millions. What was her pain compared to that?

No! She would not give in to despair. She would not! While she and Jade lived there was still hope. When the time came she would pay the terrible price for victory. If only that price could be paid in Belial blood.

# CHAPTER 19

Raum stood before a mirror, and though there was no light to reflect her image, she gazed upon her nude flesh and admired its beauty. Raum liked this body, so in an effort to preserve it longer she had etched runes of power into its flesh; the symbols burned red in her vision. The power of the Nethernight was not meant for preservation no matter how hard she tried to make it do so. The best she could do was to create an illusion of youth; for though the body didn't appear to age its internal energies were wearing out.

Raum ground her teeth in frustration that all her vast powers couldn't even keep a body from aging. The flesh of the girl Jade would fix that. She smiled at the thought. She had gleaned the girl's name through her scrying.

The beast Jade had been riding upon was still a mystery; it appearing as nothing more than smoke and shadow. But it wouldn't be long before she could see the beast also. Her power over this world was growing, and she could feel that blasted Areli

Spirit Guide's strength finally start to falter under the constant strain she was putting on him. She had to admit that for a mortal his powers were quite formidable, but in the end no mortal could stand up to her. Still, victory was all the more glorious for her having to exert herself, and when she consumed his heart it would taste oh-so-much sweeter for the knowledge that she had broken it.

The thought of it caused her body to shiver with arousal. She glanced to her bed and at the dead Belial youth that lay upon it. She had taken her pleasure from him. He had not survived the experience. She would have to have another pretty brought to her, but that would take time, and when it came to pleasures of the flesh she did not like to wait. She would punish her servants for their lack of foresight. She would just have to settle for the delicious sounds of their screams as she stripped their flesh from their bodies. She idly wondered how long she could keep them alive while she did this. It was worth exploring.

She was about to call one in so she could begin the process when a quiet knock sounded upon her door. Whoever it was, their timing was impeccable. She closed her eyes and focused on the being on the other side of the door and grunted. It was just Akecheta back from the hunt. He better have good news this time or she was going to let him take the place of her servants in her little flesh peeling experiment. At least this time he wasn't so arrogant as to enter without her first giving him permission to do so. With a casual wave of her hand the door unlocked itself and silently swung upon.

Akecheta arrogantly strolled into the room. He came to stand before her, his eyes studying her nakedness. She growled when his face remained impassive, unimpressed. She slammed him to his knees with a wave of power, bowing his head to the floor and began to lash his back with lines of dark energy, opening up his flesh and causing his blood to flow rich and red, staining the floor beneath him.

After a while she quit, her anger spent; she wasn't ready to kill him just yet. Releasing the power that held him to the floor she allowed him to rise. He climbed gracefully to his feet, giving no indication of the pain he must have been feeling. She almost forced him back to the floor to inflict further injury upon him just to see what it would take to finally crack his calm exterior. She needed him more or less whole, though, so she restrained herself.

The Belial's arts of healing were rudimentary at best and she would prefer not to waste her time patching him back up; as it was, he was just going to have to heal himself the best he could with his own arts. It was all his fault really, making her lash out at him the way she did; provoking her with his insolence.

She moved to stand close to him, and she smiled when she saw his muscles tense. Finally some kind of reaction! Looking up, she gazed into his eyes, like chips of polished obsidian, and slapped him with a strength alien to the body she possessed, sending him crashing back to the floor.

The palm of her hand stung; the pain exquisite from the now broken bones in her hand; they never having been meant to withstand such forces that she had just placed upon them. She would have to strengthen them so something like this didn't happen again. On second thought, maybe she wouldn't; the pain really was quite delicious.

The pain she had inflicted upon him had stoked the flames of her passion to greater heights, and the pain in her hand made her body ache with the want of release. She reached down and seized him by his hair to drag him across the floor to her bed, only pausing for a moment to remove the corpse that already possessed it before flinging him upon it. She then climbed upon him, straddling his hips, pleased that he was already ready for her. She took him, possessing his body, spending all her rage and passions upon him, satisfying her lusts.

Finding release in the climax of her passions, Raum's body trembled with mortal fatigue. Her hunger satiated for now left her feeling in a remarkably good mood. She climbed off of him before he too could find release; their bodies glistened from sweat and the air shimmered with the energies of their exertions.

She studied him with her eyes and other senses and found herself both pleased and annoyed at his condition. His chest still heaved from his body's expenditure, the sheets beneath him soaked with his blood from the many wounds she had inflicted upon him. She could sense his light-headedness at the loss of so much of his body's blood. Still, he had survived the experience, proving his usefulness in yet another way. Though he wouldn't be good for it until he was able to heal himself; it wouldn't be good to kill her new favorite toy just yet. She struck him again across the face, this time not putting quite so much effort into it; snapping his head to the side, and when he looked back at her for the briefest of seconds rage flashed in his eyes before his expression went blank again causing her to giggle. She grabbed his chin playfully with her broken hand, enjoying the stabbing pain.

"No, no, no," she said while gentle shaking his head back and forth, then delicately leaned forward and kissed his lips at first tenderly, almost innocently; then with increasing passion, but she cautioned herself. It wouldn't do for her to get too excited again. She punished him by biting his lip, drawing blood, which she then licked up tasting its rich coppery flavor on her tongue.

"Mmm. Yummy," she said, giggling again. Her long raven-colored hair hung down, framing his handsome yet much bruised face.

Akecheta grunted, "Master, may I now report what it is that has brought me be back to you?"

Raum sighed, and then climbed off the bed to make her way back to the mirror where she began admiring her body once more. "Is my form not pleasing to the eye, Akecheta?"

Akecheta sat up and scooted to the edge of the bed where he remained sitting, and with a weary gesture wiped his hand across his face, smearing blood, "Your form is intoxicating, Master."

Raum smiled, pleased with his answer, then turned to look at him with a pout upon her lips, "You wouldn't know it from the way you look at me."

"Master, if I fail to look upon you with the lust burning in my heart it is only because I fear to do so would seem too familiar for one of my station."

"Well, I shall forgive you if you were to look upon me with lust the way a mortal man looks upon a mortal woman." She said this with a tone that implied that if he didn't she would not forgive him. "Well I guess we should discuss whatever it is that has brought you back from the hunt; I take it you have found her." This she said as a statement, not a question.

Akecheta answered it anyway. "Yes, we've found her; she is making her way towards us."

"Good, but if you have found her why haven't you already captured her and brought her to me?"

"The Huntsmaster who found her tried, but she proved to be more formidable than we thought."

"Really? How so?" Raum said innocently.

"She used some kind of weapon the Huntsmaster has never seen before. She managed to kill seventeen of his Hounds in moments. He had to withdraw or run the risk of losing his entire pack."

Raum scowled. "It would have been better for him if he had perished in the attempt. Now I will have to make an example of him."

"I'm not defending him, but after he retreated he managed to contact the rest of the Huntsmasters and by now there should be at least six of the twelve packs on her trail, ready to attack at a moment's notice."

"Good, that's good. I want you to return and lead the attack to capture her."

"As you say, Master…"

"What is it, Akecheta? You don't sound overly confident in your abilities to capture this girl."

"I'm not, Master."

"Come here," she said, so Akecheta stood up from where he sat upon the bed and began to cross the room. Raum hissed, "On your knees! Slave!"

Akecheta immediately dropped to his knees and crawled across the floor until he was kneeling before her. "That is better," she purred. "Now tell me why it is you think you will not be able to carry out my orders."

Akecheta bowed himself before her and kissed the tops of her feet. "Master, as you commanded me I took a flyer to search for her from above and I found her moments before the Huntsmaster attacked with his hounds. I saw what she did to them and I fear that even if I were to lead all twelve packs against her it still wouldn't be enough to capture her."

Something about Akecheta's tone when he said this bothered her. "Is that pride I hear in your voice Akecheta?" She reached down and seized him by the hair and forced him to look up at her while his body remained awkwardly bowed before her. She studied his eyes, looking for a hint of what she had heard within his voice. All she found was lust; lust for her burning within them, as it should be, still... "Akecheta, you are one of the few who have dared to possess a body of an Areli warrior; tell me, were you not worried that you would lose yourself to him?"

"I was not," he said.

His simple answer gave Raum pause. Akecheta had run as big a risk in possessing this Areli's body as she did in trying to possess the body of a child of the Second Realm. "Who was he, Akecheta? Who was he before you possessed him?"

"He was no one; he was nothing. When I found him, his heart was so black with pain and rage that it was of no consequence for me to possess him," he said, panting.

"And yet you kept his name, did you not?"

Akecheta swallowed, "I did, Master."

"Why?" Raum tried to make her voice calm, even bored, as if she weren't readying herself to rip out his throat and suck the morrow from his bones if he answered her incorrectly.

"It pleased me at the time Master, and for no other reason. I shall forsake this name for another if it pleases you, Master."

Raum released his hair and patted him on his head as one might pet a favored hound. A knot between her shoulder blades that she had not realized had formed there loosened. She really would have regretted having to destroy him. This new realization bothered her; with a sharp blow delivered with a closed fist, she knocked him to the floor, and then followed her punch with a vicious kick to his ribs. She smiled as she felt them crack under the force of her blow. She moaned as several bones in her own toes snapped; the sharp throbbing pain filled her with pleasure. A low throaty laugh escaped her lips as she looked down upon him; pleased with herself. "You may keep your name for now."

"As it pleases, Master," Akecheta said, his voice a hoarse whisper as he pulled himself up once more into a kneeling position. His shoulders hunched over his right side where his ribs had been broken. "Master, in all your greatness you surely must have a way for us to overcome this girl so that I might capture her and bring her before you?"

"Do you think that I wouldn't have planned for this, Akecheta?"

"No Master, it is just that we were counting on her not being trained enough in her abilities to use them against us effectively."

Raum walked over to a chest made of hardwood and leafed in gold that rested against the wall a few feet from where her mirror stood. The chest was not locked; no one would dare steal from her let alone enter her room without permission. She reached into the chest and pulled out a large, densely woven net made from the silk of Barzel Worms that had been enhanced with the power of Netherscript, making their silk stronger then steel yet soft as down. It wasn't just the strength of the silk that would snare and hold her prize, but the cold sizzling energies of the Nethernight that were infused throughout the net's weave. The net would sap the girl's strength and keep her from pulling the energies of life from around her; cutting her off from her power source. "Use this to capture her, then bring her back to me as fast as your flyer can carry you. It will serve as a proper prison for the girl."

Akecheta grimaced. "What?" Raum said.

Akecheta pause for a brief moment before answering. "I am just not looking forward to getting close enough to the girl to use that net upon her."

"Surely you are not afraid Akecheta?" Raum said sarcastically.

"No, the thought of possibly being burned to cinders holds no fear for me," he said wryly. His voice was dry with repressed humor.

Raum glared at him through slitted eyes, trying to decide if she should be angry or amused at his returned sarcasm. She decided to be amused. If she punished him more it would be hours yet before he could heal himself sufficiently enough to be useful in carrying out her orders. Her own broken toes burned and itched as she used her host's bodily energies to speed its healing process, further depleting its natural ability to generate energy, ageing the spirit's energy core a little more. Raum had the causal thought that perhaps if she were to be easier on her host's body then maybe the body would last longer. But in the end what was the fun in that.

# CHAPTER 20

The sun was out, a rarity during the rainy season. It seemed an eternity since Jade had sat in the shade under the tree by the garden, putting off the simple work of weeding. If only she could be back there now and none of this had happened... but then she wouldn't have already bonded with Courage and she was not willing to give that up either.

Nothing was ever easy, especially when it came to her feelings. Except where Courage was concerned; when it came to him all she felt was an overwhelming sense of love and gratitude. Somehow everything would be okay as long as they could face it together.

The sun's rays shone weak through the ever-darkening landscape. A dark aerosol tar was slowly blanketing the land, making the world look dark and sooty. It made Jade's skin itch, and left her feeling unclean. She wanted a warm, relaxing soak in her bath; she would have to settle for a dip in a creek. The constant fear and tension left her little time to daydream about such things; however, for the briefest of moments she was back in her room, floating dreamily in her bath, its hot scented water caressing her skin and leaving her with a feeling of peace.

*"Jade,"* Courage's voice rudely interrupted her pleasant fantasy. *"Hold on."*

Reality came flooding back; the sensation of peace fled before it, leaving her stranded to face it alone.

Not alone; she had Courage. She had just enough time to register the world around her and tighten her hold on Courage's fur and then they were soaring over what must have been a fifty foot ravine that plummeted down into darkness. There was no hesitation or faltering in his step. In fact, it felt effortless, as if at any moment Courage could have taken flight for real.

*"Whoa, a little more warning next time."*

*"Don't worry little one. I wouldn't have let you fall."*

*"Still, that was a really deep ravine, and what if you had ended up not being able to make the jump?"*

*"Ha, I can make a jump up to three times what we just did. If I didn't think I could make the jump safely I would have tried to make a gate to the other side."*

*"Gate? Is it the same thing I saw when you were showing me how you travelled all the way from the second realm? Like the portal the demons and the Belial use to get here?"*

*"Yes and no. They are the same in that they use them to travel*

*between two far points, but that is where the similarity ends. I don't exactly know how the demons and the Belial create their portals, but what I do know is that what they do is unnatural and it creates a wound in reality. What I do is completely natural. I simply part the veil that separates two points, thereby creating a bridge linking them together."*

"Huh," Jade said while scratching her ear; thinking about what he said. "Well I can honestly say, I completely do not understand a word you just said."

*"That's okay, I didn't really expect you to. It is not a thing easily understood. If it was, anyone who is strong enough would be able to do it."*

*"Strong enough?"*

*"It takes a lot of energy to part a veil. On top of that, it takes a lot of knowledge and skill, without which you could end up anywhere, anywhere at all, and there are a lot of places you simply do not want to go. After all it wouldn't be good to open a veil that separates you and the heart of a star," Courage said. "Something like that would kill you and the whole planet you were standing on. It isn't much of a bother, though, to part a veil between two close points, so something like opening a gate between one side of a ravine and the other isn't very hard."*

"If that is true, why didn't we just open a gate between us and

Talberic?" Jade asked in frustration. "We could have been there already."

*"Hush now, I tried before I said anything to you because I didn't want to get your hopes up."*

"And?" Jade asked sharply.

*"And whatever the Devil is doing has made it extremely difficult to part the veils. It would take an incredible amount of energy to do so, and if I did it would alert the Devil to my presence here. I don't think the Devil knows that I am here yet and my instincts tell me it would be disastrous for our cause if it did. Besides, the amount of energy it would take to force a veil opening near the Devil would alert it to our exact location. There would be no hiding from it then, and I thought the idea was for us not to confront the Devil ourselves. Our job is to find the source of the curse and destroy it so that your grandmother can be freed from her burden and fight the Devil."*

*"Sorry Courage, it is just that we are running out of time and I worry that we are going to be too late."*

*"Oh Jade, remember hope brings light to even the darkest of places; never forsake it, but instead let it shine all the brighter the deeper the darkness falls."*

"Thanks Courage, I will try," she said sincerely.

*"That's my girl... On that note, do you have any ideas on what*

*we are going to do about all the packs of Hell Hounds that are surrounding us?"* Courage asked offhandedly.

"Hell Hounds! Surrounded!—what?" Jade panted; voice rising an octave with each word—the last coming out as a squeak.

*"Calm yourself, Jade; we are fine."*

"Fine? How can you say we are fine?" Jade demanded, then asked hesitantly, "How many are there?"

*"Over a hundred, maybe as many as two; I'm not completely sure,"* Courage said calmly.

"A hundred, maybe two." Jade nearly swooned.

*"They haven't attacked yet,"* Courage said a little irritably, *"and we can just do to them what we did to the last pack."*

"I don't want to do that again. It was awful, Courage, you didn't see what I saw. I didn't just kill the Hell Hounds. I killed everything. It was empty. It was dark. It was worse than this," Jade said, waving at the darkening world around them. "At least with this there is a form of life." She shuddered as she looked at that life. Sickly and diseased, it was still life. "It was nothingness, Courage, a deep pit into nothingness."

That nothingness had scared her more than anything she had ever seen before, more than the jungle, more than the Hell Hounds, more than even the Belial. For the first time in Jade's life she was scared of herself; of what she could do. It terrified her, and she had no time to come to grips with it. The one person she could turn to about this, who could understand, was dying. And if Jade failed her, she would die. All of her people would die. Grandmother had said she could last seven days. What that really meant, Jade had realized, was that she really had less time if her grandmother was being optimistic. In truth, she probably only had six days to accomplish her task. Only two days left. She wanted to scream. She wasn't going to make it in time.

Hope; she had to keep hoping. Courage was right.

She didn't realize she was crying until she tasted the salt upon her lips. *Great! I really am a bawl-baby.* Jade wiped the tears from her face and eyes and looked up at the blood-colored sun, its rays struggling down through the sooty atmosphere. Sending a silent plea up into heaven Jade prayed, *God, please help us.*

"What are we going to do?" Jade whispered. "Courage, what are we going to do? We were supposed to sneak into Talberic. How are we going to do that now? They know where we are. Stupid! Stupid! We should have never fought them. We should have kept following the guidestone."

*"Fighting was the right choice,"* Courage said. *"If we had continued on as we were, we wouldn't have traveled half the distance we have so far. And make no mistake, Jade, it is time and distance that are our real enemies here—not Belial, not Hell*

*Hounds, not even demons—but time and distance. The rest are just obstacles that get in our way and slow us down."*

"I know. Fiery hells Courage, I know, but we can't fight them; not hundreds of them, and if they truly surround us…" She let the thought linger.

*"They do,"* Courage said solemnly. *"If you were to open up your mind more you would be able to sense them for yourself. And yes, we can fight them; you have the power available to you to do so if you are but willing to take it."*

Jade shuddered. "No Courage, what I did was awful. I don't want to do it again."

*"You might not have a choice if we are going to get to Talberic in time to find the source of the curse and destroy it,"* Courage said, clearly exasperated.

"Okay, if… if I have to I will," Jade said; then her heart dropped down into her gut as a thought occurred to her. "Courage, something else just dawned on me. If all these packs of Hell Hounds have found us, wouldn't they have sent a message to the Devil about where we are?"

*"I was wondering when that would occur to you,"* Courage said, amused.

"This isn't funny Courage! We may have already failed in our quest," Jade wailed despondently.

*"You're right,"* Courage said seriously, *"I shouldn't make light of it, but I don't think we have failed, not yet."*

"If the Devil knows where we are, what are we going to do?"

*"We have options, but the best one I believe is for us to attack the Hell Hound packs and quickly kill as many as we can, then in the confusion we disappear and make our way to Talberic. After all, they know where we must be heading; I believe they have always known. The Devil must have been expecting someone to come looking for the source of the curse, which would explain why they have so many packs of Hell Hounds out-and-about. They must have been sent out hunting for whomever the Areli sent to destroy the curse."*

"Well they found us," Jade said.

*"That they did, but maybe we can get to Talberic before they expect us to."*

"Okay, so we attack, but how are we going to disappear?"

*"That's the easy part; often times when I have hunted prey I cloak myself in invisibility."*

"Can you cloak both of us?" Jade asked.

*"I can, but it would be better if you knew how as well."*

"Okay, but do we really have time for me to learn?"

*"Better now so you will be prepared to use it later if needed."*

"How?"

Courage paused for a second between his flowing strides causing Jade to grab Courage's fur to keep herself from pitching forward over his head. "Hey, careful!"

*"Sorry,"* Courage said, *"I haven't actually taught anyone how to do something like this before. My parents taught me when I was a cub, like all my kind, but I have never had cause to teach anyone else. I suppose if I ever have cubs of my own I will teach them. I guess you are my cub so it is only fitting that I teach you.*

*"A cloak of invisibility is easy; you simply take and weave the four essences together in a way that bends the light that hits you so that it instead flows around you until it reflects off an object behind you. Then allow that reflection to flow back along its course around you so that anyone who sees that light will see what is behind you instead of actually seeing you."*

"That's all, huh?"

*"Yes it is really quite simple. It does take a fair bit of energy and concentration to maintain and I have been conserving most of my energies to fight with the Devil. That is why we haven't been doing it all this time, but if I teach you then we can take turns holding the cloak and allowing the other to rest."*

"One problem Courage; I have never really used any of the essences," she said piteously.

*"Yes and you never told me why you have never learned to use*

*them. You're not like the other Areli whose powers are greatly heightened when they bond with a totem. You are a child of the Second Realm. The power of the essences has always been yours to command."*

"I know that I have always had the ability, Courage, but as a Holy Daughter I have so many other responsibilities and things I needed to learn, so this was always put off. My grandmother figured that I would have plenty of time to learn after I bonded to my totem, and it is tradition for a person to learn from their bonded how to use their abilities. Also, while I did have the ability to use all the essences before we bonded, it doesn't mean that those abilities haven't grown stronger because of the bond."

*"I believe I now understand why you got so upset when I tried to talk to you about this earlier. You think that maybe your grandmother made a mistake in not making it a priority to teach you these things earlier, and you don't want to think anything negative about her because if she really does die you will feel guilty. It's okay, Jade, even if it was a mistake, and I am not saying that it was, we are all fallen, imperfect beings; it is through our mistakes that we may learn to become better than we currently are."*

"No Courage, it is my fault. I fought her about everything. She always had to make me fulfill my obligations. I have not been a good Holy Daughter. I am not a good Holy Daughter. I have failed my people, Courage." Jade wiped fresh tears from her eyes. "I have let fear and anger rule my life, and now my people may pay the ultimate price. And if the Areli fall, there will be no one else to stop the demons from conquering this world. Why Courage, why has it taken all of this for me to finally get it? Am I really that selfish and stupid?"

*"No Jade, just young. It is good that you are taking some responsibility for your past actions. This gives you the power to change your future actions. The past is gone and can never be reclaimed but by laying claim to our mistakes we are able to learn from them. You are no longer just thinking of yourself as a victim. When a person blames all their misfortune on chance or other people, then they are effectively giving away all their power to change and grow, thus keeping themselves forever at the mercies of others, with no hope of shaping a brighter tomorrow. I am proud of you, Jade; laying claim to your problems is one of the first steps for true growth."*

"Thank you Courage," Jade said while patting him on his shoulder. Her grandmother had often said similar things to her but those had always felt like lectures, and she was good at tuning out lectures. When Courage had just spoken those all-too-familiar words it hadn't felt like a lecture, but words of wisdom and love.

She wondered why she had always had such a hard time taking correction from her grandmother. She loved her, and she respected her. She was an amazing person; so why did she always fight her about every little thing and refuse to learn the things that only Kendra could teach her?

"I'm ready to start."

*"It will be faster if we merge our minds so that I can show you directly what it is I mean and how I do it."*

"Okay," Jade said then reached out with her mind along their bond only to find Courage's mind reaching out to hers. Their minds met in the middle in a warm embrace, merging with each other. Like before, Courage's mind felt both intimately familiar and completely alien at the same time. A part of her became aware of his body and she instinctually knew that if she wanted, she could take over and use his senses as her own. *What would it be like to run with his body; all power, grace and speed, to feel herself slipping through the jungle at lightning speeds,* she wondered.

She could feel Courage's own amazement and wonder as he looked at the world through her eyes, seeing the world as she saw it; all life and light. The physical and emotional auras of all living things surrounding them glowed; he marveled as he took in a tiny fraction of the aura's as they pulsed and fluctuated. *"Jade,"*

Courage asked her, *"what do the colors mean in the trees' auras around us."*

*"They mean the trees are sad."*

*"Trees have feelings?"*

*"All living things feel, Courage, though it is often a mystery just what they are feeling or why they are feeling it. It is easy to see the sadness in these trees; I imagine it is because of the darkening land. It's like a poison that is affecting everything and the trees can feel themselves being corrupted, and they are powerless to stop it, so they are sad and scared."*

*"Wow, I don't know what I am going to do the next time I have to pee."*

*"Courage!"*

*"I know it isn't the time for levity. It's just the way you see the world. It's wonderful; in the millennium I have lived I have never experienced anything like it."*

*"Well, in all fairness, the trees don't really mind you peeing on them. In fact, they are usually grateful for the moisture."*

*"It's nice to know I am doing the tree a favor."*

*"Did you just say that you have lived over a thousand years?"*

*"Yes, why?"*

*"Holy crap, Courage, I knew that you have been alive for a long time but I had no idea it has been that long. How long do*

*your kind live, anyway?"*

*"I can expect to live at least another seven or eight millennium; some elders among my kind have lived for over ten millenniums."*

*"Wow, so even though you have lived for over a millennium you are still kind of a kid among your kind then?"*

*"Yes, and it was always annoying how much my elders enjoyed reminding me of it. So thanks. Of course I won't live near as long as you will. Your kind can live for over one hundred millenniums."*

*"Really? I can't even begin to grasp what it would be like to live that long. I wonder if Grandmother knows that that is how long someone like us can live."*

*"I don't know what she knows; maybe after all this is over I will get to have a long talk with her."*

*"She would love that, Courage. I don't know for sure but I think because we are bonded you will probably live as long as I will. I know that our peoples' totems live as long as we do even though they would normally have much shorter life spans."*

*"That is one effect I hadn't considered the bond having on me. I love it when our minds are merged like this; it feels like I am whole even though I have never thought of myself as being incomplete before. We should probably be focusing on the lesson I am going to give you. Just because the hounds haven't attacked us yet doesn't mean that they won't and I don't know what would*

*happen if they did so while we were merged."*

*"Right. Yes. Focusing."*

*"Now for starters I think I need to talk a little about the theory behind what I am about to do."*

*"A theory lesson, Courage!? Do we really have time for all that crap?"* Jade asked impatiently.

*"It's important and it will save time later. Plus, isn't it better to assume that we are going to be doing this a lot more in the future after all of this is over?"*

*"I guess."*

*"Good. That being said, one thing you need to remember is that there is no one way or right way to go about doing something. What I am going to show you is how I have learned to do it, and where I have the ability to use all the essences I tend to incorporate most of them whenever I do something."*

*"Okay, got it."*

Courage, ignoring her tone, proceeded to give a long lecture about all the possible ways a being could make themselves invisible and how each one was inferior to his method. Jade laughed when he told her about the time one of his sisters had set herself on fire when trying to make herself invisible by holding in all the light that touched her. *"You must understand,"* Courage concluded, *"that everything you do can have unintended, sometimes disastrous consequences."*

*"Okay, I am starting to get it. There are so many other methods for sensing a person that invisibility alone is not going to cut it if we are going to be undetectable."*

*"Right, that is why I use all the physical essences. Okay, pay close attention to me while I cloak us in invisibility."*

Jade felt Courage pull her consciousness into his own body. *"Now focus on my thought process,"* Courage said, *"and how I use my energies to manipulate the essences, both within and without. To handle the essence without, you need to use the corresponding essence within. Only fire can touch fire and only earth can touch earth. So let's start with the light. Feel me reach within to that place that is fire and how I use my body's energy to fuel it. Now that I have control of the essence within me I use it to reach out externally to touch the light that is all around me. Then, gently pushing, I slightly bend the light so that it flows around me. Following?"*

*"Cool."*

*"Yes it is. Now that we are bending the light around us, we can't see, so we need to let a little bit of light reach our eyes. Now we can see; however, now someone can see our eyes. So what we need to do is let the light reach our eyes but not let it reflect back out into the world. Remember what happened to my sister when*

*she did something similar. We don't want to burn out our eyes."*

*"No, we don't,"* Jade said fervently.

*"Now,"* Courage said, *"Feel me reach for that place that is water and how I use it to dissipate the heat that the light is creating. We will also do this with our entire body. Notice that I am not actually cooling our body's temperature. That would cause all sorts of unpleasant consequences for us. I am merely creating a shield that will block our body's heat from those that can see in the heat spectrum. This is really tricky because if you dissipate too much heat you become visible again to any creature that can see heat."*

*"Now, for our scent, you are going to use the essence of air to hold your scent close to your body. Remember, anything that you brush up against is going to get your scent on it too. You will need to use earth to convince whatever you come in contact with to absorb your scent so you leave nothing behind for trackers to sense. You will also need to use earth to smooth out any prints we may leave behind."*

*"Courage, my head is spinning. How on earth am I going to keep track of so many things at once? I mean, I can see what you are doing and how you are doing it. But, I don't think I can do it."*

*"Nonsense, Jade, of course you can do it. It will just take practice and patience, and before very long you will be doing it*

*just as well as I am."*

*"But when am I going to get a chance to practice, Courage; we are surrounded by Hell Hounds who could attack at any moment."*

*"Those are all valid points, but at first, I will maintain the cloak so you can continue to study what it is I am doing and you can work on doing it yourself. Don't worry, it will all work out. Now your turn. I know you have never trained with the essences but have you actually used any of them for anything?"*

*"Not really, I've never needed to. You would think I would have, when I worked in our garden; like using the essence of earth to loosen the ground to make it easier to till. But my grandmother wanted me to do everything by hand. She said it was good for me to learn to do things that way so I would have a greater appreciation for my abilities once I started to develop them."*

*"Yes, I remember the fact that you couldn't start your own fire when we first bonded. I should have taught you to do that already and been having you start all our fires. Then you would at least have had that practice at summoning your essences; even though we have been extremely limited in our ability to do even that. Let us start with that."*

Jade and Courage left his body and flowed along the bond back into hers. She found that even though she had only left it for a short period of time it somehow felt alien and strange, but then she realized that part of that feeling was coming from Courage, and it comforted her and scared her that this was all new to Courage as well. It comforted because they were in it together, it scared her because she saw herself as lost and confused and she could not believe how much in such a short period of time that she had come to rely upon Courage's strength, wisdom, and knowledge. He always seemed to know the right answer. So to experience his feelings of slight uncertainty in anything was disconcerting. It didn't take him long to regain his mental equilibrium, however.

*"Okay Jade, let us start by having you create a little flame in the palm of your hand. Don't worry, it won't burn you. When you are touching an essence you gain a resistance to it, and a flame you create with your own energy is part of you and responds to your will."*

*"That I already did know, Courage."*

*"That's good, and I apologize for repeating anything you already know. I just feel that it is best if I try to cover everything I possibly can in the time we have so I don't leave out something vital that you may need at a point in time when I won't have the ability to explain it to you."*

*"That's okay Courage. You are right. So now what do I do?"*

*"Start by thinking about fire; picture a small fire burning brightly before you. Good, you are doing well; keep picturing that*

*fire but now I want you to pay attention to me as well. Keep picturing that fire. Now I am going to show you where the essence of fire is contained within you; that special part of you that belongs to the element of fire."*

Jade struggled to picture the fire while focusing on Courage as he moved his energy throughout her body until he came to a place that seemed to resonate with the image of fire within her mind. She knew that this part of her had always been there, but she had never recognized it for what it was. It was just as much a part of her as the small of her back, and like the small of her back she rarely gave it any thought unless it itched or ached from bending over for a long period of time. Now that she was focusing on it, it was all that she could think about. And it began to itch. Jade knew that Courage was doing something to it to cause it to feel that way. She couldn't stand it anymore. It itched. But how does one scratch something that is inside? It wasn't like the back of your hand; no, it was like the place on your back where you can't reach no matter how you bend your arms. So Jade tried to mentally scratch it with the energies within her body. The part that was Courage inside of her immediately rose up to block her.

*"I wouldn't do that with that much energy while you are picturing so large a fire. We wouldn't want to set the jungle around us on fire."*

*"It itches."*

*"I'll stop agitating it now that you know where it is. Is that better?"*

*"Yes, much better."*

*"Do you still think you can find it now that the itch has gone away?"*

*"Yes."*

*"Good. Now is the time I would start talking about how to summon your body's energy to fuel the essence of fire within you, but you have obviously got that part down. One word of caution, however; most people don't have a fraction of the energy you have, so you need to be careful you don't overdo it. To put it bluntly, you are a lot stronger than you know, and with your ability to pull energies from outside sources, your abilities could be magnified countless times over. So I'll say it again; try not to overdo it."*

*"Sorry."*

*"Nothing to be sorry about. Now this time I want you to open the palm of your hand and have it facing up. Good, now I want you to picture a tiny flame dancing about an inch above the palm of your hand while channeling a trickle of energy into the part of you that is fire."*

Jade did as Courage said, squealing when a small dancing flame formed just above her palm. Jade lifted it up to hold it right in front of her eyes, studying that small flame; feeling a warm, gentle heat radiating out from it.

Experimenting, Jade extended her hand back out in front of her and pictured the flame growing slightly larger, more steady. Nothing happened. So this time while picturing the flame growing, Jade channeled a little energy and this time the flame grew to match her mental vision. Experimenting further Jade channeled even more energy into the flame but this time she maintained the same mental imagine of what the flame was supposed to be. She could feel the flame try to grow and change despite her mental image. It seemed to be straining against the bonds she had placed upon it. Almost immediately she started to feel a throbbing in her temples. So she changed the image in her head again, this time picturing instead of a flame; a spherical ball of fire twice the size of both her fists when balled up. The flame instantly changed. The slight pain in her temples went away, though this time she knew she had made the flame bigger than what the energy she was channeling could easily sustain because though it had formed into the bigger shape, the flame appeared weak and feeble. So she channeled more energy but this time she wasn't as careful and instead of only increasing it a little she let a good amount of energy flow into that place of her that was fire; pain immediately flared in her head and the ball of flame erupted in all directions in a brilliant flash of light and heat.

Startled, Jade let out a sharp yelp while the image of the flame she had been maintaining in her mind's eye fled and she felt Courage block her stream of energy, cutting her off from that place within her that was fire. The flame snuffed out as if it had never been.

*"Excellent Jade, very well done."*

Jade cautiously felt her eyebrows, checking if they were still there. Thankfully they were. Next she felt her cheeks and forehead, expecting them to be burned. Apparently she really was immune to her own fire; thankfully so, because she had just exploded a large fireball right in her face.

*"Are you all right, Courage?"* Jade asked him while checking his fur for any singe marks.

*"Of course, do you not think I can protect myself from a little fire? Truthfully I hardly felt it; I was touching the place within me that is fire just in case something like this happened."*

*"So if I am touching the place inside of me that is fire and someone hurls a fireball at me, I will be protected from it?"*

*"Yes and no. It depends on how much energy you are channeling through that essence. Touching it will provide a basic protection, but if you are hit by a powerful crafting, you can still*

*be hurt."*

*"So if I channel more energy into the essence, then I am protected more?"*

*"Right, this is why essentially you are protected from your own craftings, because you are channeling the exact amount of energy that it takes to create the crafting in the first place. They effectively cancel each other out."*

*"Courage, this is so hard!"*

*"Nonsense, you are a natural. You are already skilled at channeling your internal energies. I imagine you can do it without even really thinking about it. Honestly, it took me a long time to master it myself, but you seem to do it as easily as breathing, and you're just a cub."*

*"But I can't even craft a little flame without blowing it up in my face. How am I going to form something as difficult as that invisibility cloak you showed me?"*

*"By taking it one step at a time; now let's move on to the other essences so that you will recognize them within yourself, and you can get a feel for what it is like to channel them."*

# CHAPTER 21

Sweat beaded on her forehead and ran in streams down her cheeks only to drip off her chin. Courage had been pushing her hard. He seemed to be determined to squeeze every last drop of effort she was capable of giving in the very limited amount of time they both knew was available to them.

Jade was proud of herself for what they both agreed was an incredible growth in her skills. In one afternoon she had gone from only knowing the very basic mechanics and theories behind channeling the essences to being able to recognize all the physical essences within her and successfully channel them into different craftings of her own.

However, she was still a long way from being able to perform something as intricate and difficult as the invisibility cloak Courage insisted she was capable of learning. Channeling the essences was exhausting work, both mentally and physically. Jade was happy to cheat when it came to the physical demands of channeling by stealing little bits of energy. This didn't mean it was easy. Work was work. Then there was the mental aspect of it all, and in this she found no relief. Her abilities didn't provide her with a way to rejuvenate a tired mind the same way they allowed her to ease her sore muscles. Her mind was becoming mush, and if the Hell Hounds chose now to attack she was afraid she would be less than useless.

Jade found the place within her that was fire and began to channel a light, steady stream of energy into it while reaching out to the rays of light that streamed all around her. Delicately she began to encourage those rays of light to bend slightly around her as if she were a pebble in a stream. She created a barrier that deflected the lights rays in such a way that they were only slightly disrupted. The world of light around her went dark leaving behind only her second sight by with which to see.

She was now invisible to the naked eye. Jade would have loved to stop at this step, and had argued with Courage about the necessity of the next step because while she could no longer see with her regular sight she could get along just fine without it because of her second sight.

Courage had said that if he was going to teach her, he was going to teach it right. This was the first time they had ever really argued and it turned out that he was every bit as stubborn as she was. He finally won when he pointed out the fact that just because she could see, he couldn't, and if she was ever going to be able to hold the invisibility cloak for both of them then she would need to learn how to do it in the way that would allow him to see clearly. So she struggled on, trying to allow a little bit of light through that would let her see the world around her. At this stage she had to start using more than one essence at a time, and with each new essence, the difficulty grew exponentially. It was like counting from one to ten while at the exact same time counting backwards from ten to one. It made her head hurt.

Carefully she made a slight hole in the barrier, allowing a trickle of light to pass through. The world was growing steadily darker even though the jungle foliage was increasingly getting thinner. They had even found themselves passing through large clearings that sometimes ran for miles, allowing them to see some of the packs of Hell Hounds that were surrounding them; racing along beside them. She and Courage had had to slow down their pace despite the terrain becoming easier to traverse, because of the extra concentration her training required from both of them. Now that she was letting some of the light through the barrier, she knew her eyes were visible once more.

"Courage how do you make the hole in the barrier one way? I know you have shown me dozens of times already."

*"It's okay little one. You are a wonder to behold. It took me*

*months of practice before I was able to do what has taken you one afternoon to accomplish."*

"If that is true, it is only because I have the world's greatest teacher."

*"I am a wonderful teacher. Not even my father could conduct these lessons while running through a jungle."*

"Yes, we are both awesome."

*"I am glad to see your mood has improved enough to joke."*

"I think it's probably because I am so exhausted mentally that I have no energy left to be scared."

*"And I thought it was because I was here to protect you."*

"There is truth to that as well. I do feel much safer now that I have you. A few weeks ago I would have found a hole to crawl in no matter what was at stake."

*"You were hiding in a hole when I found you."*

"I was, wasn't I? It seems like a lifetime ago. Courage?"

*"Yes."*

"Tell me everything is going to be alright."

*"Everything is going to be alright."*

"Thank you, somehow when you say it; it seems it must be true. Now how do you make the barrier allow light in but not let it out again?"

*"Like this,"* Courage said while deftly taking over her

channeling, making the mental acrobatics required look easy. Courage altered the shared mental image they now held together in a way that Jade could not put to words, but visually made sense. Jade tried to memorize that mental image before Courage withdrew his presence with a word of encouragement for her to continue.

So Jade struggled on, this time meeting with some success. She was able to capture the image in its entirety. This was the first time she had managed to do so completely on her own.

Now if she could just get the next part. With some of the light now being trapped within the barrier, the temperature inside would steadily rise until it became unbearable. It would also light her up like the sun for all creatures that could see in the heat spectrum. She split her thought process twice more touching both places within her that were air and water. Then she began to channel energies into both of them while trying to form yet another image. This one incorporating both essences in the way Courage had shown her. This image would allow the heat from the captured light to be dissipated back out through the shield. It also formed another barrier inside the one that bent the light, shielding her body's heat.

She laid the two complete images together, forming one new one. The image held for one second, then two, then three, and with each second her excitement grew. She had done it; well, half of it.

Now, if she could only manage to use air to keep her scent close to her body, while encouraging anything she touched to absorb her scent so she couldn't be tracked. Then make it so she and Courage didn't leave prints or bent foliage by using the essence of earth. If she could do all of this, then she'd be home free. This last bit she thought a little sarcastically to herself as she became overwhelmed with the complexity of the crafting of Courage's invisibility cloak.

Jade let the crafting fall apart. Her mind rebelled against releasing the image she had struggled so hard to form; trying to cling to it like an overused cramped muscle. Jade thought that it was ironic that she had struggled for so long to create the image and hold it and now it didn't want to go away. She guessed it was a testament of how hard she had been pushing herself.

Courage seemed so far away after all the hours they had just spent together sharing each other's every thought and feeling. Jade forced her tired mind to work as she brought the world back into focus. Immediately she wished she hadn't, though she knew that that wasn't a completely rational thought. Staying and facing reality was a new tactic for her when dealing with things that she found unpleasant.

The first thing she noticed was that they were sprinting through another large clearing in the jungle and that there were dozens of creatures flying overhead. She was not familiar with them, though she had heard tales of such creatures. She had seen a large drake once. Not a true dragon, but still extremely impressive. It was something she had chosen to admire from a distance while her grandmother had talked to the warrior that was bonded to such a rare and powerful creature. The man was a Chief under Hiamovi of one of the villages that lay at the far west end of the Great Wall where it met the Impassable Mountains. If Jade remembered correctly his name was Lesharo, a man some claimed to be second only to Hiamovi in his prowess as a warrior. None dared say he was greater, but Jade recalled that Hiamovi had once speculated that Lesharo might be.

It was a powerful memory for Jade because Hiamovi seemed completely at ease with such a possibility. And in a society where everyone was constantly measuring themselves against each other, it seemed odd for a man who was supposed to be the greatest warrior among them to not care if someone was better.

She didn't know how she had gotten the nerve to ask him about it, maybe it was because Hiamovi had always been kind to her. She could still hear herself ask him why it didn't bother him. His answer had surprised her, and she still couldn't reconcile with such a foreign thought. Hiamovi had said, "It is none of my business what other people think of me, and if Lesharo really is a better warrior than me, all the better. I would love it if there were thousands more like him. For not only is Lesharo a powerful fighter, he is a good man, and I value the second just as much as the first."

She understood the importance of leaders being good men as well as good fighters. But how was it not his business what other people thought of him? Jade knew that she did, desperately so; that was why it was so terrible when she saw disappointment in her peoples' eyes when they looked at her, or even worse, disgust.

The mind was a funny thing, her resolve to face reality, as it was, had lasted a whole few seconds before her mind had slipped away into memory. Maybe it was because she was so tired mentally, or maybe it was that some of the creatures flying above her looked like some twisted version of the drake Lesharo was bonded to. Or it was just her way of coping with what she was seeing.

There were dozens of the massive flyers overhead, and each of them had a passenger riding upon their backs. Jade scanned the field around them as eerie howls filled the air. The Hell Hounds were closing in on them. They had run out of time.

They were out in the middle of the clearing, and the closest tree that she could pull energy from was over a mile away. She had never pulled energy from something so far away. She didn't think she could. So she had to settle on lesser things. They didn't hold as much energy individually but maybe if she took it from many organisms then maybe it would work. She quailed at the thought of killing so much innocence, but that only caused her to pause for the briefest of moments before she cast out her mind, connecting herself to the living things around her, drawing energies from them until they withered and died. She killed grasses, small animals, even things so small their auras appeared to her as tiny specks. She tried not to take it all, hoping that this time she wouldn't repeat what she had done earlier.

Courage had altered their course slightly, causing them to head directly towards a large pack of Hell Hounds. The Hell Hounds seemed to be coming from everywhere now. There had to be hundreds of them; more than enough to bury Courage and her beneath mountains of flesh. She went to form the energy spears she had used earlier, then stopped herself. Maybe she could use the essences this time instead.

She could always go back to using the pure energy if she needed to; if she was able to. There was not as much life here. She had to consider taking the life energies directly from the Hell Hounds and their masters, but she still didn't like the look of their sickly, mucus green auras instead of the vibrant whites and greens of life.

Courage only seemed to pick up speed as they closed in on the pack before them. He let forth a roar that shook the earth and caused the air to vibrate with its energy, causing the Hell Hounds to cease their disturbing howls only to be replaced with more nervous yowls that filled the air. Even though there was less life from which she could draw on, her blood still crackled with extra energies. She wished her mind wasn't so tired, but that couldn't be helped now. She was feeling like her mind had kicked into overdrive due to the extreme amounts of energy she was holding within herself and the added effects of adrenaline and fear.

Frantically she racked her brain for a method of attack that would not hamper Courage. Two hundred feet, one hundred and fifty, one hundred feet; Courage flew across the ground at lightning speeds. In just moments they would be amongst them.

Courage, lightning…

Lightning! Jade raised the palm of her hand, facing the oncoming Hell Hounds and pictured in her mind powerful bolts of lightning flowing from it to strike at the Netherspawn, bouncing from body to body in an ever-spreading web. With that thought firmly formed in her mind, Jade poured vast amounts of energy into the part of her that was fire.

Light and power erupted, blinding her eyes with its intensity and causing streams of tears to flow. Thunder followed instantly after, shaking the world and rattling her teeth. Her eardrums felt as if they were going to burst. Using some of the techniques she had learned while trying to form the invisibility cloak, Jade bent most of the light away from her eyes, and stopped up her ears with air thus protecting herself from the roar of thunder and the violence of the raging storm of energies that struck forth from her hand. Bolt after bolt of lightning struck among the Hell Hounds then swiftly spread out in a chain of lightning, dancing from Hell Hound to Hell Hound, flinging their bodies through the air; hurling their smoking carcasses skyward like leaves blown before a storm.

Standing in the middle of the pack was a massive Netherspawn that had probably been a Belial warrior at one point in time, but now stood over fifteen feet high. Netherscript was burned all over every part of its exposed body. The chain-lightning webbed over the demon, and each time a bolt came in contact with the creature the air flashed electric black. The demon stood protected within a cocoon formed of some nefarious energy, and though it staggered with each blow, the lightning did not touch him.

Courage never slowed as he leaped at the flesh-wearing nightmare. Jade feared she would fall off of his back but she felt a force of air that held her in place. When his body came in contact with the dark force surrounding the creature, the air flashed white; the brilliance of which was brighter than the sun to her second sight, and the concussive sound wave was felt more in the soul than heard with mortal ears. The look of surprise on the demon's face would have made Jade laugh if she wasn't so terrified.

Courage's body slammed into the demon's high upon its shoulders, carrying them to the ground where Courage proceeded to rip into it with his teeth and claws. The demon howled in agony, only to be cut off as Courage ripped out its throat. The demon's spirit tried to rise up out of the now-dead flesh, and while it should have been ethereal to the touch, only to be harmed by the essences or the Areli's magic weapons, Courage's teeth and claws shredded its spirit the same way it had its flesh. The rends in its ghostly form were filled with light that ate away at its being until it was no more.

Courage stood panting as if from a great exertion. Much the same way Jade channeled energy within her own body, she passed some of the extra energy she had taken from her surroundings to Courage. His breathing stilled. *"Thank you."*

*"No problem,"* Jade thought back at him. The battle couldn't have taken longer than a few minutes, though each minute had seemed like hours. Jade took a second to look around. She saw at least three dozen dead bodies littering the ground; ground that looked like it had been ploughed while several small fires smoldered in the damp grass. She was relieved; by using the

lightning instead of the spears made with life energy she had not destroyed all life in the area. Though the wounds to the earth were great, the auras of living things still shined in her second sight, and the life she had drawn the energies from, while looking withered and ill-used, still lived as well. She had never taken life from so large an area. She hadn't really believed she could draw life from things that were very far away. But she had, and by doing so she was able to take less life from any one thing while still obtaining a large amount of energy with which she could attack her enemies.

It had taken only a few beats of her heart for her to take all of this in, and a few beats more to realize just how many more Netherspawn were descending down upon them. It seemed hopeless. They would be buried under a mountain of flesh.

*"Courage, can you make one of those gates you have talked about by parting a veil, to get us out of here?"*

*"I could try. The Devil has done something that is interfering with my ability. Maybe if you give me enough energy I could force a gateway open. I have to warn you that we could be telling the Devil exactly where to find us."*

*"I think it already knows. We have to get out of here."*

Jade reached out with her mind further than she had ever done before, and found little difficulty in doing so; pulling energy from all healthy life around her for more than a mile in diameter. Her blood boiled with ecstasy as life flowed into her. Immediately she opened herself fully to Courage and poured all the energy she had gathered plus most of her own into him.

A wave of fatigue swept over her. The Hell Hounds were closing in. They were almost out of time. Jade could feel Courage gather the energy she had given him and marveled as he reached out and parted... something. Whatever it was resisted and Courage had to pour more and more energy into it and with agonizing slowness a hole in reality opened before them leading to a place she did not recognize. She could feel Courage swoon beneath her having expended a dangerous amount of his own energy.

A shadow blackened the sky above them. Jade looked up as a giant demonic flyer descended from above. The cry of warning died upon her lips; freezing as if she were hit by one of the bolts of lightning she had set upon the Netherspawn just moments before.

There, riding upon the beast's back, was her father. A smile as cruel and wicked as a knife slash split his face as he cast a net down upon her that crackled with a blackness that was worse than the void of nothingness. The blackness was alive and she could feel its hate and its desire to consume all life.

To consume her.

The net clung to her flesh like steel cables; the touch of it sending searing pain throughout her body. She felt herself ripped from Courage's back as she was lifted into the air. She watched in despair as the Hell Hounds reached Courage, attacking him as if they could sense his weakness caused from his efforts to part the veil. They were relentless as they piled upon him, ripping and tearing, bearing him down beneath their weight. A fire erupted, consuming all within its conflagration. A wave of force rippled the air, carrying away the ashy remains of the Hell Hounds that had been attacking Courage.

Jade looked down, helpless as she watched Courage struggle to his feet, knowing he had to be fatigued beyond all endurance. The net was somehow blocking her connection to him, leaving her feeling empty inside. In despair she cried out to him for help, but already he was growing small in the distance.

It had happened so fast. If only she hadn't frozen. A roar shattered the air, filled with all of the heartache and pain in existence. The ground beneath her seethed with hundreds more Netherspawn, all of which were descending upon Courage. In moments he would be swept away beneath the tide of their bodies. With a last roar of anger, rage, and despair, Courage turned and dashed though the opening of the veil just before it closed behind him.

They had lost each other. All that she loved would die. She had failed.

# CHAPTER 22

They should've been dead. They were definitely being ignored; like they were not important enough or dangerous enough to worry about until more important matters were taken care of. Menewa believed he knew what those important matters were.

As hard as it was for him to accept, it was the only thing that made any sense. He had always thought of Jade as weak, a coward, but he remembered how effortlessly Kendra had handled him, and she had said that Jade was just as powerful. Kendra wouldn't lie; no, she believed what she'd said and she was the one person who could really know.

Very little scared Menewa, but the more he dwelled on the incident with Kendra, he realized he had been scared. He was man enough to admit it to himself, though he would deny it to anyone else. He had decided he definitely believed Kendra, so that would mean that Jade was anything but weak. Jade, who wouldn't even go to the Training Fields to learn how to fight. She wouldn't even come down to watch others train. What was he supposed to think?

His father had told him that he was to marry Jade when they both came of age, and he had resented him for it even though Jade was a Holy Daughter. How could he be married to someone he didn't respect; how could he be married to a coward? But Jade wasn't a coward, was she? She had left behind the safety of the Great Wall and had agreed to make the trek to Talberic alone to find the source of the curse and destroy it, with only her totem by her side. As impressive as her totem was, what she was doing was incredibly brave, borderline stupid. This was something Menewa could greatly appreciate, and respect. Borderline stupid was his specialty, after all. Maybe they did have things in common.

Menewa had seen more Belial, Kaga, and hosts of Netherspawn as they continued their journey to Talberic; some of which he had never seen before. There had been several packs of Hell Hounds as well; if they had been hunting the four of them they would have been buried under their sheer numbers. How Jade and her totem, Courage, were ever going to be able to avoid all of them was beyond him.

It didn't help that they were failing at the duality of their mission. How could they not? They were told to travel as swiftly as they could while at the same time trying to distract the enemy so that Jade could sneak by them.

Both of which they were supposed to accomplish without getting themselves killed.

If they did not get to Talberic in time, then according to Alo, they would all perish. In time for what was a mystery, though Menewa believed he had figured it out. They would find Jade there at the base of the temple and help her locate and destroy the curse. But why would they have to flee and seek refuge underground? Maybe destroying the curse will cause an explosion? Alo claimed that he didn't know why, just that they had to be there.

There were too many questions. Too many ways to die; even worse, there were too many ways to fail. The thought of failing worried Menewa more than the thought of death. He was even willing to die in order for them to succeed at their mission. To die a warrior's death was a noble thing. Though Menewa admitted to himself he would much rather live nobly than die nobly.

Chaska had finally convinced them that they really couldn't fulfill all aspects of their mission. They had been trying to draw the enemy's attention but the enemy seemed determined to ignore them. Multiple times they had engaged the enemy, only for the enemy to flee the field of battle once it was clear the boys were alone. It was just slowing them down, and Chaska had argued that it was more important to be in Talberic by their deadline even though they didn't really know why. Menewa's gut agreed with his brother, and his instincts had seldom been wrong. If he was right, Jade would need them; would need *him*.

So they had turned their full attention to speed. Menewa was impressed with the twins and he knew his brother was as well. For while he and his brother had agility and raw speed, the twins' ability to manipulate the essence of earth caused the jungle foliage to give way, opening up clear pathways and allowing the twins to easily keep pace. In a race of both distance and speed, endurance was the biggest factor and that was something granted unto the twins from their channeling of the essence of earth. So in the end Menewa's secret fear that the twins would be unable to keep pace with him and his brother had changed to a deep worry that it was in fact him who wouldn't be able to keep up.

His lungs burned and his muscles ached from fatigue for they had not stopped to rest from their grueling pace. The only time they were not running, they were fighting. The fighting was occurring less and less. The land itself was growing darker until it was perpetual night. The air tasted foul and smelled rank. The plant-life looked wilted, and the jungle was filled with a quiet that chilled his bones. It was as if all animal life had fled. They walked through a tomb.

A few hours ago it had started to rain and its touch burned the skin, leaving it raw and tender. The land was growing more rocky and steep while the jungle was progressively thinning, which meant at their current pace they would reach Talberic in as little as twenty-four hours. Making the journey in under six days was a record time, as far as Menewa knew. The most important part was the memory of Kendra saying they needed to be at the heart of the city of Talberic by the morning of the sixth day or all was lost. Menewa's mind was wandering in circles, and he knew it, but couldn't seem to shake himself out of it.

They had to make it in time or the curse would take them before the Belial could. Already Menewa had noticed that something was not quite right. The foulness in the air was slowly seeping into him, worming into his bones. He had noticed, too, that Clever's thoughts seemed to be getting a little erratic, which could spell disaster in a fight. They needed both of their minds clear and focused. As he pondered these things, his optimism faltered. They could not maintain their current pace. It was impossible, even if they managed to avoid further fighting, the curse was weakening them.

They would need to rest, and soon. Menewa feared that realistically they couldn't make it by the morning of the sixth day. Had they already failed? Maybe the charm they had each been given to protect them from the curse would allow them to maintain their strength long enough to make the journey in time.

Kendra had said to use it when they started feeling the effects of the curse, but to be wary of using it too soon or the crystal would break before the curse was lifted and if that happened the curse would swiftly take them. So many ways to die; so many ways to fail.

Chaska signaled a halt, his chest heaving while acid rain and sweat coated his blistered skin. Menewa felt ashamed; he had been so lost in his own thoughts and worries that he had failed to be mindful of his surroundings or the condition of his companions. A mistake like that could cost them all their lives. Here in the heart of Belial territory any mistake was deadly. He hoped the others hadn't noticed his shameful lapse of focus.

He rubbed his hand over his arm and winced at the sting; the pain of his own blistering skin coming to the forethought of his mind. That had been one benefit to losing himself in thought. He had been able to ignore the growing discomfort and pain that was plaguing his body. To pretend his insides didn't feel dirty; unclean. His skin itched. His insides itched. He needed a bath. How could he wash away the taint he felt inside of him; would he ever truly feel clean again?

The twins approached from their lead position, which had allowed them to reshape the jungle, so all could move smoothly through the dense foliage. They were covered in welts and looked just as beaten as Menewa felt. They all looked to Chaska for he was the one that had called the halt.

"Aren't we a miserable looking bunch," Chaska said.

The twins looked at each other and shrugged, some kind of silent communication passing between them. "We have been better," Honon said.

"That is true," Honaw said after a moment of silence passed as they looked at each other again.

"Okay, right, I will get to it then," Chaska said, then immediately put a lie to his words by remaining silent for a good count of twenty heartbeats while he studied them as a group; his eyes searching each of theirs. "Feather and I have started having difficulties communicating, and her thoughts are erratic."

Honaw glanced at his brother then back at Chaska, "We have been having similar difficulties."

They all turned their eyes to Menewa and with a strange sense of reluctance he admitted that he too was having similar problems with Clever. Then he found himself saying, "I can feel it inside of me, worming into my bones." None of the others seemed to need for him to explain what he meant, and he saw each of them shudder slightly, silently.

"I think it is time," Chaska said, pulling out his charm from under his shirt. The crystal sparkled in defiance of the darkening world. Chaska took a small particle-blade from the sheath strapped to his forearm and pricked his finger. A small drop of blood pooled on the tip. Replacing the knife, Chaska took the crystal in his hand and smeared his blood across it. A look of relief bordering on ecstasy crossed his face. Menewa studied his brother. Chaska's breathing had slowed. The muscles in his face relaxed; even the welts seemed to shrink and his skin lost some of its redness.

The twins had followed suit and were reaping similar benefits from the charm's magic. His bother and the twins looked at him expectantly. His hand trembled though he didn't know why; he took his own particle-blade and pricked his fingertip, replaced the knife in its sheath, then squeezed his finger until a large drop of blood beaded upon it. Taking the crystal in his hand he smeared the blood all over its surface. The blood soaked into the crystal, turning it ruby-red. As the blood soaked into the crystal, Menewa could feel a wrenching inside of him, as if a part of him were being pulled into it. Whatever part of him had been pulled into the crystal was taking the taint, the darkness with it. He could feel the darkness flow out of him like blood from a wound. A sigh whistled through his lips; the relief had been immediate.

"*I am feeling better, boss,*" Clever sent her thoughts to Menewa.

"*Me too Clever. The charm Kendra gave us is working.*"

*"Didn't she say those would only last so long?"*

*"She did. So now we are going to have to hurry the rest of the way to Talberic before the charm fills with the curse and brakes. If that happens then we are as good as dead."*

*"Don't let your feathers get weighted down by thoughts like that, boss. We will make it. No one is swifter in all the Areli as the two of us."*

Clever was the only one in the world that Menewa felt comfortable sharing his true feelings, doubts, and fears. He had shared his insecurities about failing his people, and about his inherited position among them. Chaska would be chief one day, but Menewa would be the leader over the warriors; answering only to the council. Most days he felt he was up for the task, but there were moments, moments like today, when he doubted everything. He had no secrets from his totem.

*"Are we swift, Clever? I don't know. We have been running and fighting for days and we have had almost no rest. I am exhausted; if we had to fight right now I don't know if I could channel a decent crafting to save my life."*

*"Of course you could. Menewa, your brother has been trying to get your attention."*

*"Fire and feather, Clever, why didn't you tell me earlier?"*

Clever chuckled.

"Sorry Chaska, I was talking to Clever."

"Menewa, you need to work on your ability to pay attention to the world around you. You can't lose focus like that," Chaska said, then pointed his finger at him, "and talking to your totem is no excuse."

"You are right, Brother, I will do better." Menewa said, his face blushing from embarrassment at being reprimanded by his brother in front of the others.

"Good, we were just discussing how long we think these crystals will last, and how much time it is going to take us to get to Talberic," Chaska explained.

Honon grunted, "From what Kendra said I don't think that she really knows how long the crystals will last. She seemed to think that they wouldn't last very long, however, so we have no time to waste. If we don't get to Talberic and help Jade so she can destroy the curse…"

"My brother's right," Honaw said. "We have no time to waste. Our totems don't tire easy so I am thinking that if we all take turns riding on them we should be able to increase our speed and make it to Talberic in time."

"Your totems will let us ride on their backs?" Chaska asked.

"Normally they wouldn't, but they know the situation and are willing to let you."

"Tell them we are honored," Menewa said, and he meant it. He hadn't considered that an option earlier because most totems would be completely unwilling to do something like that even under the present conditions. Totems were completely loyal to their bonded, but they still possessed free will, and even though they had bonded to an Areli they also tended to retain an element of their wild natures. Totems were an independent lot. Clever had told him "no" many times. But the possibility of riding on Honon and Honaw's Rock Bear Totems would allow them to rest in intervals, making it possible to continue on at their current pace. They would make it.

*"Please, heavens above, let us make it in time."*

# CHAPTER 23

The war was not going well. Better than expected, but not well. They were still holding, still fighting, but they were losing. Messages that had been arriving hourly and what Alo was able to show on the prognostication map painted a terrible picture. The hardest villages hit were the ones furthest from the center; furthest from Kendra and her protection from the curse. Even using the Dragon Throne, her reach could only extend so far, and the more she weakened the shorter that distance became. But they held for now; son of fire, they held for now.

Still, while the reports and the map painted a terrible picture, it was Kendra who showed Hiamovi the true bleakness of their situation. Kendra, who had served by his side faithfully his entire reign as High Chief, and for the entire reign of his father, and his father, and his father before him; Kendra, who until a few days ago had looked young and vibrant. Now she looked... old and tired, and that terrified him. *"What kind of creature is this Devil that it could render Kendra into such a state?"* he thought to himself.

Approaching quietly, Hiamovi moved to kneel in front of the Dragon Throne, before Kendra. It was right that the High Chief kneel before the Holy Daughter; especially when she was bleeding her soul for his people. Gently, reverently, he lifted her hand up off of the armrest and held it in both of his. His hands dwarfed hers. She had always seemed larger than life, filled with power and confidence, and yet her hand had been small and delicate— graceful.

Now it felt fragile, brittle, as if even his gentle grasp might fracture it. Her eyes were far away, seeing things that he could never see, and he was grateful to her, for bearing this burden so that his people could continue to fight; to live. He would gladly take the burden from her if he could, though he knew his shoulders were not strong enough to bear it. The burdens he already bore were crushing him. Still, his strength was hers if she would but take it. "Kendra... Kendra, come back to me. I need to talk to you." His voice gentle; yet persistent.

He searched her eyes, waiting for them to focus. Moments passed before he gently whispered her name again; squeezing her hand in his as firmly as he dared. "Kendra, come back to me, please." The word please was filled with sorrow, and pain; the pain of seeing a loved one die.

Slowly, Kendra's eyes drew back from that far distant place to focus on his. Her eyes were so unlike anything he had ever seen before; the mark of a Holy Daughter, beautiful, mysterious. They fascinated him. Eyes alien and strange yet filled with a love and compassion that a son might see in his mother's eyes.

"Kendra, please I beg you, take some of my strength that you might preserve yourself."

"Hiamovi, you call me back for this? I told you, I will not take strength from you. I have told you this at least a half dozen times already. You need it to lead our people." The words of reprimand were spoken gently, taking the sting out of them.

"Then take the strength you need from others! If we lose you, we lose everything!" he said vehemently.

"I remember when you were a young boy; all passion and fire. But it was a boy's passion, a boy's fire. Now you are a man, and you haven't changed a bit in that regard; except that now you have a man's passion, a man's fire. But you know what I love about you most? I love your compassion. Your love for our people, both as a whole and individuals; you are a symbol of what it is to be Areli. We are a people at war; a people of death and violence, but we have kept our heart, our humanity. We are worth preserving."

"Kendra."

"No, I will not take the energy from our people. Why would I when I have spent all this time preserving them against this curse.

That's a little counterproductive, don't you think?"

"I am only asking you to take what you need. Just take a little from each of my warriors here. Or even better, let me take you outside so you might take the energy from the jungle; heaven knows we have enough of it to spare."

"There is merit to what you are suggesting, but you do not understand. You say take only what I need, but what if I need it all? There is something you do not understand about what it means to be a Holy Daughter. Our bodies are programed to preserve themselves at all cost. Let me give you an example: If you go without food for even a few hours your body starts to crave it, and after a while it can consume your thoughts. When you finally do eat, because you have gone so long without food you are ravenous and it becomes easy to overeat; to consume more then you need. Your body needs fuel to create energy so it drives you to seek out that fuel, to crave it; even to fight for it." Kendra held up her hand seeing the objection in his eyes. "I see that that was not a strong enough analogy for you, and I guess the simple lack of food poorly illustrates the situation I am in."

"When you were a boy you almost drowned. I remember because I was the one that pulled you out of the water, and as I remember it, you struck out at me in panic, trying to climb atop me so that you could breathe. Do you remember that?"

"I do. To this day I am ashamed of how I acted. As a little boy I thought myself brave, until that day. That was the first time I ever truly felt fear; I responded poorly."

"Do not be so hard on yourself. I was never in any danger, and you were just a little boy, but more importantly, your body was in survival mode. It was simply trying to do what it could to preserve itself. We all have that survival instinct born into us. You couldn't breathe. Your body needs air to live. So your instincts took over. The important thing to remember is how desperately you needed to breathe and what you were willing to do to get it."

"I remember."

"Good, because for me taking energy from the things around me is like breathing; it is completely natural, and I do it without ever really thinking about it. In fact, I have had to train myself to only take energy from things that can easily withstand it. The more taxed my body becomes the more energy it naturally tries to take. It is much like when you run for a long time. After a while you find your body struggling to take in as much air as it possibly can in order to maintain itself. Hiamovi, what I am doing is like running the entire length of the Great Wall while holding my breath. My body is now so starved for energy that it is almost as desperate a battle to keep from pulling in all the life force from around me as it is to fight the curse. If I let go of my restraints for even an instant it could be devastating to all life in this area."

"Kendra, there must be something we can do?"

"Hope is not lost, Hiamovi; there is breath in me yet."

There was a quiet knock on the door. A grizzled warrior put his head in and looked around the room, spotting Hiamovi still kneeling before Kendra. "We are not done talking yet; this will take but a moment," he said, and then squeezed her hand before releasing it and rising to his feet. "Come in, Honani."

Honon and Honaw's father slipped in and shut the door behind him. He had to walk around the war table to reach them. Stopping halfway around it he paused and looked down at the table; studying the map. His face showed no surprise at what he saw, only bleakness, and a cold determination. He turned from the map, squared his shoulders, and marched across the floor with all the pride, majesty, and arrogance of an Areli warrior. A small Spiked Ironwood Badger lumbered along at his heels. A stone bear would think twice before tangling with one of those. Hiamovi knew that Honani's sons felt the same way about him, though the father loved his sons and the sons their father. Spiked Ironwood Badgers could launch their spikes at both predator and prey alike with enough force to punch clean through their bodies; even bodies with skin as tough as stone.

Hiamovi notice two black ribbons bound to Honani's right arm;

an Areli sign for mourning. It seemed Honani did not believe he would see his sons again.

The old warrior came to stand before him and Kendra and saluted them, hand over heart. "High Chief Hiamovi, Holy Daughter Kendra, I have come to report that the villages that stand sentinel at the far ends of the Great Wall have been overrun. The Belial and their Kaga masters are pouring into the jungle behind us. It is just a matter of time now before they are able to completely surround us. I have also come to report that a large host of Belial are now gathering at the edge of the jungle before us.

"Finally! Some good news!" Kendra said.

He snapped his head around, looking at Kendra. "Tell me Kendra, how in heaven above and earth below is that good news?"

"Because those Belial are going to help me save as many of our people as I possibly can; in fact, the more the merrier."

Hiamovi and the grizzled warrior Honani shared a look, then gazed down at Kendra in consternation and confusion. "Tell me," Kendra asked, "how many days has it been since Jade left for Talberic?"

"It is the evening of the fifth day," he said.

"The Belial will attack tomorrow morning. As Alo foretold it; then—then they shall feel my wrath!" Kendra exclaimed.

# CHAPTER 24

Pain was absolute. It tore at her soul; her very essence of being. She was lost in the nightmare that had been plaguing her since all of this had started; though this time she was without Courage to protect her. She couldn't fight off the darkness; she didn't know how. The darkness caressed her, burned her, scorched her, and ate at her; it flayed her. Her screams ripped forth from her throat over and over again, hurled out into the darkness, only to have the darkness hurl them back at her, mockingly, scornfully, contemptuously.

Time was paradox. Floating in and out of consciousness, seconds passed like hours, hours like eternities. No time passed at all; yet in the moments of lucidity she could count out the minutes if she tried from the beats of her heart. Her heart fluctuated and fluttered—each beat erratic.

Her mind, frenzied, played over and over the moments before and after her capture. At the same time it desperately tried to hide from what had come later; from where she was; from her frequent visitor; from the truth. It had been her father, yet not her father, who had cast the net upon her.

The father she had known had long raven black hair that was always pulled back in a warrior's braid, but this thing that wore her father's face kept its head shaved. Tattoos covered his face in a hideous demon mask. Tattoos that flowed and swirled across every exposed part of his skin, seeming to form a language that was just beyond her knowing. They seemed to mirror the darkness of her dreams. They made her want to vomit.

She knew that this thing could not be her father; her father was dead. But this thing walked and moved as her father had; its voice was her father's voice. Her father's eyes had always held love for her, even in his dark days before he had left to hunt Belial, to seek his vengeance. Those same eyes that had held a deep gentle love for her now looked back at her with a cold and raging hunger that scared her; a hunger she could not understand.

Her father—no, the Kaga—came to look at her often, for he seemed to be standing before her most times when she regained consciousness. One time she had seen a beautiful Belial woman standing nude before her; gazing upon her as if she were some kind of insect.

She could see between screams that the net she had been captured in hung from a hook suspended from a steel chain that was attached to a gibbet, leaving her dangling several feet above the ground. People and creatures of nightmarish nature would sometimes pass by her, though they seemed to try to avoid her, and as they passed her by they would avert their eyes, as if it was she and not them that should be feared. Their behavior towards her only added to her confusion.

Her skin was blistered and bleeding from the contact with the fine steel-like mesh of the net. No part of her could penetrate the barrier the net created. If she tried to force her fingers through the webbing, the black pulsing energy made them feel as if the skin was being stripped from her bones. But that was not the true agony; the pain that left the inside of her throat torn and bloody from her screams. For the first time in her life she was truly cut off from the world around her. Whatever black energy was woven throughout the net blocked her ability to reach out and take the living energies from around her. Each time her body tried to reach for it, it was as if the black power slashed her soul and pierced her mind. No matter how hard she tried to keep herself from reaching out to that blessed life, she eventually failed, only to have her soul cut again, and the more her soul was cut the harder it became to stop herself from reaching out.

So she fled into the depths of her being—hiding from the darkness, hiding from the pain. Deeper and deeper she fled; past the places within her that were the essences. She fled until, time, space, and self became irrelevant; fleeing ever deeper until she came to that place within her that was her center; her core.

It was cold, lifeless, giving forth no light. She found herself to be incomplete. Her soul had no fire; though the longer she resided here she found that her core wasn't as cold and lifeless as it had at first appeared. It was like entering a dark room only to find that as one's eyes adjusted, light was present after all. The longer that she was in her core, the more she could sense its warm, gentle glow. It wasn't enough, and what it meant she didn't know. She would ask her grandmother.

She clung to the hope that she would see her grandmother again. That all wasn't lost. That her grandmother, her people, weren't dead already. Hope—it was like the light of her core; so dim that at first it appeared to not exist at all. But in the name of the light, it was there—IT WAS THERE! She clung to it tenaciously; refusing to yield it up to that awful beast of despair.

Here in the center of her being she found relief from the torments of her flesh, and indeed there was a sense of peace that she had seldom found in her life, but the peace was not absolute. Even here she could not completely rid herself of the anguish of self-recrimination though while she resided here there seemed to be a buffer between her true self and the pain, allowing her to think clearly. To be analytical. To problem solve. To nurture hope. She knew that if she left this place she would be plunged right back into the oblivion of thought that existed within the pain, and feared that she might not be able to find her way back here. If only she could take this place with her, but Jade knew it didn't work like that. If she couldn't take it with her, could she somehow leave part of herself here? Maybe that way she could somehow keep that buffer between her and the pain. If she was able to control the pain, maybe she would be able to figure a way out of this.

Alone. She was all alone... Heaven above, she needed Courage. What happened to him? Was he still alive? The instant she was captured in the net her sense of him was cut off, and though they had only been bonded a short time, his absence left a large gaping wound within her. Thinking about her time with Courage brought some comfort as long as she didn't dwell on their separation. She remembered how they had meshed their minds together and she had instinctively left a small part of herself back in her body. Maybe something like that would work here. Now if she could only remember how she had actually done it before. It was odd that now she would have difficulty doing it after she had done it before with no thought whatsoever. Then it dawned on her that Courage had been secretly helping her, guiding her, so gently that even though they had shared thoughts it was only now looking back at it that she was able to see that he had done it.

Time was irrelevant here; she didn't know if minutes had passed or days; light, she hoped it hadn't been days. Time and again she tried to leave part of her consciousness here in this place while the rest of her journeyed out, back towards the surface of her being, but the second she started to leave she would become increasingly aware of the pain that awaited her and she would flee back to her center. Ages passed, seconds passed; no time passed at all, and still she drifted here at the core of her being. The longer she was here the more peace she felt in both her heart and mind and the more she started to become aware of the different parts that made up her soul.

She looked at the different parts of herself and slowly she began to understand. She was seeing the four chambers of her soul —physical, emotional, spiritual, and intellectual.

She didn't spend too much time dwelling on the mystifying parts of herself, but instead went back to the elements of herself that were more familiar. She looked at herself, really looked, *"Man I am a mess"*, she thought. The physical part of her that experienced pain radiated a deep purple so intense that it seemed to give off a form of heat, though she knew that it wasn't really heat that she was feeling. She studied the pain, then looked at her chamber of emotion and found that she could identify various points of pain within that as well. The pain had a similar feel, and she could now see that they were connected. She moved back and looked at herself as a whole—looking for similar connections; indeed there were, and in that moment of time she saw that everything was connected. The essence of her being, each and every bit, was connected in a complex and beautiful web that formed the reality of her. From this distance looking down upon herself—now that she knew what to look for—she could see those points of deep purple that was her pain.

The pain was threaded throughout the four chambers of her soul. She mentally reached out to one of the points of pain; immediately she withdrew. When she had touched the point of pain, it had been brought into sharp focus once more and the intensity of it had almost overwhelmed her. She dared not touch it again, and the more she studied the problem she began to realize it wouldn't be as simple as leaving the part of her that was pain here in this place for it was spread throughout her entire being.

Maybe... Maybe she could isolate it somehow. Block it from the rest of her. Every part of her was separate yet connected. What was it that was connecting them? The answer came to her when she went back to studying the four chambers. She saw a brilliant flash of light in her intellectual chamber at the same instant she had the realization that it was the spiritual chamber that connected everything together. It was spirit that made up the strands of delicate steel that connected the individual pieces of her.

She thought of cutting the strands that connected pain to the rest of her, but felt a sense of doom steal over her as she contemplated such an act. Pain was a necessary part of her; it wouldn't be good to remove it completely—would it? The thought of cutting away any part felt wrong. What would happen to that part after it was cut away? Could she ever reconnect it? Would that part die, and be lost forever? No, severing the strands of spirit that connected the pain to the rest of her she felt was a very bad idea.

She began to look for the bond she knew connected her and Courage. Once she found it she tried to follow it to where she knew Courage's presence would be, but ran into a solid wall of filth that separated them from each other. She tried to push through it, but felt herself begin to convulse at its touch. The bond hadn't been severed, but whatever that wall was, it blocked her from Courage.

If her bond was able to be blocked, then maybe she could form some kind of barrier between the pain and the rest of herself. She reached into her chamber of spirit and took up its essence; the essence of her. The sensation this caused was unlike anything she had ever experienced. It was as if she held herself in the palm of her hand. Taking her spirit essence, she moved to one of the points of pain and formed a barrier around it; she moved on to the next point of pain, and then the next.

After repeating this process several times, she allowed herself to drift a little out of her center back into the web that was her; the pain immediately came back, but it was less, blessedly less. It was working. She moved back into her center and at once set herself to blocking off all the points of pain with an almost feverous intensity.

There were so many of them, and she had no idea how long she had been here residing within her center; minutes... days... Blessed light, let it not be days. She paused in her efforts and looked out at the work she had done. She hadn't blocked off all of the points of pain but she had managed to get a majority of them.

With fear and trepidation she left her center, and felt a gasp of euphoric joy escape her dry cracked lips at the sweet absence of pain. Peace stole over her; then with a deep breath of sulphuric air, Jade opened her eyes to a world of nightmare. She didn't close her eyes to it, or cower away from it in terror; no, she looked upon it and found calmness within her heart. That did not mean she felt no fear, but it did not control her. For this moment, at least, she was fear's master.

She had found a way to overcome her pain, and control her fear. Notwithstanding the severity of her and her people's situation, she was feeling quite proud of herself; something that she had seldom felt in her life up to this point.

The Kaga who wore her father's face stood before her. "You surprise me," he said. "I didn't believe you would be able to master your pain. I am proud of you."

Jade grunted as if she had been punched in the gut, "Now that I have mastered my pain, you try to torment me in another way; you who wears my father's face."

"Oh, but Jade, I am still your father; just a better version of him."

"You are not my father! My father is dead!"

The demon looked up at her with a sardonic smile, "Your mother was beautiful; beautiful in every way. I loved her so much. You know, even now, I can feel the pain of losing her. The demon that possessed me tried to strip that all away from me, but I did not let him. It is important to feel pain sometimes; it allows us to appreciate the times we are free of it. Pain reminds us of our humanity."

"You have no humanity, and you are not my father!" Jade whispered desperately.

The demon went on as if he had not heard her denial. "A part of me feels that I should have never left; that I shouldn't have abandoned you. A part of me wishes to ask for your forgiveness."

Tears streamed down Jade's face. The calm she had felt just moments before had been shattered. If she hadn't already blocked away so much of her pain this would have unmade her. As it was, this thing's words were crushing her heart. A rage started burning deep within her.

"I might have been able to forgive my father," Jade said vehemently, "BUT YOU ARE NOT MY FATHER!" she screamed, her throat cracking again, causing blood to run down the back of her throat. The bitter taste of copper caused her to gag, ending her screams.

The gold irises of her eyes began to glow from the heat of her fury as she gathered together all the energy remaining in her body. She hurled it out of her in a desperate attempt to destroy this creature that tormented her so. Her raw energy slammed into the barrier of the net and rebounded back at her with tremendous force; her vision blurred and blood began to leak from her ears.

Jade curled up in a tight ball and sobbed. She sobbed for the loss of her mother. She sobbed for her father's abandonment, and the creature he had now become. She sobbed for the hole within her where she knew she should have been able to feel Courage. She sobbed for the little girl within her who would have given anything to see her father again and to hear these words this creature now spoke to her while wearing her father's face, and above all she cried for the hope she had clung to so tenuously; hope that was now slowly slipping away.

Her grandmother was dying, if she was not already dead. She hadn't been strong enough. Her father, who had always been mighty in her eyes, was now a Kaga. He hadn't been strong enough either. What hope did she have if two of the strongest people she had ever known were too weak to stand against such power? She was nothing. That was what she was. Maybe if she still had Courage by her side, but he was gone too; she was truly alone.

Despair rose up within her like a fire and consumed the last of her hope, and there she lay, huddled in upon herself, tormented in body, mind, and spirit. Her body felt weak unto death; death would be a release. She would be reborn to a new life; hopefully a better life, but there in the depths of her desolation she found that she still had a desire to fight, and with that revelation she found that she was slowly able to rein in her emotions and quiet her sobs.

She remembered Hiamovi once saying that a true Areli warrior would continue to fight even when hope was gone. Well, hope was gone. She had failed, but there was breath left in her yet, and so she would fight. She would die, but in the end she would die a true Areli warrior. Peace claimed her heart once more; a peace born of knowledge; knowledge of who she was. For as long as she could remember she had lived in fear; fear of loss. This fear had crippled her. It had buried and crushed her beneath its weight. She surprised herself with her ability to see the irony of it all. For in the end she had lost everything, but in so doing she had found the greatest thing she had lost all those years ago—she found herself, and she liked what she had found. She was a fighter; a warrior. She was Areli.

She knew there was no hope in getting out of the net she was trapped in; not without some form of outside help, but she could still fight back. She had her mind. She had her words. Her grandmother had once told her that those were the greatest weapons a person possessed, and after the way her father—no, the demon's—words had cut into her soul, she had a better understanding of what her grandmother meant. She was not a master of words, and her mind was growing fatigued, but they were the only weapons she had left; so she would use them.

"You say you're my father, but my father wouldn't have trapped me in this net. My father would be trying to help me."

"But I am helping you, Jade."

"How? How is this helping me?" Jade demanded. New tears of rage and frustration stung her eyes and left burning trails down her cheeks.

"I don't expect you to understand, but after your soul has been re-forged in the fires of possession you will thank me. Then we can be a family again and together we will rule this world as is our right."

"You mean to destroy me!"

"You will not be destroyed, but made anew," Akecheta snarled.

"Father, help me... Tell me where the source of the curse is located. Please, Father, let me go so that I might destroy it and our people can have a chance to survive; to live," Jade pleaded.

Large gusts of wind tore through the great square in front of the temple dedicated to the Belial's Dark Gods, setting the net Jade was trapped in to swinging gently back and forth. The stench of the wind smelled of sulphur and sickness, a wound that had been left to fester and rot. It smelled of despair. Jade watched the creature her father had become take in a deep breath of the tainted air, then slowly let the foulness escape his lungs as if he were savoring the sweetest perfume.

"The Devil Raum, I think, will tell you where the source of the curse is. Maybe, if you ask her nicely, she will. I can feel her approaching. She holds such incredible power," he said, a look of hunger flashing across his face; "Power that will soon be yours to command, Jade. You must do something for me, though."

"Only if you promise to let me free," Jade said desperately.

"Fine," Akecheta growled, "I will promise to set you free, but know this. If you fail to do as I ask she will destroy you while you hang, helpless, in that net, and you will never get the chance to free the Areli from the curse, and they will all perish."

Jade took heart in his words. Not because he said he would free her. She wouldn't believe that until he had actually done so; after all, what did a promise mean to a demon? No, what gave her heart was that he had said that her people would perish in the future tense. That meant her people still lived, still fought. The knowledge of this brought back a small particle of hope. She had been fishing for information like this; afraid she would be denied it if she had asked for it outright. And so she had engaged this creature, hoping something would slip.

*"Too bad he didn't let slip the secret to getting out of this cursed net,"* she thought. It was vastly unlikely he would let that information slip, but the little he had told her helped to steel her resolve.

Jade could see a nude woman skipping down the stairs of the temple, heading in their direction. It was the same woman that she had been vaguely aware of earlier before she had been able to overcome her pain. The woman seemed so carefree as she skipped down the last few remaining stairs; looking childlike and innocent.

At least, she would have appeared so if Jade couldn't see the wicked smile plastered across her face that contained all the lust and rage of the world. Like the demon that had possessed her father's body, she too had tattoos and symbols burned into her flesh. The symbols on her body glowed crimson and black in Jade's second sight, and again their meaning seemed just beyond her reach. She shuddered at the thought of understanding what those symbols could possibly mean, ignoring them the best she could.

Still skipping, the woman approached Jade to stand next to the creature that had been her father. Jade could suppose that the woman was beautiful, or she would be if not for all the tattoos and symbols. The woman looked up at her with a ravenous hunger that Jade could not understand. A look she hoped to never understand. The woman noticed that Akecheta was still standing. A low, vicious growl escaped her lips and Jade could tell she was gathering some form of energy with which she was going to lash out at him. The Kaga met the woman's gaze then slowly lowered himself to the ground to prostrate before her. She put her foot on his head and began to grind it into the pavement. After several brutal seconds she stopped with a look of satisfaction upon her face. Then her focus returned to Jade and when their eyes met, Jade could see her doom.

"You are an attractive young thing. That pleases me. Though I will be honest I would still take you for my own even if you were ugly; after all, it takes so little effort to reshape a form into something more pleasing."

Jade spit at her—more blood than saliva. When the spit came into contact with the net it sizzled and popped until it was completely gone. The woman laughed, low and sultry. "My, my, such temper. It's really misplaced, you know. I have come to set this world free. I'm to be its savior."

"You are no savior," Jade said with scorn and disbelief. "You are a creature of hell that has come to enslave and destroy this world, but in the end it will be you that will be destroyed."

"Such brave words from someone who can't even free herself from a simple net," the woman said flatly.

Jade stared down at the woman, trying to gather her thoughts. She didn't know why she was provoking this monster but she couldn't seem to stop herself. She didn't *want* to stop herself.

*"Maybe,"* Jade thought, *"it would be better if she killed me."* Jade didn't think she could be possessed once that happened, and death looked to be the better end; this thought was driven home as she contemplated the fate of her father, who she could see was still laying prostrate upon the earth in a posture of subservience, though his fists were clenched in what looked to be rage. The import of the Kaga Akecheta's behavior towards the woman did not escape Jade.

"What is your name, Devil, that I might know who it is I am going to destroy."

"I am Raum, Lord of the Nether, and you are a Child of the Second Realm. In a very short time your body and all of its powers will belong to me. Do you think it is coincidence that it is you and not the other, the one named Kendra, who is here before me? I planned this whole thing, and you have been kind enough to play along so brilliantly. I might have been sent here to conquer this world, but it is you, your body, that I have really been after." Raum laughed. "And now I have you."

"Yes, you have me. So why haven't you tried to possess me yet?" Jade asked provokingly.

Raum look pleased at the question. "That is simple, and it is what makes this so fun. First, I must break your body of its strength, and then I get to break your spirit. The Nether that is woven into that net is doing the first, and the complete obliteration of your people should be sufficient to do the second. In the end, it is you who will be begging me to possess you."

"Never!" Jade screamed.

"That's inevitable, and once you have been broken you will have no will, nor any desire to resist me. In fact, I think I shall wait until you do beg me. Oh, what fun," Raum said then clapped her hands in delight. Without turning to look at him she snapped, "Akecheta rise!" Once Akecheta had arisen, Raum commanded, "Go and oversee the end of these Areli. Take your flyer and head to the central village where even now my armies are preparing to strike. You should be able to get there by morning. Take part if you wish, but once they have been eradicated from this world I want you to return and tell us all the wonderful details."

Akecheta turned and looked to the sky. After several moments a giant creature came into view. Its size grew with each passing second as it drew nearer, until it landed before them. Its wings stirred up dust into the air as it approached swiftly, causing Jade to cringe, expecting it to crash into them. At the last second it pulled up and its clawed feet touched the stone gently. The beast was all teeth and talon with a stinging tail like a scorpion. It looked as if at one point in time it had been a drake, much the same way a Hell Hound started its existence as some kind of wolf. It definitely had scales like a drake, and Jade could see that its talons had left gouges in the stone. Black oily smoke boiled out of its mouth, adding its essence to the corrupted air, and Jade instinctively knew that the smoke was toxic.

Akecheta leaped up upon its back. The beast shook its body in protest but made no other attempts to displace its rider. Akecheta patted the flyer on the neck almost affectionately. A look of contentment settled on his face. The simple act disturbed Jade immensely, for she had seen her father in that gesture, and the thought that some part of her father might still exist somewhere buried deep down in the monster was horrific.

That monster made eye contact with her and a brief smile turned the corner of his lips. With a yell the beast took flight and quickly soared off into the distance. Her father might have been in that gesture, but it was the monster that was leaving to slay her people.

"What was that look that passed between you too?" The devil Raum asked; a curious, childlike expression on her face.

Jade was surprised by such an innocent question. She looked down upon this woman and squinted, trying to see the creature that must rest just beneath her flesh. Whatever dark energies that had been woven into the net were distorting her second sight, and the harder she strained to see through it the more her vision blurred. She could see the same dark energy that was woven throughout the net coursing and surging around this woman's body. This was the source of the corruption that had come into their world.

"You're not nearly as impressive looking as I thought you would be."

"Why, am I not beautiful?" Raum asked as she pulled her long luxurious hair over her shoulder and began examining it. She cupped her breast. "Are these not large enough?" Then she smacked her hand hard across her belly, "Is not my stomach firm, and my loins inviting?"

Jade drew back, mortified. "That's not what I meant."

Raum smirked at her, "Isn't it? It is true that this form will not stay pleasing for much longer. This mortal flesh cannot survive my dark arts. The best I can do is slow down its decay; that, my young beauty, is why I need yours. With the power your body possesses, I will be able to stay young and vibrant forever. Not to mention how powerful I will become once I combine the powers of the Nether with that of the Terrestrial. There would be none who would dare challenge me. I will rise up and take my rightful place as a High Ruler of the Nether Realm and I shall destroy the one who sent me for he has forever been a thorn in my side. It will be I who is finally able to conquer the rest of the Third Kingdom and bring it under the dominion of the Nether Night. It will be I who finally finds the way to rend the Veil to the Second Kingdom. The name Raum shall be feared by millions of worlds!"

"I shall die before I let you possess my body!" Jade screamed.

"It is true," Raum said calmly, "that it is better to possess the body of a living being than that of a corpse; for a corpse produces no energy with which to add to our own, and they quickly become useless. But I do not think this will be a problem with you because I don't intend to kill you. I intend to make a deal with you."

"I will never make a deal with you," Jade stated emphatically. "You are a monster. You are worse than a monster."

"It is bad to say no to a deal when you haven't even heard the offer yet."

"There is nothing you could possibly offer me that would convince me to make a deal with a creature like you."

"Oh, really? I would imagine you would be willing to make a deal if it meant saving the ones you love."

This made Jade pause for a moment, but only a moment, before she answered, "Everyone I love would rather die than live as a slave to you, or see our world destroyed."

"Those terms are agreeable," Raum said while absently toying with her hair. "Once you surrender your body to me I will remove the curse and withdraw my forces. I will then leave this world and see to it that all other demons and Belial do so as well. With the power I gain from our union I will be able to enforce my will that this world be left alone and your people shall forever live in peace."

Raum's words were like daggers to her brain. They tore and cut away at her consciousness; rending what little strength she had left. The trials of the last week, the talk with the one who had been her father, and now this, left her feeling as if parts of her were slowly being stripped away until nothing remained.

She was being undone. The net was sapping her strength, and soon she would either slip into that peaceful abyss of death with hope to be reborn into a better world, or she would lose all her ability to resist this monster and it would take possession of her. Either way, her people were doomed. "How can I believe that you would keep your word?"

"You don't," Raum said flipping her hair back over her shoulder, "But I will."

"You expect me to doom countless worlds just to save my own?"

"Those worlds will all fall in time anyway. It is inevitable. What remains to be seen is whether-or-not yours shall fall and your people be destroyed with them. It is within your power to deliver them from this fate, but I warn you," Raum said with conviction, "if I have to take your body by force then the agreement I offer you is void and I shall make this world suffer more than any other. This I promise you."

Jade shuddered. "I need time to think."

"Don't think too long, pretty; your loved ones don't have the time," Raum said, then turned back towards the temple, leaving behind a very troubled and frightened young girl.

# CHAPTER 25

How could he escape air; air that burned? The dilemma plagued Menewa, and he knew his brother and the twins were wondering the same thing. The crystal talismans protected them from the worst of it, but they all had raw soars that oozed blood, staining their cloths.

The four boys had forgone armor so they could move faster and with greater stealth, trusting their magical craftings to protect them from their enemies' weapons. It had been nice not dealing with the extra weight of the armor, and even without the armor it had taken everything he had to make it here to Talberic on time. Still the extra protection from the noxious air would have been blessedly welcome.

For awhile, Menewa and Chaska had maintained their shields of hardened air while Honon and Honaw shielded their bodies with a thin layer of living rock. This had worked, but it was difficult to maintain such shields over extended periods of time, especially when one was already exhausted from days of hard travel and brutal fighting. They had all finally dropped their shields so that they could better conceal themselves as they approached their final destination; choosing stealth over protection.

The toxic vapors in the air blocked out the sky, preventing it from showing the dawning of a new day. Menewa wondered if, when the sun did come, would he even be able tell? The darkness did have its benefits; for though the air scorched their skin and lungs, it provided concealment. Here in the heart of Belial territory, each of them had learned to be masters of concealment. Menewa and his brother could manipulate the light and air to conceal themselves, while the twins blended into their surroundings by using their earth magic's to create camouflage, making them all but invisible. Even knowing they were there, Menewa had a hard time seeing them. Still, sneaking them all into the heart of Talberic was going to be a problem.

Their crystal talismans hadn't failed yet, praise the light, though they were now blacker than midnight. It was a potent reminder that they had little time left. He had taken the talisman off for a few seconds to see what would happen and immediately started feeling weak and nauseous, and an irrational fear and rage swept over him, clouding his thoughts. Hurriedly he placed the crystal talisman back on and let out a sigh at the relief it brought.

Chaska was incensed that he had done it without telling the

others that he was going to do so, and chewed him out under his breath for the next hour until he finally apologized to Chaska, knowing that his brother was just being overprotective. He wouldn't have been nearly as mad if it had been one of the twins, but Menewa let it go to keep the peace, and instead told them what had happened so that they would know what to expect if their talismans failed before they had accomplished their goal. They all understood that if the talismans failed they wouldn't last long enough to finish their goal, so it was important to hurry. They could feel the hand of time pressing down upon them.

Menewa found himself on edge as he looked down at the camouflaged forms of the twins. Both had their hands to the ground, hardly seeming to breath as they searched the area for any caves that they might flee to after they had helped Jade.

The twins both stood up at the same time. It was easier to see them when they moved, though they still blended into their surroundings almost flawlessly. Not all earth crafters could do that. It was a unique gift from the bond between their Rock Bear totems. Every totem not only enhanced the use of the basic essences, but they often had distinct gifts shared only between the bonded and their totem. Rock Bears had a natural ability to blend into the jungle and because of this the twins had this special ability too.

"We found a suitable cave not far from here," Honaw said, then added as he patted his totem on her massive shoulder, "but Aylanna says that there is no opening to the surface, so we will have to make one."

"Aylen agrees," Honon said. "It is good we came with you. If there is one thing Rock Bears are good at, it is finding nice cozy caves to sleep in." Aylen grunted then butted her head into Honon's back, knocking him forward a few shuffling steps. Honon looked back at her, clearly annoyed. "I am getting to it; there is no need to get pushy. Anyway, what Aylen wants me to say is that this particular cave runs down under the city so if you want we can travel through the cave and come up inside the city. It shouldn't be too hard to find Jade, then get back to the cave before whatever is supposed to happen, happens."

Chaska clapped his hands together. "Great that solves several problems at once. So where is this cave?"

The two Rock Bears turned and started walking off, heading in what Menewa believed to be a southern direction, though he was a little embarrassed because he was not completely sure. Between the over cast early morning sky and his weariness, he had gotten a little turned about. *"Clever, what direction are Honon and Honaw's totems going?"*

*"They are moving in a south-westerly direction. Why boss?"*

*"Oh, just checking to see if you are paying attention."*

*"Ha, if you say so."*

*"Hey, Clever do you see any Belial in the area?"*

*"No, but I am having a hard time seeing under the jungle canopy in this area. However, I have been flying over Talberic and for a city as big as it is, there are not many people about. It almost looks deserted. I did see a couple of nasty-looking beasts walking the streets, so be careful. I don't think you would want to run into one of them."*

*"Clever, you know that after we help Jade we are all going underground, right?"*

*"Are you sure we all have to? You know that I hate going underground."*

*"Yes, I am sure, so you had better start preparing for it mentally because it is going to happen."*

*"Aagg, all right. But I expect a treat later because of it."*

*"If we all come out of this alive I will be happy to shower you in treats."*

*"I am going to hold you to that. So there is no going back on your word."*

*"I wouldn't dream of it,"* Menewa said.

*"I don't know, you still owe me a treat for the other day."*

*"Don't worry I haven't forgotten that one either."*

One of the She Rock Bears turned and grunted at them. "I

guess Aylanna wants us to follow her," Menewa stated.

Honon laughed, "That's not Aylanna; that's Aylen."

Honaw slapped Menewa on the back, propelling him toward the retreating bears. "Don't feel bad, no one else can really tell them apart, and Honon is just having a little bit of fun with you; that really is Aylanna."

Chaska moved in beside Menewa, something he was only able to do thanks to the abilities of the twins, for the jungle had become dense once more as they came within a mile of Talberic. None dared to create a light by which they might be able to better see where they were going. Fortunately, Honon and Honaw's totems didn't seem to have any difficulty seeing in the dark under the canopy of dense jungle trees. After a little time traveling in the eerie silence, the jungle opened up before them as they walked out onto a rock shelf looking down on the city of Talberic.

Menewa had heard descriptions of this city from elder warriors who had been brave enough, or foolish enough, to venture here into the heart of Belial territory. Those elder warriors had described the city as a place of squalor and riches. The rank and file of the Belial lived in small stone dwellings haphazardly built, forming chaos-riddled and crooked streets, teaming with Belial brats fighting for survival and dominance. The weak and crippled were sacrificed upon the altars atop their temples, which were large pyramidal structures built to honor their dark gods—gods that walked among them in the form of Kaga.

The Belial believed that possession by one of the beings from the Nether was the greatest blessing that could be bestowed upon them by their dark gods and was sought after zealously. For possession meant power. Possession meant wealth. Possession meant transcendence, and only the most vile and depraved were granted such an honor.

The city itself was built from black marble, streaked with silver veins, which could have only come through the Dark Portal. The city appeared a dark blur in the distance and seemed to float in the smoky fog that blanketed the land. Menewa lifted his hands and formed a curved lens with condensed air in the hopes that he would be able to better see the city they were about to enter, but it was useless. The dark vapor made it impossible to see anything beyond the basic shapes of things, and with the streets so obscured he couldn't see if there were any people walking about. It frustrated him that he couldn't see what they were walking into.

Casting a thought to his totem who was currently flying high overhead, circling the city, he asked, *"Hey, Clever, can you see the city well enough from up there to tell me anything?"*

*"Only what I told you earlier; it's just too obscured. I think if I get closer I will be able to see more."*

*"Okay, just be careful."*

*"Don't worry boss, I doubt that anything down there can see as well as I can. I should be able to see them long before they could ever see me, not to mention my outstanding cloaking ability."*

*"Just don't get cocky. We have no way of knowing what sort of things are down there."*

*"Is there anything particular that you want me looking for?"*

*"Yes, I'm thinking we need to know exactly where Jade is. Alo said that she would be at the base of a temple. If you are able fly over and search the ground around the base of those temples, maybe you can locate her so we will know exactly where we need to go. Also, I think it would be a good idea to let her know that we are close and that she can be expecting us shortly."*

*"Good thinking, I will also look for the best routes after I locate her,"* Clever said.

*"Do that. We are going to enter the city through an underground cave, and I don't know where we are going to come out, so I will need you to be our eyes in the sky. Is Feather up there with you?"*

*"She is. You know, she's really snooty. She barely says two words to me, even if I ask her a direct question. And you can forget about her talking to anyone besides Chaska. If it wasn't for her temper, I would think she was a Snow Owl. She's Miss Perfect Ice*

*Queen."*

Menewa chuckled to himself. Calling a Fire Eagle a Snow Owl or better yet an Ice Queen was looking to get a giant fireball hurled at your head. *"I hope you didn't actually say that to her. Did you?"*

*"You know me better than that, boss. I would never actually say that to her. She'd peck my flaming eyes out. No, what I did say was that her feathers look lovely today. She couldn't say thank you, do you know what she did say to me?"*

*"What did she say to you?"* Menewa asked while smiling to himself.

*"She flaming said, 'I know'. Can you believe it? Miss Ice Queen can't even take a complement properly. She could have at least said back to me that mine were looking lovely today, too."* She sounded a little sullen and hurt.

*"Well then let me be the first to tell you that your feathers are looking especially beautiful today. They're radiant even in this darkness,"* Menewa said, then added, *"I'll tell Chaska what you are doing. I don't know what he was planning to have Feather do, but maybe she can help you search. Seriously though, try to get along. What we're doing is far too important to be caught up in personal conflicts. With both of you searching I am confident that you will be able to find Jade, no matter where she is in that city."*

"Menewa, pay attention, you are going to be left behind, and we have no time to wait for you," Chaska said, clearly annoyed.

"Sorry, just talking to Clever," Menewa said, becoming truly aware of his surroundings once more.

"You really need to work on being able to communicate with your totem without losing focus of your surroundings," Chaska said, "It's going to get you killed one of these days if you don't."

"I know and I'm working on it. It is just that when we are talking I get so wrapped up in the bond that I forget to pay attention."

"Do you think I don't understand that?" Chaska said, "Because I do; I had to learn how to keep myself from getting tangled up in the bond while communicating, too. We all have."

Menewa fumed at his brother's reprimand, especially because he knew what he said was true; getting lost in the bond like that out here was a sure-fire way of getting oneself killed, along with one's companions.

"Both of you are wasting time," Honon said, exasperated. "Let's get moving. Aylen and Aylanna are already to the bottom of the rock-shelf."

Honon stepped over the edge of the rock-shelf and started walking down its shear face as deftly as a mountain goat; always seeming to find a solid foothold to place his feet. Moving to the edge, Menewa was able to see that not only were Aylen and Aylanna at the bottom, but Honaw was only a few steps behind them. Honon had obviously been holding back, waiting for them to follow. Menewa looked at his brother and laughed at his look of chagrin.

"Race you to the bottom," Menewa said, and then leaped out over the ledge, falling hundreds of feet to the jungle floor below. Honon laughed as he heard him zip by. Menewa looked up to see how close behind his brother was, but all he could see was a slight distortion to the air just a few paces above him, for he too had cloaked himself in invisibility.

The fall was freedom, and for just a moment he was able to forget the sooty air that burned like acid and the curse that was killing his people. For the briefest of moments he could forget that his body burned and itched and bled. He could forget the fatigue that ate at his bones. He could forget about the growing worry for Jade and the confused feelings that he had started having for her.

The wind whipped in his ears as the ground came rushing towards him. Channeling his energy, he began a crafting, sending air jetting out beneath him to slow his fall to a safe speed. Flexing his knees for impact, his feet hit the ground, causing a shock to run up his legs. He heard his brother land just seconds after he did. He craned his neck, looking up at the height he had just leapt from, and crowed softly in triumph. It was the highest height he had fallen from and the fact that he remained unharmed made him proud.

Even in his exhausted state he had accomplished something noteworthy. He had done it without doubting that he could for even a second.

All that was visible to Menewa of his brother were his eyes, the color of freshly churned soil, similar to his own. "You are crazy, brother," said Chaska.

"True," Menewa replied back, "but then again, so are you."

"Well," Chaska said, "at least now we won't have to listen to Honon complain that we are holding them up."

Menewa chuckled quietly as they waited for Honon to descend the rock-face. Honaw joined in and Menewa could tell that he was amused by Chaska and his antics.

"Chaska, while I was talking to Clever we decided that it would be a good idea for her to fly low over Talberic so she can see through this noxious gas and better search the area around their temples to find Jade," he said, waving his hand in the general direction of the city, "so that once we leave the tunnel we will be able to go right to her." He shrugged. "I don't know what you planned on Feather doing but it might be a good idea to have them search together."

"I am already having her do just that. By the way, what has gotten into Clever? Feather says that she's being unreasonably ornery with her today."

Menewa laughed, "Clever said roughly the same thing about Feather."

Chaska and Honaw joined in the laughter; though they all kept it to a low volume not wanting to alert any potential enemies that might be in the area.

Still laughing Chaska said, "They fight like sisters! Honaw, do you and you brother ever have similar problems with your totems?"

"Aylen and Aylanna? No, not at all; they are very close. You know they are twins like Honon and I? Though I must admit that Aylen can be a little temperamental sometimes; especially for someone whose name means happiness," he said.

Menewa heard Aylanna emit a grunt that sounded remarkably like laughter while Aylen grunted in annoyance.

Less than a minute later Honon reach the bottom of the cliff.

"Nice of you to catch up," Chaska quipped.

"Not all of us can just jump of a ledge and fall hundreds of feet only to land as delicately as a rose petal lands upon the water," Honon said seriously.

They laughed more at Honon's poetic words. The laughter was

good. It helped counteract the darkness. And it was good to know that laughter could exist even in times such as this. Menewa felt that evil could never truly win when good men and women could laugh and hope and love. The last thought caused him to blush as his thoughts turned to Jade. Fortunately for him, his face was still veiled behind a cloak of invisibility.

The thought of Jade caused Menewa to feel a sense of urgency that had been plaguing him relentlessly over the last few days. "So where is this tunnel that will lead us into Talberic?" The warm laughter died at his words, leaving behind only the darkness once more. Menewa felt its loss as a physical thing and now wished he could have allowed himself to enjoy it a little longer despite the sense of urgency.

"We can enter it here," Honaw said, while tapping one of his Cold-Iron Mauls on his hip.

"Really? I don't see an entrance anywhere." Menewa gazed around the area.

"Menewa, you have ashes for brains," Chaska said. "If you had been paying attention earlier you would know they have to open up a pathway for us to enter."

Swallowing a retort, Menewa smiled, "Let's get going then."

"Sounds like a plan," Honon said, clapping his hands with a loud crack; reflexively, the rest of them jerked and quickly scanned their surroundings to make sure no one had been close enough to hear it. There wasn't, and that too bothered Menewa.

*"Shouldn't this place be crawling with Belial and Netherspawn?"* he wondered. It was a question he had no answer for.

Honon and Honaw knelt down, placing the palms of their hands to the ground while their totems came to stand beside them. Moments later the ground shook quietly, though it seemed to Menewa to be as loud as thunder. A sloping tunnel appeared, large enough for the massive bears to fit through comfortably.

Menewa was the first to enter the tunnel; forming a white ball of light that floated a foot above his head and just in front of him. The others followed quickly and the ground shifted, closing the entrance behind them as if a giant maw swallowed them whole.

# CHAPTER 26

Menewa shuddered. He hated being underground; all that rock was suffocating. He knew it wouldn't be so bad if he was able to manipulate the essence of earth, but he might as well try to fly to the moon. If the tunnel collapsed he would be crushed and there would be nothing he could do about it. He was completely dependent upon Honon's and Honaw's skills, and while he trusted them, depending upon someone else's skills didn't sit well with him.

There was also the problem of navigating the tunnels that seemed to run everywhere. The twins both claimed they were from ancient lava flows. He supposed that was possible because not too far down into the earth he could sense a powerful and intense source of fire, though it seemed sluggish—almost asleep. While he felt hopelessly lost, the twins seemed to know exactly where they were going, never hesitating before taking a tunnel.

He wiped sweat from his forehead and cheeks. He was sweating like a blacksmith standing at his forge in the middle of the dry season, though the air was relatively nice, even cool compared to the world above. The toxic vapor that had burned their flesh in the world above was blessedly absent here and the relief was almost euphoric. The air smelled of rich soil in the cavern, reminding him of growing things—of life.

They took a few minutes to eat; just enough to satiate their hunger. The odds of dying were quite good and it would be a shame to die hungry. The meal was a cold one, as they did not dare to take the extra time to heat anything up. Not like there was much that needed heating anyway. Still it would have been nice to have a hot drink made from Jinti berries and some mint leaves. He almost regretted not taking the time to do that—almost.

He assumed they were making good time, at least that was what the twins were saying. They claimed that they were actually under the city now. Now they just needed to find Jade and locate the best place to return to the surface.

Something was bothering the twins, Menewa knew, but he figured they would tell Chaska and him if it was important. Chaska was of a different mind-set on the matter and asked, "What's bothering you two?"

"Besides the obvious?" Honon said, causing Honaw to chuckle.

"Besides the obvious," Chaska agreed.

"We figured that there would be a lot more people moving

around above us."

"You're saying that there isn't that many people or other things up there?" Menewa asked, feeling a sense of relief. He had been envisioning them returning to the surface only to be buried under a swarm of Belial bodies and other demonic creatures.

Chaska was obviously thinking the same thing because he asked, "Isn't that a good thing?"

"I suppose it can be seen as a good thing for us," Honaw said, "but do you remember how many Belial were on the Prognostication Map? If only a few are here in the city, that must mean they are throwing everything they have right now at us. How long can our people last against those numbers, especially when you figure in the curse?" Honaw lifted up the crystal talisman; its obsidian color seeming to suck in a little of the light his brother and him had summoned. "Judging from what Menewa experienced when he took his talisman off, we would succumb to the curse within the hour if our talismans failed. How many of these talismans are there? I know that the Holy Daughter said that the further we got from her and the closer we came to the devil the less she would be able to protect us from the curse so we can hope that our people are faring better than we would be, but you know that they must be hurting and weak. We are just worried that even if we are successful here that there will be no home to go back to—that our people will have already been over run. That we are already too late."

Chaska was quiet for a moment before answering with a calm, firm authority. "Brothers, take heart. We are Areli. We have fought against the darkness from before our records of time even began, and we will continue to fight them until that day comes when we are finally able to drive them from our world completely. I can feel that day approaching. This is not our darkest hour, but our finest. For it is in the darkest of times that the fire of our hearts burns the brightest, and with that fire we shall burn away the darkness; for it is the nature of light to overcome darkness. We will prevail." At that moment Menewa saw the man his brother was becoming. He could see the guiding hand their father had had upon him; shaping him into a man worthy of being High Chief over their people.

"Yes of course Chaska," Honon said. "You are right."

Honaw stepped up to Chaska and gripped his shoulder in his hand. "We will follow you wherever you lead, Brother."

When one of the twins stood close to his brother Chaska, who was considerably bigger than Menewa himself, he was reminded of just how massive they were. The twins were doubly dangerous for they were smart too, and not for the first time Menewa was grateful to have them upon this quest. Their aid had been invaluable during their journey here and now they were providing the ability for them to stroll into the heart of Talberic through this underground tunnel; even if being underground made his skin crawl.

"This is a good thing," Menewa chimed in. "If everyone is away attacking the villages, then there will be less people here to prevent the destruction of the source of the curse, and once the curse is broken our people will rally and throw back the Belial and their Kaga masters. Like Chaska said, all is not lost," he paused for dramatic effect, "In fact, I think we have them right where we want them. It couldn't have played our way any better."

Clever's voice sounded in his head, *"We found her, boss."*

When his eyes focused again he could see a wide grin splitting Chaska's face. Feather had obviously told him the good news too, and he was now telling the twins. *"Clever, where is she; is she all right?"*

*"She looks to be in really bad shape boss, but the good news is, she looks unguarded."*

*"So she's been captured, and that's why we have been sent on this mission. We're meant to free her."*

*"Looks that way," Clever said.*

*"Does she know that we are here? Did you reveal yourself to her?"*

*"I had to drop the cloak of invisibility for her to see me."*

*"That was risky, why didn't you just talk to her and let her know we are here?"*

*"I tried boss. You know it's hard for us totems to talk to anyone we are not bonded to, but for some reason with her it was impossible. I tried until my brain cramped with the effort. Feather couldn't do it either."*

*"What did she do when she saw you?"* Menewa asked.

*"At first she didn't notice me. I literally had to flap my wings in front of her face to get her attention, and then I still don't think she recognized me right away, but when she did she cried out and immediately began to cry. It broke my heart to see her like that."*

*"You did amazing, and we are going to get her free; now if we only knew why we are going to have to flee after we set her free. I would think that she would need help finding the curse and destroying it. Wouldn't she be more likely to succeed if we helped her?"*

*"Menewa,"* Clever said, her mental tone deadly serious, *"I was with you when Alo told you what would happen if we didn't flee, and I am not prepared to die just yet."*

*"It is an honor to die for our people, Clever, and you know it."*

*"You misunderstand me. I did not say I was unwilling to die for you or your people. What I am saying is that death is permanent and once you are dead you can no longer help your people,"*

Clever said, and then continued on in an unusually patient tone. *"Death is easy, fire of my heart, life is hard. It is far easier to die for a cause then to live for one. To die for a cause is a singular choice; a singular sacrifice. It is one act of selflessness before the end, but to live for a cause means you will be tested and tried every minute of every day. You do not face one choice but an endless string of choices that will challenge your commitment and your beliefs. It is not one sacrifice but an entire lifetime filled with them."*

Her words rang in his ears, speaking to his heart in a way that only she could. He had named her Clever because the first thing she had said to him was much like this—brilliant and to the point. There was no doubt in his mind that she was the smarter of the two of them. She often played down her intellect and joked around with him; calling him boss, usually sarcastically. In her relationship with Feather she was clearly the younger sister who desperately wanted the approval of her older sister. Still, in just about any other circumstance he could trust her intellect far more than he could trust his own.

These thoughts went through his head as he weighed the wisdom of her words and found them to be a pearl of great price. *"So boss, we are going to follow Alo's directions exactly, and I know that means I am going to have to go underground."* Clever said to him seriously, but then went on in a more joking tone; *"I will even forgo my treat."*

*"You'll get your treat,"* Menewa promised.

*"Good! I was testing you. If I don't get a treat for it, I will be furious with you."*

Menewa pulled back from his connection with Clever and the world snapped back into focus. At the look on his brother's face he groaned internally—he had done it again. He had gotten so tied up with his connection to Clever that the world around him had disappeared completely. If his brother or the twins had meant him harm he would be dead right now. Menewa ground his teeth—he would do better.

"Sorry, I will do better," Menewa said. The others grunted in acknowledgement and let it drop at that, though Menewa could tell his brother wanted to say something more, but didn't, and for that he was grateful. "So what have you told them?"

A little exasperated Chaska said, "I was telling them that Feather and Clever have found Jade, and that she is trapped in some sort of net. Feather said that the net crackled with some kind of black energy that made her feel sick, or at least sicker, the closer she got. She's already feeling sick from the toxic air above."

Menewa felt a little annoyed with Clever—and a little proud. Not once did she complain about the pain she was feeling from the environment they had been forced to move through the last several days. He knew she hurt and itched every bit as bad as he did, but she would never complain. Of course he hadn't complained to her either, and he wouldn't unless she complained to him first.

Chaska continued speaking, "They revealed themselves to Jade but were unable to speak to her. Feather did say that once we get back on the surface it should be easy for her to guide us to Jade, and I am confident that with the reduced population here in Talberic we should be able to get to her undetected."

"Couldn't we just follow one of these tunnels and come up right by her so that we don't have to take the risk of being discovered?" Menewa asked, though he felt uncomfortable proposing to stay below and subject himself to the smothering sensation that would creep upon him at odd times.

The twins looked at each other—just a glance, but there was an edge to it. Honon said, "It would take more time to find her from under here then it would from the surface, and we can feel time running out—we can feel it in our bones." Both twins unconsciously touch their talismans.

"My brother speaks truly," Honaw said, "but that is not all of it. There is darkness ahead. A darkness that swallows our earth-sight —can't you guys feel it? With every step we take, we are approaching our doom."

His words hung heavy in the air. *Maybe I'm not just being claustrophobic,* Menewa thought. *Maybe it is something more.* It was an excuse to leave the underground tunnels and it was good enough for him. "So we go back to the surface?" he asked, trying to keep the hope from his voice.

"We go back," Chaska agreed. "Take us to the best place to surface."

"We are already here." Honon said, "We will be able to come up into an alleyway where none should be able to notice us—and before you ask, Aylen and Aylanna already checked the area above; the way is clear."

Chaska nodded then crossed his arms, taking a stance of extreme relaxation. Menewa knew it was a ruse, and that his brother was on edge, ready to spring into action. Following his brother's example Menewa assumed a similar position. To his surprise, acting relaxed actually caused him to become more relaxed. It was a weird experience. He looked at his brother and grinned.

Honon and Honaw did whatever it was they did, and the ground shifted forming an opening to the surface. With supreme effort Menewa kept himself from sprinting, allowing the two She Rock Bears to climb out first, followed directly by the twins.

"After you," Chaska said, waving him forward.

Menewa didn't need to be asked twice. He winced when the air from the surface once again touched his skin—burning it anew. Fighting through fatigue, Menewa gathered up his body's energies and channeled to form a crafting that pulled away the toxic air, and then formed a barrier that would filter out the vapors, only allowing clean air through. All of this took effort and would further deplete his body's store of energy, but at this point he didn't care.

Talberic was every bit as disgusting and dirty as he thought it would be. Refuse and human waste filled the alleyway, adding to the already overwhelming stench of sulphuric vapors. They squeezed into the alleyway, trying to place themselves in a battle-ready position in case there was some Netherspawn that had somehow gone undetected. The twins could only sense something if it was touching the ground, so an airborne attack was still a real possibility.

Menewa could feel his brother form a dome that would conceal the party from above. It was an impressive crafting; Menewa wondered where his brother found the strength to do it. Then to his shame, he noticed that his brother had forgone protecting himself from the harsh climate in order to shelter the group as a whole. The pride he felt in his brother only highlighted his shame.

Gritting his teeth, Menewa forced his crafting out away from his body until the whole group was protected. He had no idea how long he would be able to hold such a crafting but he would be flamed if he gave out before his brother did. Menewa caught his brother's eyes; a big grin upon his face that said—I know exactly what you are thinking; challenge accepted. Menewa flashed a grin right back at him, knowing that his heart would have to explode from the effort before he would give in now. Considering the effort he was now putting into the crafting, it just might. It was worth it when he heard the twins groan in relief.

He knew that the twins could protect their skin by using an earth-crafting to coat their bodies with a thin layer of living rock, but they could do nothing to protect their lungs. Several times he had watched one of the twins cough into their hands only to wipe the blood that had been filling their lungs onto their shirts. Something he and Chaska hadn't had to deal with; it took only a little bit of energy to filter the air that went into their lungs, even if they couldn't always protect their whole bodies.

The twins faded into the color of their surroundings; matching the subtle dark shades perfectly, and in the gloom became almost invisible.

Menewa looked to his brother's crafting, seeing that it was indeed sheltering them from view on all sides and wondered why the twins would spend the extra energy to mask themselves with their camouflage when they did not have too.

The twins must have read his question from his expression for one of them answered it. "When we camouflage ourselves, we become invisible to anything that can see in the heat spectrum. If anything can see through your brother's crafting they won't see us."

The other twin add, "If they attack they will be surprised to find not two but six of us to fight, giving us a great advantage."

It was a good idea; no, it was a brilliant idea, Menewa thought.

He could feel Clever through their bond circling high overhead, and guessed that Feather was with her by the way his brother looked to the sky.

"Feather says she can lead us to Jade from here," Chaska said.

"Lead away," the twins said in unison.

They began a trek through a far ranging warren, and if it hadn't been for Feather and Clever guiding them from above they would have been hopelessly lost. Menewa could feel the time slipping away and each second that passed brought them closer to disaster. The Fire Eagles were not alone in the sky above, either; groups of winged nightmares carrying Kaga would launch themselves from the interior of the city, only to circle then fly off to the east— toward the Areli. So for extended lengths of time communication between Menewa's and his brother's totems would be disrupted as they struggled to avoid detection—fear and excitement poured through the bond during these stretches of time as his Clever outsmarted and outflew the winged monstrosities that shared the skies above.

The boys were not alone on the ground either. Many times they came upon a group of Belial, Netherspawn, or both, that couldn't be avoided; fortunately they were able to sneak up and assassinate them before any call of alarm could be sounded.

During one of the brief interruptions in aerial communication, the boys were forced to confront a Kaga. The Kaga walked down the middle of the ally with a strong confidence. It was the master here. When it noticed Chaska and him, seeing through the cloak of invisibility, it gave no cry of alarm, but simply strode forward, pulling two Life-eater Blades from their sheaths borne upon his back, confident that it could easily dispatch the two boys.

The Kaga had retained the shape of a man (though his face had a snake-like quality to it) and wore black metallic armor with curved razor-edged spikes along the vambrace of each forearm— deadly weapons in their own right, but nowhere as deadly as the Life-eater Blades it carried; even being near such blades weakened the strongest of warriors. The blades danced in the possessed hands, each blade striking with a viper's speed. Arrogant and proud, he slithered in for the kill.

Menewa had been right. The look of surprise that flashed across the demonic face was priceless as the twins and the two She Rock Bears attacked from the sides. The fight was fierce and relentless, but the Kaga never called for help, even after they had freed it from its physical form.

The demon-spirit thrust his arm into Honon's chest, piercing his armor of living rock. Honon's anguished cry slashed at the air, and he would have perished then and there if it hadn't been for Menewa plunging his Cinderblade into the demon-spirit's back; his blade's energy tearing at the essence of the demonic being. In the end they were able to slay the fiend, and in the stillness that followed Menewa could hear Honon's ragged breathes. Honon waved them off, indicating that he was fine.

They left the two Life-eater Blades where they lay, not daring to pick them up. The nausea and weakness they'd felt every time the blades had come close to striking them was enough to quell their curiosity.

They approached a set of three Belial temples that rested in the heart of Talberic, thrusting hundreds of feet into the sky to dominate the city's heart, and Menewa knew that their vile sacrificial altars would rest upon each pinnacle. The opulence of the buildings they now passed in comparison to the squalor of just minutes before sickened him and was just another example of the difference between his people and these demon worshipers.

There were no poor among his people, for they were their brother's keepers and they actively sought the welfare and betterment of their fellow brothers and sisters. He knew that his were a proud people but their love for one another was greater, and this love demanded action. No Areli could stand by and enjoy their wealth while another of his people went without. Indeed, the constant war left many of their people crippled beyond repair by either magic or technology, but they were not shunned for their inability, but instead they were showered with love and riches and hailed as heroes, and were helped to find new ways in which they could serve.

Nausea aside, Menewa was impressed by the sheer scope and size of the temples ahead, along with the morbid beauty of the buildings that surrounded him—he would have never believed a people such as the Belial could have built anything so... He couldn't think of the right word for it. He had expected the squalor and the putrescence they had passed through earlier, but not this dark grandeur.

Stretching out before them was a massive square empty except for the girl in the distance, blurred by the dark vapors, hanging in a net from a gibbet.

His heart leapt in his chest, and he had to restrain himself from rushing recklessly out across the open ground to free her. His overwhelming fatigue was momentarily forgotten.

"That is a lot of open ground to cover," Honon said while probing the spot where the demon-spirit's hand had penetrated his flesh.

Chaska stared out across the open ground. "Feather says she sees nothing from above—that the way is clear. What does your earth-sight tell you?"

"It tells me," Honon said, "that there is no living thing out there, but I can see Jade in that net."

Menewa immediately got what Honon was implying. They could all see Jade, but Honon couldn't sense her with his earth-sight. It was possible that there could be things out there they could neither see nor sense. In a way they were walking blindly into the unknown.

Menewa could see the same conclusion in his brother's eyes, but it was overshadowed by determination. The same determination was reflected in the twins' eyes; they had come too far and had been through too much to balk now. Their people were depending on them. "Let's go," Chaska said, leading the way.

Menewa followed his brother, eyes firmly fixed upon Jade. He didn't understand his feelings for her anymore, but he had been told that she was the key to their survival. She was to be the people's hero, but she was trapped in that net and unable to get free. He would set her free so that she could save them all. If she was to be their people's hero, then maybe he could be hers. The thought of it made him smile.

# CHAPTER 27

The sun had broken over the horizon and its early morning rays were warming Hiamovi's back in what promised to be an oven of a day. The rainy season was ending. The day would've seemed hot even if he was in the far northern land of ice and snow. His mind was wandering and he mentally slapped himself, refocusing his attention, only letting one errant thought float away from him—*yes the day would still scorch even in ice and snow for battle was always broiling.*

The darkness to the east was marching towards them and had begun to overshadow the village. If today went badly, it would be the last day the sun would shine down upon them.

If the day went badly, it would be their last day period.

Indeed, if they lasted through the morning it would be a miracle. It was a day of miracles, though; he could feel it in his bones—hope.

Standing on the Great Wall he had a view that stretched for miles—miles upon miles that were filled with the hordes of Kaga,

Netherspawn, and Belial warriors. Dark winged nightmares filled the skies, capable of raining death from above. Some looked like demonic bats. Others looked like drakes that had been twisted by their dark magic; still others looked like winged scorpions with pinchers that could cut a man in half and a stinger that could pierce a body clean through—stingers that dripped poison.

Several of his archers had taken shots at them with little effect; even the ones with Shadowbolt bows would find their energy bolts detonating against powerful shields that the Kaga had erected around them and their winged Netherspawn.

The Belial and their Kaga masters were gathering for a full assault. From what he could see it would appear that their enemies' strategy today would be a simple one—bury them with numbers. *And the light knows,* he thought, *they have enough of them to do just that.* Still, before the day was out he would be able to kill a lot of Belial; any day he got to do that was, by his definition, a good day. Even if it was likely to be their last. But by the peace of the light, he would cling to hope. Alo had said there was a chance, and so there was a chance.

The hordes of Belial hadn't started attacking yet, though he didn't know why they waited. Maybe it was the fact that every hour their numbers continued to grow. As it now stood, it looked as if there were a million of them. He knew this wasn't true; their real numbers were more like one hundred thousand to one hundred and fifty thousand, but the light only knew how many of them were actually Kaga.

Hiamovi looked along the battlements of the Great Wall, mentally counting his people. There couldn't be more than ten thousand. The war raged up and down the full breath of the Great Wall, stretching his people's numbers thin. It was unfair; it should have done the same to the Belial, but with their massive numbers they could afford such a stratagem.

Hiamovi chuckled to himself. Thinking something was unfair was a luxury of youth. It was what it was. He had ten thousand to stand against ten times their number. He also had to admit he was looking forward to the wrath Kendra had said she would unleash upon them. He knew that Holy Daughters were far more powerful than a normal Areli warrior, but few could actually claim to have seen one fight. Sure, he had seen several visions from the time of the Holy Mother passed down from generation to generation, and the might of the Holy Mother in those visions was truly breathtaking. He knew that the Holy Daughters were not as strong as their predecessor, but the strength she displayed in fighting the curse hinted at power unimaginable to him. She was currently with Alo, waiting for some sign of Jade before she would move against the Belial herself. In her weakened state she had to be carried by young Areli warriors. He would have been carrying her himself if he wasn't needed here upon the Wall.

He signaled his archers to stop shooting their Shadowbolt bows at the enemy flying overhead, not wanting them to expend all their weapons' energies before the real fighting even began. Still, something would have to be done about those winged nightmares and their riders for his warriors were vulnerable to their attack. He could probably use the energy cannons for they were more than twice as strong as the Shadowbolt bows, but he would need them to even the numbers for all the ground troops. He also figured it would be a good idea to focus them on the Kaga once they had been identified. Many were easy to identify for they had changed their human forms to better reflect the demon's spirit that inhabited the bodies they had taken for their own, but others had kept their original forms, making them harder to locate until they used their powers.

When the time came he would take care of the flyers. While he was anxious to see exactly what Kendra could do, he knew his people were looking towards him to see just what he was capable of. He looked forward to showing them. As High Chief he almost never got the chance to confront the enemy directly, and it had been years since he had been able to unleash his fury upon the Belial. He would remind them why they should fear them.

Approaching rapidly was a massive winged flyer. It was easily twice the size as the ones that were already circling overhead, and looked to be more drake-like in nature, though it had a tail like a scorpion as well. He watched it land among the Belial body and shortly after that, they attacked.

They came pouring over the open ground like ants, causing the earth to shake with the tread of thousands upon thousands of feet. Hiamovi lifted his arm and signaled his warriors to begin attacking. Fire rained down upon the Belial even as waves of earth lifted up and crashed down among them, crushing and rending their bodies. Giant blades of air sliced through the hordes, sharper than anything save Particle-blades. Bolts of lightning streaked from the sky while others formed small twisters of fire and superheated air. Watercrafters sucked all the moisture from large groups of Belial Warriors leaving behind dry and shriveled corpses. Shadowbolt bows hummed as the arrows exploded into the Belial followed by even bigger explosions from the energy cannons that were targeting the obvious Kaga.

The attack was not one sided. Death fell upon the Areli too, coming from the flyers above, killing warriors they could not afford to lose. Black-lightning struck at the energy cannons, destroying them, while Netherfire consumed Areli—freezing their bodies only to have them shatter into tiny pieces moments later. In desperation, many of the windcrafters worked in conjunction to form life-saving shields, protecting them from death from above.

Hiamovi thrust his hand in the air, Sparks resting on the other, and closed his fist while channeling his body's energies through that place within him that was fire, bringing its essence to bear. He seized the energies within the bruised clouds above the demonic flyers and used it to hurl bolt after bolt of lightning into their midst —killing some; the winged nightmares falling to the earth, carrying with them their Kaga riders, their physical bodies destroyed to reveal the evil contained within. The other flyers were forced to back off from their attack upon the Wall momentarily, allowing his warriors to go back to harassing the horde below.

Time marched incrementally while the battle raged. Hiamovi called out orders using aircrafting to carry his words to the ears of his warriors who then carried them out like the veterans of war that they were. Several Kaga had gained the Wall, leaping over a hundred feet into the air—propelled by their dark arts, further disrupting the Areli's ability to fight back.

Kaga were not the only things to gain the Wall, for several of the Netherspawn, creatures that Hiamovi had never seen before amongst the Belial, were able to run straight up the Wall as if it were flat ground. These creatures would spew acid and poisons while attacking with spikes, claws, fangs, and stingers.

Large mammoth-looking Netherspawn pulled war-machines manned by Belial warriors. The retort from these machines split the air like thunder as they hurled massive iron balls that exploded upon impact against the Great Wall, causing craters and fissures that the Wall struggled to repair. Hiamovi wasn't too worried about them. The Wall was strong, and he didn't believe that it would be destroyed by such weapons; at least not before they were completely overrun. The weapons disturbed him, though, because it was yet another thing he had never seen the Belial use before— some strange technology.

Where was Kendra? Hiamovi knew she had said she must confer with Alo before she acted against the Belial. But they were losing, and quickly. Kendra had sworn she would visit her wrath upon the Belial. Hiamovi didn't know just what she was capable of doing, but at this point anything she could add to the battle would help.

The flyers were circling overhead once more, and this time they had been joined by that giant monstrosity that dwarfed the others. It was time for him to take to the skies and show these flaming goat kissers the error of their ways. In the absence of Alo or Kendra he turned to Honani and commanded him to direct the battle on the Wall. Honani nodded his willingness and turned back to the enemy.

With a cry of rage Sparks launched off of his arm and took flight. Hiamovi gathered his power. Two wings formed of the essences of fire and air sprouted from his back, extending twenty feet in each direction even as he pulled a massive two handed Cinderblade from its scabbard. With a yell filled with a rage that mirrored his totem's, he took to the sky. His wings beat with slow powerful strokes, and his heart beat in his chest with adrenalin and fury.

Together he and Sparks burst into blinding blue flames, causing the nightmarish flyers and their riders to cry out in pain; they tried to turn and gain distance from these two living infernos that scorched the air. Sparks, the faster of the two, already flew among them, casting potent fireballs that burned and battered the shield barriers erected by the Kaga riders. Some of the fireballs hit with such force that the flyers were flung dozens of feet, but despite the raw display of power by Sparks, it in no way compared to the awesome might of Hiamovi—High Chief of the Areli Nation.

He tore through the Kagas' shields with a brutality that left them dazed and confused. His Cinderblade burned white as molten steel and sliced through the armored shells of the flyers as if the blade were parting silk. With a flick and a twist he would remove one flyer's head only to pirouette in the air to remove another's wing, claw, or tail. The violent blue flames of his body burned to ash all that he came close too. He danced amongst them in the air, lighting up the ever darkening skies with his radiance; with a grace and splendor that left all who witnessed it stunned at its beautiful ferocity. A dozen burned and smoldering corpses rained down upon the Belial armies below.

Many fled in fear, but others turned to focus their attacks solely upon him. Black lightning flashed from dozens of Kagas' hands, splitting the air, causing it to roar in pain. With speed born of instinct Hiamovi dodged and twirled, performing aerial acrobatics, avoiding all but a few of the deadly bolts. The ones that hit, he was able to deflect with curved and slanted shields. Sparks wasn't as lucky, having taken a direct hit that she was only partially able to redirect. Hiamovi cried out in shock and pain as he felt Spark's wing break. Then his world turned red as his rage overflowed all restraints. Not caring if he stripped his soul of all his life energies, the blue fires that covered his body exploded outward in a solid wave of fire and air that consumed all in its path for hundreds of feet in every direction.

The demon-spirits that had not been consumed in the fires of his rage fled in panic—all save one. It was the one that had been riding the massive drake-like flyer. The Kaga now floated in the heart of a broiling cocoon of black energies—its flyer having been incinerated; its ash mingled with the others as they floated to the battle field below. The cocoon split, then spread to form ebony wings.

The fires that had engulfed Hiamovi were now extinguished and fatigue weighed him down, trying to pull him back down to the earth below; if he died right here and now he would be pleased, though; having taken so many Kaga and Netherspawn with him. But he couldn't stop now; the job was unfinished while even one remained. So gritting his teeth, he steeled himself to do battle once more.

Hiamovi's wings beat slow and steady as he used his arts to hold him stationary in the air—facing off with the Kaga before him. It did not close fast in a sudden rush to finish him, but instead they drifted closer together almost lazily, each reading the other for signs of injury and weakness. Hiamovi knew he was showing both —Spark's broken wing was bothering him, but there was nothing he could do about that for he was exhausted. Never before had he done something like what he had just done; indeed he hadn't known he was capable of such a feat.

A growing apprehension built within his chest as they slowly circled one another—not at the thought of death; he had long since lost all fear of that. No, the apprehension that was rising up within him was from a sense of horror.

That face. He knew that face. A face of a man he had loved as a brother. Under the demonic tattoos and cruel smile was the face of his best friend, Akecheta. He wanted to weep. He couldn't give in to fatigue just yet. He had to free his friend from such an awful state. His knuckles turned white and popped as he tightened his fists around the hilt of his Cinderblade.

His blade was as exhausted of energy as he was. Instead of shining like molten steel it was now the color of banked coals. He should retreat and have this battle another time when things were in his favor, but the demon had possessed his best friend's body, and there might not be another day. Dredging up strength from the depths of his being, he prepared himself to give battle once more.

"That was impressive Hiamovi. You have grown in strength since last we sparred," Akecheta said, "but you will find that so have I."

"You have stolen my friend's body," Hiamovi said, "prepare for me to cleanse it of your filth."

"My friend, always so serious. I would have thought Alo would have been able to loosen you up a little more over the years."

"How is it you have stolen my friend's memories?" Hiamovi demanded from the Kaga before him.

"I have stolen nothing," Akecheta growled. "You have fought against us for millennia yet you know next to nothing about us." His ebony wings beat fiercely; a look of anger flashing across his face. "I am who I am. I was once Akecheta, Areli warrior, but now I am so much more. I am Akecheta, Kaga, General of the Armies of the Nethernight; and this world will be but the first to fall to me."

"So you say," Hiamovi said, "but it shall not be. Prepare to fall to my blade, demon." He could feel Sparks slowly start to feed her own strength through the bond into him. Hiamovi sent a mental warning to his totem—who had made it back to the Wall safely—to not give too much for he was worried about her broken wing.

*"Darling, I will give as much energy as I please,"* Sparks sent back to him.

Despite everything, Hiamovi allowed himself to smile inwardly even as he engaged the Kaga Akecheta. *Light save me from all the stubborn women in my life,* he thought. Sparks did not reply. She wouldn't want to break his concentration, though he could sense her biting her tongue to keep herself from doing so.

Gritting his teeth, blue flames sprang into existence once again. They were just in time, for at that instant Akecheta unleashed a torrent of Netherflame. Even sheltered within his flames, Hiamovi felt so cold his bones could snap. Pouring more energy into his crafting, the cold lessened. He could picture right where the demon was in his mind's eye. Striking out, his sword connected with the wall of force that protected the Netherbeing. Racking pain seized his muscles as he was hurled away from his prey. The world spun, and he felt as if he was going to vomit as he let the blast carry him clear of easy retaliation. With supreme effort he regained control of his flight, only to see Akecheta swoop down upon him with a Light-eating blade. It was Hiamovi's turn to go on the defensive, by forming a net of solidified air laced with tightly controlled lightning, which he then cast over the descending form of his adversary.

Akecheta's shield of black energies clashed violently with the net, and the shriek of pain and rage that escaped Akecheta caused Hiamovi to chuckle. The trick was keeping the net supple, allowing the lightning to sap all the strength from the victim. It was evil, but effective, for Akecheta struggled in vain to find any purchase with which he could attack the net to free himself. Indeed, Hiamovi believed it would have worked if he had been fresh into battle, but he was burning through Spark's borrowed energy and their combined strength was failing. So when Akecheta's struggling settled and he instead focused on using the dark energies of his shield to eat away at the net, Hiamovi was forced to release his crafting or fall from the sky—all his strength spent. He could barely maintain flight, and his blue fires extinguished once more. He had overreached and now he was going to fall to this monster. Akecheta knew it, too; Hiamovi could see it in his eyes.

The Akecheta Hiamovi had known was the kind of warrior that preferred to finish his kills with the blade over a crafting so he positioned his blade waiting for his enemy's final move. Akecheta's attack came fierce and swift, but was interrupted as a good half dozen blasts from energy cannons detonated upon his shields. The world flashed white.

Hiamovi spun out of control and plunged to the ground below, having been caught-up in the concussive force of the blasts. Clinging to consciousness, he tried to gather the shreds of his body's energies, but he had done too much, too fast, and had nothing left within him. Sparks energies' too were desolate; she had given all that she could.

He smiled. It was a good death—a warrior's death. Chaska would make a fine leader.

The world slipped away into blinding darkness.

# CHAPTER 28

Jade wept when she saw the totems Clever and Feather. The presence of the two totems could mean only one thing: Chaska and Menewa were near. *"How did they get here?"* She thought. She had watched them leave the village a little before she herself had, not knowing what their mission was. They must have headed directly to Talberic to have gotten here so fast. Had Alo known she would be captured and would need someone to help her escape, or were they a backup plan to destroy the curse in case she failed?

She bristled at the thought that they had been sent as a back-up plan, but then again she was trapped here in this blasted net. Swallowing her pride left a bitter taste in her mouth. It didn't matter why they were here, it only mattered that they were, and their totems had found her. She had tried to communicate with them but had been completely unable to. So she had no idea how long it would take the boys to actually reach her.

*"Heaven bless the light,"* she thought, *"let them get here before that devil returns."* The thought of having to face that thing again

made her throw-up in her mouth, and its foul taste left her wanting back the bitter taste of her swallowed pride instead.

She could sense that morning had come, though there was no real sign that it had. No rising sun or even a lightening of the darkness. This place truly had been cast into eternal night—the fate of the world if she failed; as if she needed another reminder.

She composed herself as best she could, not wanting the boys to see her cry. She wanted to appear strong before them. She *would* be strong before them. She scanned the area with her first sight. She felt blind having her second sight denied her. She was capable of seeing in the dark quite well, and even more so since she bonded with Courage, but her vision still was not strong enough to pierce this light-eating darkness very far.

So she was startled when the darkness moved. She prayed that it was the boys and not someone or something else. She believed that nothing here—no man, Kaga, or Netherspawn—would touch her, not when the devil wanted her for itself, but that didn't stop her from feeling vulnerable. Knowing that the devil was out there and that it wanted her made her feel even more helpless. She shuddered at the thought of the deal she had been offered, and to her shame, how much she had considered it.

The shadows of movement coalesced into new hope as Menewa strode out of the vaporous darkness, followed by his older brother

Chaska and the twins Honon and Honaw and their two She Rock Bear totems. Despite her determination to not cry, tears flooded her eyes and she quickly wiped them from her cheeks before they could betray her.

"Flaming light, Jade, you look like hell," Menewa said, smiling up at her.

She wanted to laugh and burn him to ash with her eyes all at the same time. "And you look like you haven't bathed in a week," she retorted.

He must have seen the smolder in her eyes for he blushed crimson. He didn't look away, but instead he straightened his shoulders and met her gaze with a challenge of his own. What that challenge meant, however, she had no idea. Her ability to give such a sarcastic retort surprised her for only a week ago she probably would have been completely unable to form a coherent response to such a statement.

"Are you okay?" Chaska asked her, clearly concerned at her appearance.

She had no way of getting a good look at herself, but judging from the bloody welts that covered her arms and legs, and the bruised tenderness of her face—she was a mess. The boys looked no better than she felt.

"No, not really," she answered truthfully, "but that won't stop me from doing what I must."

"Well said, Holy Daughter," Honaw said while his brother nodded in agreement. "We're here to get you down."

Menewa was already examining the gibbeting. He went to touch the net. "Don't," Jade warned, "I don't know what would happen but I don't think you guys should touch the net with your hands."

"Well, how in the four elements are we to get you down then?" Menewa asked.

"I have an idea," Chaska said, "Honon, Honaw, can you guys cause the steel chain to break without touching it?"

"No problem," Honon said, looking at his sibling

"The honor is all yours Brother," Honaw said, shrugging.

Honon looked at the chain and a second later it cracked, dropping the net. Before she could crash into the ground she was caught-up in a cushion of air and gently set down upon the ground.

"May I?" Menewa asked his brother.

"Sure."

With a look of concentration Menewa stretched forth his hands and began to make odd movements as if he was unhooking the net with his hands. Two hands formed of dirty air took shape and began to mimic Menewa's hand movements. With swift dexterity the hands of air pulled the net open, freeing Jade from her terrible prison.

She stood on shaky legs as she stumbled out and away from the net only to fall in Menewa's arms. His arms felt strong yet tender as they held her in their warm embrace. Then they both collapsed to the earth together as Jade realized with horror that she had begun to draw what little life energies that remained within his body into herself. Forcing her body to stop was one of the hardest things she had ever had to do in her life. She trembled at the thought that she had just about killed Menewa, and reflexively jerked away when the others came to help them up off the ground.

"Don't touch me! Please!" she said as she scuttled further away from them. "I don't think I can stop myself again."

The boys looked at each other, confused at her outburst, not realizing the danger they were in. "I'm sorry," Jade pleaded, "Tell Menewa I'm sorry." With a sob Jade hopped to her feet and fled, fearing she would lose control and kill them all. The boys' cries of alarm and concern flogged her onward. The energy she had stolen from Menewa was a soothing balm to her battered body and lent speed to her feet.

Fearing the boys would follow after her, she gathered up what energy she had stolen and began to form the crafting for the cloak of invisibility that Courage had taught her.

Freed from the net she could once again feel the guidestone pulling on her, and it was in this direction that she fled. It wasn't until the steps of the temple rose before her that her footsteps faltered.

She was fleeing in the very direction the devil had gone.

She stopped before the temple steps, panting from the burning in her lungs. She could feel the guidestone urging her onward—pulling her toward those steps. Courage's voice sounded in her mind with the force of thunder *"Jade!"*

*"Courage!"* she wailed in relief and hope. *"Courage, where are you?"*

*"I am coming little one! Hold on, I am coming."*

*"You have no time to wait for him, Jade. You must hurry."*

"Alo? Alo, is that you?" Jade asked.

*"Yes, it is I. Now hurry, you must climb the steps of the temple. You will find the source of the curse sitting upon the sacrificial altar at its top."*

*"What about Courage!?"*

*"You don't have time to wait for him. Hurry Jade. RUN!"* his voice thundered.

So Jade ran, climbing the steps in a frenzy, her heart pounding within her chest. She could feel what little energy she had left burning away in her veins. She released the cloak of invisibility, having no energy left to maintain it, leaving her exposed as she climbed desperately to Alo's urgings. She passed several openings that led down into the heart of the temple. She faltered as she climbed the last step of the temple and fell to her knees in her fatigue; heart palpitating, she threw up stomach acid onto the stones before her. With a weariness born of misery she forced herself to her feet and began to stumble towards the altar that lay only a stone's-throw away.

As she approached she could see what could have only been a young Areli boy, barely old enough to have gone on his spirit walk, laid upon the sacrificial altar. The miasma of evil that permeated the air nearly overwhelmed her. Symbols burnt into the boy's flesh seemed to open up into the Nether itself while black liquid ran like tears from the boy's eyes—eyes that had become two pits of eternal darkness.

Jade wept for the boy, and hoped that he would be reborn into a better, more peaceful life. Now that she was close to the boy she could feel that while his body radiated evil, it was not its true source. That originated from the stone goblet that rested just above the boy's head. Just being in the cups presence Jade was able to feel its evil seep into her making her feel dirty inside. She had a powerful urge to bathe though she knew she could never scrub away the feeling of filth that was seeping into her pores.

*"What do I do?"* Jade asked, holding the guidestone in her hand as if that would somehow make it easier to talk to Alo.

*"Jade, your grandmother Kendra is here with me. I need you to do exactly what she tells you to do."*

*"Grandmother,"* Jade said, sobbing in relief. *"You're still alive; are you okay? I worried that you would be dead, but I was afraid to ask,"* she said in a rush.

Kendra responded with a sense of irony in her voice, *"Yes I am still alive Granddaughter, and I love you, but right now I need you to focus. Can you do that for me?"*

*"Yes Grandmother."*

*"Tell me everything you see. Don't leave anything out no matter how small or insignificant it may seem."*

Jade started telling her grandmother everything she could see, feel, and hear; trying to leave nothing out. After she was done her grandmother asked several discerning questions that helped pull her attention to things she had missed. The sense of urgency she had felt when she was climbing the temple stairs had stayed with her, and even now her heart thundered within her chest, threatening to bruise itself against the inside of her ribcage. She had the distinct feeling that the devil was near and was getting closer.

It wasn't just her; she could hear fear and sorrow in both Alo's and her grandmother's voices. It felt like they were saying goodbye even though they didn't say the words.

*"So what do I do, Grandmother,"* Jade asked, *"to destroy the*

*curse?"*

*"You described a symbol that was burnt into the flesh of the boy that was interwoven with his birthmark of the Heaven's Script for totems. I want you to dip your finger into the stone goblet and use its contents to scribe that symbol on yourself exactly where and how the one on the boy's body is."*

Jade cringed at the thought of it, but steeled her resolve and dipped her finger into the stone goblet. Immediately her finger felt as if the skin was being eaten away. She jerked her finger out, fully expecting to see nothing remaining but bone. It was red and blistered and swollen but the skin was still there. Taking her other hand she pulled down the neckline of her garment, revealing the top of her left breast, and began to trace the symbol as her grandmother had instructed her to do.

The pain was excruciating, but with a little concentration she was able to control it with the techniques she had learned while held captive within the net. A wave of dizziness swept over her and she only remained standing by gripping the edge of the stone altar, and despite blocking the pain, her muscles cramped and spasmed. She could feel the symbol she had drawn on herself eating away at her.

Through gritted teeth she said, "It is done, now what?"

There was a pause before her grandmother answered, her words colored with pain and sorrow, *"Drink from the cup."*

Trembling, Jade reached for the stone goblet. It was heavy and required her to use both hands, nearly causing her to fall. Looking down into the goblet, Jade saw her death.

"Grandmother, is there no other way?" she whispered.

She heard her grandmother gasp with the effort of holding back tears. *"No, there is no other way."*

*"If I do this will our people be saved?"*

*"If you do this we will have a chance. That is all,"* her grandmother answered truthfully.

*"I'm scared."*

*"I know. I love you,"* Kendra said sorrowfully.

Jade knew that that was the closest her grandmother was going to come to saying goodbye.

"I love you too," she said, and then drank from the cup. She felt herself fall to the ground, her body convulsing. The liquid from the cup burned her insides as if she had drunk molten lead. She could feel her insides melting. She screamed only to vomit blood. She clawed at the stones beneath her; her fingernails tearing from the flesh of her fingers. She couldn't see. She couldn't breathe. She knew her lungs were filling with blood—drowning her. Then the pain began in earnest as it invaded each cell of her body, leaving no part of her being unmolested. Her nerves split and burned, contracting her muscles with such force that they ripped from her bones.

She could hear Courage's voice calling her as if from a far of distance as she felt her consciousness spinning down into oblivion —the darkness consuming her soul.

"GOD! HELP ME!" She cried out with the last of her strength. Then on the brink of the abyss she felt her body respond.

The Light of Life flooded into her, combating the darkness, trying to heal her body even as the darkness tried to destroy it. The two fought for dominance within her. The light wasn't enough—it was losing. She needed more. So she reached out and took it. The Heavenstorm raged.

# CHAPTER 29

For the first time in Courage's existence he felt helpless. In what was to be their moment of escape Jade had been snatched from his back, and he had been unable to stop it from happening. He had failed her. The worst part was that he could no longer sense her through their glorious new bond. They had been heading towards a place called Talberic, and he assumed that was where she had been taken. He took heart in the fact that she was still alive. He knew this because even though he couldn't sense her through the bond; the bond itself still existed, and it wouldn't if she had been killed.

So he headed in the direction he hoped would take him to Talberic. He believed that the devil must have missed the ripple in existence when he had parted the veil to escape from the hundreds of Hell Hounds and their masters. If it had noticed, it hadn't attacked him directly. The dark energy that lay upon this land made it difficult to part the veil, and it had only been possible for him to do so because of all the extra energy that had flowed into him from Jade and her manipulation of the life energies around them.

While Courage couldn't open a pathway through a veil he could feel the devil do just that over and over, and he could only assume that it was using those openings to send hordes of Belial to attack the Areli. He couldn't pinpoint exactly where the pathway through the veil opened to, but he believed the devil was sending Belial and their demon masters beyond the Great Wall the Areli had built. If he was right, the Areli were in for a terrible surprise when they realized that they were completely surrounded. There was nothing he could do about it right now so he tried not to dwell on it.

Any enemy he had come upon while he was running—in what he hoped was the right direction—he destroyed with a terrible ferocity, taking his rage and frustration out upon them, rending the flesh of some while others burning to ash. Even with the distraction of killing Belial and their Kaga masters the night and his journey were interminable. Courage could feel the rhythm of the world and could tell that dawn had come, though there was no lightening of the sky above. The toxic vapors that grew thicker as he travelled were only a small annoyance that he blocked with minor effort. The thickening of the toxic vapors he took as a good sign, however, for he believed that it indicated that he was drawing closer to the devil where he would find Jade.

Courage knew that Jade would be a great prize for the devil, and the consequences of a devil successfully possessing a terrestrial body would be devastating, and have far-reaching effects. The first would be the destruction of this world, with all its inhabitants being destroyed or enslaved (better to be destroyed, for the righteous would be born again to a better life in a new world). The thought of Jade being possessed enraged Courage and he swore he would face this devil and destroy it if possible. There was another darker, more selfish thought—what would happen too him if Jade was possessed?

The jungle had grown thicker once more as he had traveled westward, and while he was able to maneuver through even the densest of jungles it did slow him a little. Courage sensed through his earthsight a large city and he sent a prayer to heaven, "In the name of the light, please be Talberic."

Then it happened—awareness of Jade came flooding back. The relief of it nearly caused his legs to buckle. With that awareness Courage could feel her thundering heartache and sorrow. Pain also laced her body though she had somehow learned to block it using her body's spiritual energy. That was his girl.

Suddenly he felt horror sweep through her. *"Jade,"* Courage called, but she was so caught-up in whatever caused that overwhelming sense of horror that at first his calls went unanswered. Gathering his consciousness Courage thundered, *"JADE!"*

"Courage!" Jade wailed in relief and hope. *"Courage, where are you?"* she cried.

*"I am coming little one! Hold on I am coming,"* he said. His legs were already carrying him through the jungle; he could feel where she was and he flew towards her like a tempest sweeping over the land. He could hear Alo talking to her again, urging her onward toward her final destination.

Over the last twenty four hours Courage had come to suspect just how Jade was supposed to break the curse. If he was right, it was extremely dangerous and the odds were that Jade would die, and the world with her. It would also leave her completely open and vulnerable to possession by the devil, which might have been its plan all along.

Courage roared at Kendra's words, and his body quivered as Jade painted the Netherscript over her heart. *Jade wait*, he pleaded in his heart. He was coming. What he could do… he didn't yet know, but there had to be a better way. Still, Courage felt pride swell up within him as he sensed Jade lifting the stone goblet to her lips and drink with the firm belief that she was going to die to save her people. Her love for them gave her the strength, and the courage, to overcome her fear.

If Courage had been a lesser being, just the feedback through the bond would have driven him insane. As it was it stunned him into immobility. He was distantly aware of his body sliding across the ground and hitting a tree, partially uprooting it, with bone-breaking force. He was being pulled down into oblivion along with Jade.

Then…then the ecstasy hit in a swirling vortex as life energies tried to fill the void that the Nether had created. It bled through the bond, infusing Courage with more energy than he had ever even believed possible. He felt the bones that he had broken when he slammed into the tree being knit back together. With all the skill and discipline Courage had learned over a millennium of life, he reasserted control over his body, but it had taken him precious time. Each second thundered in his mind along with Jade's tormented screams.

On trembling legs he rose from the ground. The juxtaposition between ecstasy and pain threatened to rip away his soul. Light rolled off him in waves, destroying the darkness that was consuming the land. With a casual ease that just moments before had been impossible, Courage reached out and sundered the veil between him and Jade. Through the hole in the fabric of reality, Courage could see the devil standing over Jade with a look of triumph as she bent over and placed her hand on the Netherscript

Jade had drawn over her heart. Radiating outward from the devil was darkness as deep and blighted as the Nethernight.

With a roar that shook the earth Courage stepped through the parted veil and prowled towards the devil; his muscles bunching and straining against the powerful energies coursing through him —demanding release. The light that wafted from his body grew in intensity with each step he took, fighting against the darkness. All the while, a towering vortex of energy poured into Jade as her body brutally stripped away the life essence of every living thing in an ever-increasing sphere and it was accelerating rapidly.

****

Kendra wiped tears from her eyes, her hands bony and frail. No matter how hard she tried she could not stop their tremors. Even still, a sigh of relief escaped her lips as the curse was lifted up off of the Areli people, freeing her soul from the burden of sustaining them.

"It is done according to my vision," Alo said, "now it is up to you if we are to survive this." His eyes filled with compassion; an expression reflected thousands of times in the mirrors of the Hall of Visions.

Alo had been able to briefly summon an image of Jade as they talked to her; instructing her on how she was to break the curse.

*"On how to destroy herself,"* Kendra thought bitterly.

The few moments after Jade had drunk from the cup screamed in her consciousness. She could see Jade's body reacting violently to the curse she had absorbed in her own body, and even now a storm of death raged across the land as her body consumed all life in an effort to stave off death. If Kendra didn't act swiftly they would all die, and even then nothing was certain.

Alo stood and reached down, taking her hands to help her up. There was a gentleness to his grip and Kendra could see in his eyes that he knew just how delicate and frail her hands had become. With great pain she allowed Alo to pull her to her feet; every joint in her body throbbed with sharp, burning pain. She steeled herself as she looked at her image in the mirrors. She looked ancient; her skin a thin brittle parchment. Her hair, what was left of it, was steely grey. She was thin, emaciated.

Two male Areli stood at the entrance to the Hall of Visions— one a warrior; the other a blacksmith. They looked torn; both of them Kendra knew wanted to be at the Wall fighting, but both also knew what an honor it was to have been chosen to attend the Holy Daughter this day.

"Matoskah," Alo called, "Carry the Holy Daughter to the top of the Great Wall. Pa-akanti, take the Dragon throne; she will need it. If you are not fast enough, we will all die."

Both Matoskah and Pa-akanti blanched but then sprang into action. Pa-akanti was already heading for the door with the Dragon Throne while Matoskah carefully picked Kendra up; cradling her in his arms. She rested her head against his shoulder as he rushed out the door to catch up to the nearly sprinting Pa-akanti who bore the massive Dragon Throne effortlessly before him.

Even running, Matoskah moved with an easy grace that almost lulled Kendra to sleep. She was so exhausted and his arms were so strong. She felt safe; which was something even a Holy Daughter needed from time to time.

Upon exiting the building they were greeted by two pacing totems. Matoskah's giant Frost Bear from the far north, and Pa-akanti's Steelback Bison from the vast savannah that stretched to the east of the Megiddo Jungle. The two totems joined the frenzied yet uneventful journey through the village to the Great Wall.

Matoskah and Pa-akanti reached the top of the Great Wall at the same time. Both acted as if they could have continued on indefinitely. Kendra, however, could see in Pa-akanti's aura a slight darkening of his physical energies, indicating fatigue. Then she saw it; a slight flutter in his aura indicating a leaky heart valve. It would be so easy for her to fix if she didn't feel as weak as a day-old pup. If they survived this, she would have to remember to track him down and heal him. It wouldn't kill him anytime soon;

however, she would have normally advised him to refrain from vigorous exercise until she could attend him. That wasn't going to happen so she would just have to let it go for now.

She looked down to where she knew Sinopa walked beside her. He looked as mangled and run down as she did. He wasn't a powerful totem. He was small and his elements of fire and earth were modest even for his own kind, but his heart was as big and courageous as the fiercest of warriors and he would carry on to the end with a quiet dignity that steadied her trembling heart. She let her arm dangle down in a gesture to comfort her closest friend and he gently nipped her finger with a playfulness that defied the darkness that threatened to consume her heart—pushing back the fear of what she was about to attempt. She knew that the light of her life was likely to be snuffed out like a candle in a storm. At least the Belial would face the same fate. A small smile curled the corners of her lips; maybe, just maybe those Belial that came to destroy would in turn save.

Once they had gained the top of the Great Wall Kendra was able to see a small group of Medicine Women working desperately over an unconscious form. They were pumping his chest and breathing for him, while channeling complex healing craftings.

As they grew closer she was able to see the prostrate form of Hiamovi. Kendra could tell that he had exhausted his body's energies beyond endurance and that his heart had stopped.

She wanted to wail in despair. Like fixing Pa-akanti's leaky heart valve, Kendra found that in this too she was unable to help. All it would take was for her to gift a little energy into Hiamovi's body, giving it the energy to restart his heart, but she had nothing left to give. No, his fate rested in the hands of the Medicine Women frantically working on him. She had trained them well. She prayed they would be enough.

Pa-akanti set the Dragon Throne to face the Belial armies. The noise was deafening. The concussions caused from the energy cannons thumped deep within her chest. Matoskah carefully set her down before the Dragon Throne, facing her out over the battlement so she could take in the battle raging all around them. He kept one hand on her for support. She smiled at him gratefully. She knew that he had chafed at having to sit out the battle while his brothers and sisters fought, but she also could see the pride swelling in his breast at having the opportunity to serve her in her time of need. If they survived Kendra believed that he would tell his children and his grandchildren of the time he had carried the Holy Daughter in his arms; then stood beside her, lending her his strength on the day of the Heavenstorm.

She wasn't as strong as Jade. She could only take energy from that which she could see. Fortunately for her she could see for miles from her vantage point. It was very unfortunate for the horde of Belial and their Kaga masters below. She could feel in her bones the Heavenstorm raging towards them. She had just moments to act.

Stretching forth her hand, she cast her mind out to all living things within her sight; excluding the Areli and their totems. Then she grasped it in her fist and took it. Raging life stormed into her, setting her blood boiling. With each beat of her heart she felt renewed. The liver spots and blemishes faded, leaving behind smooth youthful skin. Her body tremors ceased and she felt her muscles grow firm. Her scalp itched as her hair grew back to the length she preferred it.

She looked down at Sinopa and saw him go through a similar transformation. Light began to radiate from both her and Sinopa's bodies. At first the light was dim but it quickly became blinding—blazing like the sun.

All the Areli around her fell back in astonishment and fear, shielding their eyes lest they go blind. She had forgotten what it felt like to hold so much raw power. Her body's exhausted core flared back to life, trying to match this new power coursing through her, adding to her strength. The ecstasy slammed into her along with the power. It was like every good thing: a delicious meal, the sun kissing your skin, standing in a furious storm and feeling its majesty, a cool drink of water after hours of intense labor, a child's smile, the raging passion found in a lover's arms. It was all these things and so much more.

A wave of darkness unfolded before her second sight, leaving behind only the now-disembodied Kaga; their auras somehow even darker than the absence of life. To the Areli around her, the world before them crumbled to dust that was then blown and twisted about from the furious winds that had arisen. They shouted in joy at the destruction of their enemies, though they became more reserved when they saw all the demon-spirits remaining. Surely if the Holy Daughter could wave her hand and turn all things to dust then she could also destroy the demon-spirits. To them the battle was almost over.

*"How naïve they were,"* Kendra thought sadly.

She had pulled all the energy of life before her for a dozen miles. She would have vomited if it wasn't for the fact that she was able to exact retribution on more than a hundred thousand Belial.

*"In the name of the Light of Heaven,"* she thought, *"let it be enough."*

She then sat on the Dragon Throne and closed her eyes, linking her spirit to all living Areli. What she was about to do was a lot like what she had been doing when protecting them from the curse. She began to stream her body's energies along the invisible threads that now connected them; infusing them with a portion of her energies. Then she channeled the energy through the individual Areli, forming a shimmering white and green cocoon around them.

*"Just in time,"* she thought. Bracing herself, the Heavenstorm hit. Its approach had been hidden due to the dead zone Kendra had just created before them, but when it did hit, it was like being struck by the detonations of a thousand energy cannons simultaneously. Thousands of her shields crumpled under the initial blast of the Heavenstorm, killing her beloved people in the same fashion that she had just done to the Belial.

With a scream of rage and defiance she strengthened the shields and waited—waited for salvation to come.

\*\*\*\*

Courage stalked his prey. A prey more deadly than any he had ever before hunted. But the life energy bleeding through the bond made him stronger than he had ever imagined. He recognized the danger of addiction that something like this posed. Jade blazed brighter than the sun at noon and he only slightly less so, but as brightly as they shined the light did not pierce the void that had sprung up around the devil before him. The light destroyed the darkness and the darkness ate at the light. Courage had forced the devil to back away from Jade. Stepping over Jade, he continued his pursuit while the devil cursed him.

Courage formed a protective shield around Jade to protect her from what was about to happen. The devil tried to slip past him several time in order to get at Jade.

"I will rip your soul from your body and devour it whole," Raum snarled then channeled the Nether in its pure form, trying to engulf Courage.

Courage felt the light buckling under the onslaught. Drinking deep of life, Courage met the attack and threw it back at the devil, causing her to scream in rage.

Courage roared. Light spewed forth from his mouth, shredding the darkness that shrouded the devil, causing her to scream not in rage but in pain. The ground quaked under the strain of the two mighty forces contending for dominance. Buildings collapsed and reality trembled under the brutal attacks they hurled at each other. After one such attack, Courage pounced. His claws tore into her flesh; rending, and slicing.

Then he bit off her head.

A powerful burst of Nether energy exploded forth from the devil's decapitated corpse, hurling Courage through the air. He slammed into the side of one of the neighboring temples. Bones crunched upon impact and his vision swam. Steeling his resolve, he forced himself to his feet and spit out the head. Its acrid taste stung his tongue and throat. He swiftly healed himself then launched himself into the air—brilliant white wings forming as he flew—carrying him across the distance with tremendous speed.

The devil approached Jade and was preparing to possess her body once more—her true self revealed. She was a towering figure, standing well over ten feet and obviously female. She would have been beautiful if not for the hate that twisted her ghostly visage, and the ram's horns curling out of her head. Actually he didn't really mind the ram horns all that much. He had assumed her form would be hideous and was slightly disturbed to have his presumptions proven wrong. The talons that extended from her fingers were sufficiently wicked, however.

Courage knew that if she was successful, all was lost. So he left nothing back, throwing himself at her shadowy form. Flesh cannot harm spirit but energy could and Courage was bursting with it— radiating it—his claws sheathed in effervescence. Courage tore into the devil, leaving wounds infected with light. Courage did not go unscathed for the devil's talons had also left riven wounds in his flesh filled with the poison of the Nether.

The two separated and began circling each other. Courage used the precious moments to heal his grievous wounds for if left unattended they would consume him. The devil had obviously done the same thing for the light-filled wounds slowly closed up with darkness.

The world bucked and trembled from the forces the two beings brought to bear against each other. This time instead of physical attacks they both attacked each other mentally. Courage could feel the devil's dismay as she felt the veracity that made up his soul. His purity repelled the devil more violently than all the powerful energy he was able to bring to bear against her. Still, the touch of her mind left him feeling tainted.

Alo's voice rang within his mind, *"Courage! We perish!"*

*"What would you have me do, Spirit Man!?"* Courage growled in response; shaking his head as if an annoying bee buzzed within it. *"Don't distract me!"*

*"You have no more time with which to slay the fiend. We perish, Courage!"*

*"What would you have me do?"* he roared back again.

*"You must end this now,"* Alo replied desperately.

*"How?"* Courage demanded.

*"The guidestone; Kendra and I prepared it to work as a prison. You have the ability to part veils. You can open a veil into the heart of the guidestone. The curse enters this world through the devil. If you trap the devil in the guidestone it will sever the connection to Jade and end the threat to her and save us all."*

*"Do you know what you ask, Spirit Man? I will have to enter*

*the prison and keep the veil closed from the inside. We shall both be trapped, and at the best it will only postpone the inevitable."*

*"I know, but it will give us time to recover. Time to prepare; and when it is time, you shall have Kendra to stand beside you and Jade as you fight. Please, if we are to live it is the only way."*

*"So be it."*

Courage gathered the energy that was storming through him and formed ropes of energy that flowed out of him and wrapped around the devil. He tried to yank the devil towards him, causing her to pull away. In the time between seconds, Courage pounced, ripping a veil into the heart of the guidestone behind the devil. Courage slammed into the devil, hurling them both through the veil.

\*\*\*\*

The Heavenstorm raged, and her people died as one shield at a time failed. The energy Kendra had seized drained away under the storm's unrelenting hunger. She poured more energy into maintaining the shields but if she did too much she would never last long enough for the storm to end and all would perish.

Death was a part of life even for a nation not at war, but no matter how long Kendra had lived she could never get used to it. With all her powers she should have been able to save her loved ones. It was unfair that she should live when they would not. It wasn't until the curse struck that she realized she, too, could die. Kendra knew that the Holy Mother hadn't been truly immortal— she could have died. The vision memories showed her that much, but Kendra had never felt her own mortality until the curse had struck and for the first time she found her strength insufficient.

Each and every death tore at her, and it was worse being linked to each of them through the Dragon Throne for each death felt like her own. When the shield failed and their life energy was sucked away, it was her life energy that was sucked away. Their screams of pain and terror rang within her mind, causing her to weep tears of liquid light. Each tear that stained her cheeks shimmered a little less, the light of life fading away as the Heavenstorm raged. Another Areli died; his screams adding to the anguished refrain.

"No more!" she cried in defiance.

Abandoning her strategy of a careful retreat against the might of the Heavenstorm, Kendra gritted her teeth and sent a surge of energy through the bonds connecting all Areli—strengthening the shields. For a minute they held, and then another, and another, but with each moment that passed, the energy Kendra had taken burned away until all that remained was the energy from her own core. She would not stop though. She would not let another of her people fall. Not before her.

The new youth that had been returned to her began to fade once more as she fed her own life's energies into the fires of the Heavenstorm. She knew this time she was going to die, and she was ready for it.

Sinopa had jumped up onto her lap and she hugged him to her chest. The love and peace she felt from him soothed her heartache. They grew old together. She would not enter the void alone. The storm raged, rapidly eating away at the shields that they maintained with their lives.

There was a way to preserve her people even beyond her death; for a time, at least. Maybe it would be enough. All she had to do was be willing to die eternally—to truly cease to be; to convert her soul back into the pure Light of Heaven. It would be enough. It had to be. *Please let it be,* she prayed.

Sinopa, dear Sinopa, had read the thoughts of her heart. She saw the clarity of his thought as he relinquished his rights to exist and poured all the potential of his soul into hers. The pure Light of Heaven entered into her and it was love. He had seen her heart and gave his life for hers, and it was enough.

Not another Areli died until the Heavenstorm ended.

# EPILOGUE

Alo sat in the Hall of Visions, watching his visions come to pass. In each mirror he saw the lives of his loved ones and his people play out. He watched Menewa, Chaska, Honon, and Honaw leave the deep caverns that riddled the earth beneath Talberic. The city was now destroyed by the titanic battle that had taken place between beings not meant for this mortal sphere.

He watched as Menewa climbed the steps of a temple, the only building still whole, towards what was becoming his heart's desire. Menewa walked into the blazing sun and picked her up; a look of tenderness and awe painted upon his countenance. The guidestone glistened around her neck.

Alo looked and saw the clouds in the heavens part and the noonday sun light up the land—a land devoid of all life for hundreds of miles. A land that was prowled by bodiless Netherbeings. He smiled as he saw their pain at being fully exposed to the light with no mortal frame to protect them.

He watched as the Light of Heaven healed and restored his

people, making them whole once more. He watched as Hiamovi stood on shaky legs and made his way over to comfort Kendra, whispering something in her ear that made her laugh through her sobs. Alo ruthlessly squashed the jealousy that began to burn in his chest.

They had entered the darkness and had come out the other side. It had been the sacrifice of a young Areli that had cursed them, and it was only through Sinopa's sacrifice that they had been saved—fulfilling the law.

Alo allowed himself to relax. Hope had won. Then his mind flooded with new visions, and that hope choked and died. The worst was yet to come.

*Heaven help them,* he prayed.

The End